SOMEWHERE BETWEEN RAINDROPS

Book 2 of the
AMBER LEAF TRILOGY

a novel by

SANDRA H. ESCH

A LAMP POST BOOK

SOMEWHERE BETWEEN RAINDROPS
     BY SANDRA H. ESCH

ISBN 10: 1-60039-200-8
ISBN 13: 978-1-60039-200-9
ebook ISBN: 978-1-60039-725-7

www.lamppostpubs.com

SOMEWHERE BETWEEN RAINDROPS

BY

SANDRA H. ESCH

ACKNOWLEDGEMENTS

What a privilege to write. Writing a novel is like watching a favorite movie over and over and over again. With each revision, the landscape changes, the characters change, and the twists and turns of the plot are modified, offering an endless opportunity for entertainment at the keyboard. And laughter. And tears.

If that isn't reward enough, there are also the rich exchanges with fellow writers, new friendships, encouragement, stimulation, and remarkable support.

My heartfelt thanks to my publisher, Brett Burner at Lamp Post, who made this amazing journey possible. Thanks, also, to my editor, Hannah Demers.

Special thanks to my Writers Critique Group—Martha Gorris, Ann Larson, Jean Mader, Mary Kay Moody (thank you for the above and beyond feedback, Mary Kay), Maria Sainz, Diana Wallis Taylor and others who passed through our group—as well as fellow writers Sue Duffy and Bev Nault.

More special thanks to Bonnie Aase-Roach, Cindy Belshan, Tom Cafone, Pam Coley, Roselyn Collver, Marilyn Damian, Ann Fletcher, Del and Marianne Glanz, Lorraine Hooks, Fran Jenkins, Lois Kuehnast, Lori Lobnitz, Alice Muilenburg, Sonny Okland, Ellen Sheldon, Patti Tzannos, and Nadine Washburn for their generous input and amazing encouragement.

A word about mentors. Great mentors are gifted—generous in thought, word, and deed. That said, my heartfelt thanks to Natalie

Jensen Baker. Nat, when it comes to mentoring, you walk where the air is thin and the sun shines bright. I can't thank you enough for taking me under wing and believing in me when becoming an author was nothing more than my dream.

Finally, thanks to my cousins, Margaret Farr and Shirley Ravenshorst; my sisters, Ardena Okland and Lois Williams; and my niece, Sheila Okland. And thanks, Fred, for your heartfelt encouragement and for keeping me on the straight and narrow by tirelessly proclaiming, "you still have way too many words."

We are not retreating…
we are advancing in another direction.

— *General Douglas MacArthur*

CHAPTER ONE

AMBER LEAF, MINNESOTA—LATE MARCH 1945

Honestly, what kind of person steals flowers from a cemetery?" Jo Bremley lamented. "Wasn't last week's desecration enough?" She slouched back on her heels, emptied the air from her lungs in one long soulful breath, and surveyed the damage. The clay pots on the spokes of the wagon wheel flanking her husband's headstone had their geraniums stolen. Again. All eight of the blooms. She swiveled around and scoured the small rural cemetery. Floral droppings should have made a striking trail of red. But they didn't. Whoever sheared off the flowers didn't drop so much as a petal.

Kneeling beside the grave, she pressed another geranium deep into its violated pot, brushed a disheveled lock of hair from her forehead, then stroked the tender blades of grass cloaking Case's grave. "Someone stole your flowers again, Case. It's great knowing there's life out here so you aren't all alone, but somehow there has to be better company than flower thieves. Sure wish I could catch the culprit. But what are the chances of that ever happening?"

Casting aside her grief, she reached out to her husband's shiny headstone and delicately traced its carved letters with the tips of her fingers.

CASE BREMLEY
Loving Husband and Father
July 2, 1918–November 8, 1943

She stared at the stone for a long while, talking to Case the same way she'd been talking to him this past year and a half—as if he were still among the living. "Tryg stopped by the boarding house to see Big Ole Harrington yesterday afternoon. I literally bumped into him in the hallway. Of course, I just happened to be carrying a basket full of dirty laundry." She squeezed her eyes closed, heat rising up her fair cheeks. "There I was, all decked out in my cotton shift that looks like it was sewn from an old cheesecloth. Cardigan hanging on me like an overused hand-me-down. Hair tucked up in a scarf. No makeup. And there he stood...crisp, clean, wearing the finest threads available to man, and smelling like he'd just taken a bath in a tub of Old Spice. I wanted to collapse into a fetal position, but I didn't. I made sure I held my head high."

Jo squeezed down the lump rising in her throat, and then continued on. "I've got to get away from him, Case. I know he was your best friend, and I know the accident that put you here wasn't entirely his fault. But the pain I see in his eyes and the grief that overtakes me the few times we've run into each other are tearing me apart. Makes me want to rethink our dream of moving to New York," she said thoughtfully. "You with that job waiting for you at Haskins & Sells and me wanting to get into the fashion industry. One of these days I need to make our dreams come true." Jo looked up as if she could see her husband peering down through a cloud break. "But I don't know if I'm ready yet. I can't leave you, Case. I just can't."

A sudden breeze flicked a smattering of cut grass onto the headstone. Jo gently wiped it away with her handkerchief and polished the stone until it reflected its original high gloss. She then returned to busily repotting geraniums.

Not five minutes later, the whirr of a car's engine droned through the cemetery. Tires crunching on gravel. The harsh shriek of tired brakes. She looked back. A lone soldier was struggling to get out of the backseat of an old taxi. Suddenly that familiar ill-at-ease feeling overwhelmed her again, accelerating her heartbeat and tempting her to flee.

The man in uniform collected his crutches. With a push of his full weight, he appeared to test the ground for softness. He snatched a bouquet of daisies from the back seat, mumbled something to the cab driver, and then hobbled through the rows of headstones. As if he could feel Jo watching from afar, he turned and briefly locked eyes with her.

Sad eyes.

Eyes like Tryg Howland's.

Jo plucked a blade of grass and picked at its jagged tip as if tearing away at it could remove the conflicting feelings that tore at her heart. *Tryg Howland.* While her husband was sniffing the underbellies of tulips, Tryg was still sniffing the clean Southern Minnesota air.

With the flat of her hand, Jo lightly patted Case's grave. Then a curious thing happened. She found herself rambling pensively. "A soldier just arrived, Case. I wish you could see him. From a distance, he looks a lot like Tryg. Has that same Bing Crosby look, only his hair is dark and thick. He's been wounded, too, just like Tryg when he first came home with that broken leg of his. Just think. It's been nearly a year and a half already. I heard he wanted to re-enlist, but they wouldn't take him. He still has that bad limp." She hesitated for a moment. She had to spill what was chewing away at her insides. "You know, sometimes I get the feeling he regrets that he didn't die on the battlefield."

She pinched her eyes closed, repulsed by another thought that came too easily. *If Tryg had died on the battlefield, you would still be alive.*

While stuffing the last geranium into its pot, she heard a light commotion and looked up. The wounded soldier was climbing back into his taxi. He slammed the door and the rickety cab disappeared through the side gate, a whirling puff of gray smoke from its muffler pushing it down the lonely stretch of gravel road.

She lowered her gaze again to Case's grave. "The soldier just left. I don't want to imagine what that poor man has been through. The war is winding down in the European Theatre. Looks like we're winning there, but Japan is still putting up quite a fight in the Pacific. I can't wait until this ugliness is over with once and for all."

A distant rumbling beckoned Jo's attention. She looked toward the far western sky, where thin bolts of lightning danced to the peal of soft thunder. A cool breeze picked up, moaned through the pines, and swiftly permeated the air with the strong aroma of ozone. She pulled her sweater tight around her thin frame to stave off a sudden chill. "Looks like a nasty storm's heading this way. Guess I'd better get going."

Jo stood, but thought better of it and knelt once again at the foot of the grave. "Oh, Case, I wish you could speak to me. I don't know what to do." She tugged off her work gloves. "I've given so much thought these past months to the dim future Brue and I have here in Amber Leaf without you. We have a few good friends, sure, but no lifelong friends. When Brue gets older, I might be able to find a job working as a clerk in one of the local retail shops, but there aren't any fashion industry positions, not in a small factory town like ours. My job at the O.M. Harrington House? It just isn't the same anymore. Too many of the old-timers have left, heading off to other pastures that I doubt could be as green. The place has drained of life, lost its pulse. And bumping into Tryg every now and then also makes me want to get out of town. Maybe life would be better that way—better for him, and better for us, too.

Jo shivered at the thought of the soldier she'd seen hobbling through the cemetery. Even he, a complete stranger, reminded her of Tryg and how his careening a car into a ditch during a blinding snowstorm had unintentionally destroyed her life. Reminded her that Case was no longer here. The words, "and would never be ever again," rolled softly off her lips. That could not be fixed. Ever.

Tryg was a storm she couldn't outrun.

In a way, the timing for a move would be ideal. New York was her best hope for a new and healthy beginning.

But not this soon.

A fierce gust of wind momentarily knocked her off balance as the sky gave way to a dark shade of midnight pierced with brilliant flashes of lightning. The surrounding black and barren fields ripe for spring plowing quivered beneath the scintillating light. "I've got to get out of here. This storm is closing in way too fast. It's gonna be a bad one."

She grabbed her gardening tools and raced to her car.

She had another storm to outrun.

Before reaching the end of the gravel road, a torrent of rain dumped on her old '31 Chevy like water splashing from a bucket. She pulled the car over to the shoulder and stopped to wait out the downpour while troubling thoughts washed over her like the deluge of rain. She thought about the money she saved. She stashed away enough to last at least a couple of months in Amber Leaf. But in New York City? And what about the unknowns? What if she and Brue were miserable there? What if a good job was impossible to find? How humiliating to return to Amber Leaf a failure. Then what? If they did decide to leave...Jo shuddered at the thought. For now, at least, a move to New York felt too final.

The heavy car listed in the wind and the rain turned to hail. It pinged loudly at the windshield like marbles thrashing a tin pail, while an accompanying cold draft rippled her arms with gooseflesh. And still the thoughts kept coming. Brue needed to grow up around family. Cousin Shirley lived there. Relatives were close by to enjoy the holidays with. But would Brue be happy at a new school? Would Jo and Brue make friends easily in a big city or would they merely get lost in a crowd?

Jo slapped the steering wheel. She knew what she needed to do. She needed to hold on to her dream, keep working hard, keep saving, and then one day—a year down the road, maybe two—she and Brue would leave Amber Leaf. With little opportunity here, only memories, New York offered the best hope for a brand new life.

CHAPTER TWO

J o restrained a smile. The puffy-faced old man was sitting alone at the far side of the O.M. Harrington's great room, lost in his world of literature, looking innocent, almost childlike. Bushy eyebrows hooded his deep gray eyes, which were gliding across the pages of a book made small in the largeness of his hands. Soft murmurings trembled through his thick lips. Around him, a handful of guests meandered about. Some shuffled cards near the bay windows overlooking Harrington Park. Some chattered quietly over steamy cups clattering on fine china. Some simply warmed themselves near the fire. Although Jo was vaguely aware of their presence, it was the old man who dominated the room.

They called him Big Ole. Not all that long ago, Jo had found him formidable. It took courage for her to even say hello to the man. Not anymore.

He looked up, a grin tugging at his ample cheeks. "How long were you planning on standing there?" he asked. "Don't tell me you need an invitation to come in."

Jo straightened the barrette in her seven-year-old's long blond hair and guided her forward. "Not at all. It's just that I've never seen you taking time to relax before."

Ole tucked a bookmarker snugly between the pages of his thick novel and closed it. Then, with a nod toward the radio and in a deep voice unusually pleasant to the ear, he said, "I took a few minutes to get caught up on the war news is all...and indulged in a little reading during the commercials while I was at it. Just haven't made it back to my office yet." He shifted his gaze to Brue. "You playing hooky from school today, young lady?"

Brue grinned. "Hunh-uh. We have Easter vacation this week."

"Well then, how about if we have another one of our little history lessons while your mother slips into the back room and works on the laundry? Would you like that?"

Jo watched for a moment as Brue and Big Ole settled in on the settee nearest the blaze dancing on the hearth—two adversaries turned friends. Harsh encounters. Hurt feelings. Simmering emotions. They'd had them all. But now they were the best of friends.

Brue snuggled up next to the old man, her midnight blue eyes gleaming. Big Ole taught her about current events, but gently, in a way a child understood—the names of the Allied countries and American generals, why the leaders of the big bad countries needed to be stopped, and how our brave soldiers were carrying out a well-developed plan to stop them.

As Big Ole reached into his pocket, popped open a small tin, and offered Brue some peppermints, Jo proceeded to the laundry room, where she gazed wearily at the immense task before her. Taking in a deep breath, she tugged up the sleeves of her cardigan. Time to dig in. Laundry work was backbreaking, but it definitely paid the bills.

Less than five minutes later, Jo jumped when Brue tore into the room, brimming with excitement. "Mom, Mom! You got a telephone call. It's long distance, person-to-person."

Jo gulped, her heart thumping unrelentingly. "Who is it? Do you have any idea?"

"Hunh-uh."

With Brue scurrying along at her heels, Jo journeyed down O.M.

Harrington's long hallway at a brisk pace, wondering who in this war-torn world would call her at work—long distance, person-to-person nonetheless. Whoever it was, it had to be serious. She anxiously finger-primped her hair as if she was about to make the acquaintance of someone important. But she wasn't. She only had to pick up the phone.

Big Ole stood at the registration desk and handed her the receiver while Brue sidled up next to him. They both watched with no small amount of interest.

Jo swiped nervous palms against her apron, then picked up the receiver and held it warily against her ear. The other hand she drew toward her stomach, where apprehension whipped like cream. She glanced around the great room, at the crackling blaze on the hearth, the brocade settees, and end tables aglow with small lamps, then out the far windows toward Harrington Park, where she feared she would much rather be at the moment. "This is Jo Bremley."

"Go ahead, ma'am," the operator said.

"Jo? It's me. Shirley."

Jo's breath caught. Shirley's husband. He was fighting in the Pacific Theater. He hadn't been wounded had he? Or worse? "Shirley? Is everything okay?"

Shirley lowered her voice. "Are you in a place where you can talk privately?"

Jo glanced into Big Ole and Brue's concerned eyes then twisted the telephone cord around her forefinger, her gaze slicing toward the hardwood floor. "Not really."

"Okay. Just listen, then, and I'll do all the talking," Shirley said, sounding far too cheerful to be the bearer of grim news. "Sorry to call you at work, but we're on our way out to an early dinner and the theater, so I can't call later tonight. I've got great news."

"You do?"

"Remember how you and Case were planning on moving here to New York?"

Jo nodded into the phone.

"Well, guess what? You still get to come. I got you a job, sight unseen, at JD Barrister's. It's an upscale dress shop just a few blocks from here. They're looking for a seamstress who can also interact with buyers and assist customers. Sounds perfect, doesn't it? I think you might even be able to work your way up into management, in time."

Suddenly feeling like a traitor, Jo rotated toward the windows. "You *what*?" she asked guardedly into the mouthpiece.

"I said I got you a job, silly. Isn't that the best news you've heard all day? But you've got to jump on it. The owner needs to fill the spot right away. She can only give you a couple of days to think about it. Then she needs to advertise. I'll give you a call again on Friday. Gotta go. Bye."

Jo held the receiver for a long moment before gently cradling it. She then glanced into the questioning eyes of Big Ole and Brue, but said nothing. They appeared to sense this wasn't the time to ask questions and said nothing either. Turning on her heel, Jo hurried back to the laundry room, her thoughts in a dither.

For the next ten to fifteen minutes or so, she pulled out and tripped over more pieces of soiled linen than she plunked into her baskets, mindlessly pressing dirty laundry into her wicker basket. Her dream surfaced again, this time with intensity. But she needed to make an immense decision in a bite-sized window of time. Was that even feasible? A move to New York. Being close to family. Getting into the fashion industry. Not having to bump into Tryg Howland anymore. She glanced down at her basket and sighed when she noticed she'd kneaded the tight lump of soiled linen as if it were bread dough.

A short while later, Brue poked her small turned-up nose through the door. "Mom, Big Ole wants you to stop by and see him on your way out."

"Do you have any idea what about?"

"Hunh-uh. He's in his office." Brue pulled her thick hair back and gingerly stepped farther into the room. "Mom?"

"Yes, dear?"

"Who called you long distance? Was it Cousin Shirley?"

Jo nodded, then tossed the towel she was holding aside and drew Brue into her arms. "I'll tell you all about our conversation on our way home, okay? But for now, why don't you go and warm yourself by the fireplace in the great room? I won't be much longer."

Jo shoved several heaping baskets of soiled linen by the door then headed toward Big Ole's office, her heart thumping twofold harder and faster than her footsteps. He wanted to know about the telephone call; she was sure of that. Nothing got past him. In a few minutes, the discussion would be nothing more than a memory, but knowing him, getting past those first few minutes would be the hard part. She stopped immediately outside his door, inhaled a deep breath, then peered in.

Big Ole's office bespoke richness with its shiny wooden floors, floor-to-ceiling wall of French windows, and a bookcase lined with leather-bound books. But the clutter of papers and pencils concealing the top of his large chestnut desk, full ashtray, and the stench of lingering tobacco smoke made the mere thought of entry far less intimidating.

He appeared to be studying a note on a small piece of paper.

Jo shifted her weight from one foot to another as she waited. When he finally looked up, he simply peered at her as if he was looking over bifocals. "Mrs. Bremley. Come in, come in."

Jo drew her shoulders back and plastered on a confident smile. "I understand you wanted to see me."

"You understand right." With a wave of his hand, he indicated a black leather chair at the far side of his desk. "Please. Have a seat."

He reached into his center desk drawer, pulled out a cigar, and carefully removed the cellophane. With his attention on the cheroot, he said, "Is there anything you wanted to share with me?" He raised his bushy brows until his penetrating gray eyes met hers. "Any advice you wouldn't mind taking from an old-timer?"

Jo's foot swung involuntarily back and forth, a nervous gesture that she certainly preferred to do without at the moment. "I take it you figured out what that phone call was all about."

"I believe I did, yes. Would you be interested in knowing what tipped me off?"

Jo nodded circumspectly.

"You. Your response. Turning away. Giving your daughter and me your back. Speaking a little too quietly into the phone. Smacks of guilt, doesn't it? Of course, there was also that tearing off for the laundry room without a word of explanation." He swiped a match against the bottom of his shoe, the stench of sulfur suffusing the air as the match burst into flame. He held the fire to his cigar and inhaled until it glowed. After a few quick puffs, his warm expression chilled unexpectedly, his gaze burrowing into Jo's. "Shirley. Isn't she that cousin of yours who lives in New York?"

Jo nodded again.

"I see. Are you planning on moving there then?"

"I don't know yet."

"Well, let's say that you do decide to go. Will you be running *to* New York or will you be running away from Amber Leaf?"

"You certainly aren't afraid to ask probing questions, are you?"

Big Ole leaned back and rocked in his chair. A grin blossomed on his face, plumping out his already plump cheeks. "At my age, my dear young lady, why should I be?"

"That's fair enough, I guess," she said reluctantly. "I certainly hope I'm running to, not from. I have to tell you, though, when Brue told me I had a long-distance, person-to-person call, the memory of my last long-distance call backed up on me with a vengeance. I can still hear the static exploding through the wires. That awful snowstorm. The accident. Losing Case."

"I understand that only too well. But what's in New York? Other than your cousin, that is."

"Case's dream," she announced proudly. "We were planning on building a new life there. You know...before the accident."

When Ole lifted his chin and peered down at her, she knew she was in for a whole new round.

"Ahh. I see," he said. "Case's dream, you say?"

"Excuse me?"

"Case's dream? Not your dream?"

Jo's stomach constricted. She thought for a split moment then said, "They are one in the same, aren't they? As for me, I've always wanted to get into the fashion industry. They're holding a great job for me there, sight unseen. I'm not sure what to do yet. This is all happening way too fast. Almost sounds too good to be true."

Ole took his time inhaling a sizable amount of smoke, then playfully emitted small puffs high into the air. "Love this fine tobacco," he said, his eyes smiling at his swirling artwork.

With the exception of cherry tobacco, Jo found the smell of tobacco smoke less than pleasant. "It does have a nice fragrance...for a cigar," she said politely.

"What about Tryg Howland? Are you thinking about running away from him, too?"

Jo stared at Big Ole until the shock subsided. Enough of that! Gripping the arms of her black leather chair, she squared her shoulders. "What makes you so sure I'm running away from anything?"

"You are."

Jo gulped. "Excuse me?"

"You're running away from Tryg. Your deceased husband's friend."

The words, "You mean the man who took my husband's life," passed through Jo's tightening lips before she caught them.

"That's a bit harsh, don't you think?" Ole stared at his cigar as he tapped the slightest bit of ash into his ashtray. "Think about how you phrased that. I prefer to think of him as the wounded soldier and best friend who, anxious to get home, was driving your husband's car during a blinding snowstorm and slammed on the brakes to avoid hitting a deer."

Jo pushed back in her chair. "I'm sorry. I don't know where those words came from. It was an accident. I know that. It's just that whenever Tryg sees me, he relives it. I know he does. I can see it in his eyes."

"He relives it? Or *you* relive it?" Big Ole got up and paced toward the windows, giving Jo his back. "The two of you aren't the only ones who've been down that road, you know."

"What is that supposed to mean?"

He shot back a cursory glance. "My wife."

Jo blinked, then leaned forward. "I'm afraid I don't understand."

Ole slipped his hands into his trouser pockets. Rocking from heel to toe, he gazed out toward the park. "She didn't need to die either," he said, a hint of hurt coursing through his deep voice.

"Wh—"

"I said she didn't need to die either," he repeated sharply. He turned and glanced again at Jo, but only briefly. "I know precisely how you feel. I hated her doctor just like you hate Tryg Howland."

"But I don't hate Tryg," Jo fired back, her voice strong. "And this isn't about Tryg. It's about a wonderful opportunity to begin a new life in New York."

Big Ole ignored her comment and continued on talking toward the window as if she hadn't said a word. "Hated him for his quick and arrogant diagnosis. Hated him for not taking the time to question himself. Hated him for not paying better attention. Hated him for letting her die. He was way too confident. Insisted she'd eaten something that didn't agree with her. She hadn't. She had appendicitis. Her appendix burst. She died."

Shock rippled through Jo, not so much from Ole's words, but at finally feeling at one with someone who really understood. "I'm so, so sorry. I knew she died. I just never knew how or why. How did you get over it? Or haven't you?"

Big Ole strolled back to his chair and plunked down. He slowly rubbed its leather arms, his eyes frozen in a thoughtful stare. "I found out that the doctor tried drinking himself to death. It took a while. But when it finally dawned on me how much he was suffering, too, I knew I had to help him through his torment."

"But why you?"

"Somebody had to," he said, sounding surprised at her question.

"That was unbelievably charitable. So did he ever get past himself?"

Big Ole nodded. "It took time...for both of us."

"But, about Tryg," Jo said. "I don't hate him."

"No?"

"No. Absolutely not."

Jo stared into the silence that followed until it occurred to her that Big Ole was intent on drawing her out. "Why are you doing this?"

He looked at her hard and strong, drawing in another long puff of smoke and slowly blowing it out, but still saying nothing.

"Okay then," she said softly. "You want to know about it, I'll tell you. Whenever I see Tryg now, all I want to do is run. I don't know how to overcome my feelings. But I wouldn't call it hate. Jealously, maybe, but not hate. After all, Tryg is building a great new life. Meanwhile, Case's life...my future with him...it's all been stripped away."

Ole leaned forward, his chair groaning beneath his weight. "And you've been reduced to taking in laundry to eke out a living while Tryg Howland is flourishing with his new law practice. That's the bigger part of the problem, isn't it? And you see no way out. Other than running away to New York, that is."

Jo flinched, suddenly feeling exposed, as though her emotional clothes had just been ripped off.

"Seems unfair, doesn't it?" he asked, as though he felt a need to speak for her. He then said in an empathetic voice refined by experience, "It is. It is unfair."

"But I don't like the way I feel—small. It's not right to be like this."

"You'll get past it," he said warmly. "You're in a very difficult spot right now. Maybe in the greater scheme of things you still have more forgiving to do."

"Forgive what?" Jo asked incredulously. "Forgive Tryg for having a law practice?"

Big Ole grinned and tapped a finger against the arm of his chair. "One day you'll figure it out."

"I'm not sure I want to figure it out."

"If you do decide to go," he continued, "I want you to know that we're sure going to miss you around here. Your work has been stupendous."

Jo sighed. "That's very kind of you to say."

"Not kind. True. And, again, if you do decide to go and find you need anything when you get to New York, I'm here for you any time, day or night."

"Thank you, Mr. Harrington. For everything. I don't know what I would have done without the work from the boarding house these past months, saying nothing about the good friends I've made here. There's a big part of me that just wants to stay where I can bask in the comfort of the familiar, where I know what I do and don't have."

After expressing a painfully conflicted goodbye and gathering up Brue, Jo crossed River Lane and stepped onto the path cutting through Harrington Park, all the while fighting the heaviness in her chest. Big Ole certainly had done a number on her. *Maybe in the greater scheme of things I still have more forgiving to do? Forgive what?*

She stopped for a moment, glanced back at the O.M. Harrington House, and considered his words. Would she be running to New York—the city that never sleeps? The city with its quaint horse-drawn carriages in Central Park, the Tavern on the Green, Statue of Liberty, Empire State Building, the subway, Rockefeller Center. Weren't they wonderful places to see? Wonderful places to go? Wonderful places to become a part of? And what about her new and promising career?

Or would she really be running away from Amber Leaf?

CHAPTER THREE

Jo jumped when the telephone rang. It was Friday morning. Precisely ten minutes before eleven. She needed to buy a little more time, just a few more hours, to make sure she was making the right no-turning-back life-changing decision. Inhaling a deep breath, she picked up the receiver.

"How soon can you get here?" Shirley asked without so much as a hello.

"I need a little more time, Shirl. I promise I'll call you back immediately after the Good Friday Service."

At eleven o'clock, Jo tugged bobby pins from her hair and prompted Brue to get ready. In keeping with the colorless designs of a world devastated by war, where everyone made the best of what they had, Jo slipped on her black tea-length skirt and conservative square-shouldered ivory jacket. Somehow it didn't look or feel quite right. She riffled through her closet and stumbled upon an old blouse that had seen better days. She plucked off its rhinestone buttons. Moments later, she donned a lovely new jacket, confident that no one would see the safety pins holding the swapped rhinestone buttons in place.

Stepping up on her tiptoes, she caught her reflection in the mirror high above the kitchen sink and ran a brush through her chocolate shoulder-length hair. She was painstakingly positioning an ivory felt beret asymmetrically at the side of her hair when Brue bounded in.

"How does this look, Mom?"

"Turn around. Let me see all of you." Jo retied the sash in the back of Brue's dress. Wearing a black sweater, patent leather shoes, and gloves, Brue's knee high socks barely offset the white collar trimming her charcoal woolen dress. "You look absolutely lovely," Jo said.

She pushed up on her tiptoes one last time to catch her reflection, pinching her fair cheeks for a little added color. She tugged on long black gloves, then turned and stared at her handbag before reluctantly picking it up and heading out the door. She always looked forward to attending Village Church, but not today. Everything felt surreal. If this wasn't Good Friday, she might have given serious thought to staying home. If she did decide to move to New York, that charming small house of worship would be the one place in Amber Leaf she would miss most of all.

At a quarter to twelve, Jo and Brue walked the winding, shade-mottled paths through Harrington Park. Village Church sat on a small hill immediately bordering the south side of the park. Jo slipped her arm around Brue's shoulder—under today's uncertain circumstances, that was more of an instinctive gesture to seek support than to guide. They slowed down for the last few steps, walking in sync as they gazed up at the bell tolling somberly in the belfry.

She and Brue settled in on the same wooden pew where they always sat, fourth row from the front, far right side. As they exchanged pleasant smiles and handshakes with those sitting around them, it occurred to Jo just how important these warm and kind parishioners were to her.

In his capacity as elder, Big Ole approached the lectern. The congregation settled down, but not Jo. His words the day before yesterday comparing his life's situation to hers still troubled her. He forgave a negligent doctor for his wife's death, and Jo forgave Tryg for Case's death. But Big Ole Harrington shared a long and full life with his bride while Jo's marriage was sliced short by decades. *And Ole thinks I might have more to forgive? Forgive Tryg Howland for prospering?* Jo reached forward and placed her church bulletin in the hymnal bookrack, wondering for a fleeting moment if Big Ole was right.

When he subtly raised his huge hands for the congregation to stand and they all joined in the a cappella singing of the Doxology, a wave of goose bumps fluttered Jo's heart and prickled her flesh, beginning at the nape of her neck and descending all the way down to her toes. When the congregation was seated, the organ resounded and he alone sang *When I Survey the Wondrous Cross*. His baritone voice, so deep and resonant, sounded as if it were booming straight from the majestic gates of heaven—fairly apropos for a Good Friday service. As he sang, Jo was struck by how strong and genuine their bond was and how through their turbulent relationship he'd jarred her into feeling again. The memories they made these past months cut stress fractures across her heart like a five hundred piece jigsaw puzzle.

Big Ole returned to his pew.

After a thoughtful moment of reverent silence, Tryg stepped up to the lectern to read the scriptures. Striking sable hair combed to perfection. Height on the tall side of medium. Well dressed in a black pinstripe suit and gray vest with a sheeny silver handkerchief protruding from his coat pocket. The light from the narrow windows reflected cleanly off his wire-rimmed glasses, which only added to his intimidating, bigger than life demeanor. He exuded intellectual confidence, his brown eyes looking at the world with sharp attention. He was a born leader and every bit as commanding as Big Ole Harrington, but in a quiet sort of way.

Jo watched him open his Bible. Big Ole was right about one thing. She had issues with Tryg. While he had a career, she had a job. While he basked in riches, she floundered in poverty. While he moved forward with his life, she felt mired in a dead-end existence.

At that precise moment she knew what she needed to do. She slipped off her gloves, folded them neatly onto her lap, and wrapped her arm around Brue, drawing her close. Jo's breathing relaxed. She finally felt at peace.

She and Brue were moving to New York. Jo will make her own way and join ranks with the Trygve W. Howlands of this world if it is the last thing she ever does. She will be a lady and dress her daughter in fine clothes and one day return to Amber Leaf as a genuine success.

Tryg asked the congregation to stand. As he read, an instant and inexplicable ripple of weakness worked its way through her, beginning at her feet, threatening to buckle her knees as it rose upward. She quickly righted herself, standing ramrod straight, then inhaled a deep breath, forcing herself to maintain her composure. This is no time for second thoughts. No turning back. Not now.

Immediately following the scripture reading, Tryg returned to his pew farther back in the sanctuary, and Pastor Calvin Doherty approached the lectern. Jo smiled inwardly. He may be Pastor Doherty to the congregation, but after getting to know him so well during their days at the O.M. Harrington, he will always be Calvin to her.

He opened his Bible and said, "Mr. Howland read about Christ's crucifixion from the twenty-seventh chapter of the book of Matthew. I want to concentrate on five of those verses, verses fifty through fifty-four. Follow along with me in your Bibles if you would, please."

Calvin paused as if to collect his thoughts and then continued. "Jesus, when he had cried again with a loud voice, yielded up the ghost. And, behold, the veil of the temple was rent in twain from the top to the bottom; and the earth did quake, and the rocks rent; And the graves were opened; and many bodies of the saints which slept arose, And came out of the graves after his resurrection, and went into the holy city, and appeared unto many. Now when the centurion, and they that were with him, watching Jesus, saw the earthquake, and those things that were done, they feared greatly, saying, Truly this was the Son of God."

Calvin gripped the sides of the lectern and his expression grew increasingly sober. "Imagine with me for a moment what it must have been like to be there. To actually experience Christ's crucifixion. Can you feel the violent shaking? Hear the rocks breaking? See the saints swirling up out of their graves? Now imagine your intensity of fear if you realized you'd just mocked, scoffed, flogged, struck, spat upon, and then crucified Jesus, only to learn that He is the true Son of God."

Jo sat dumbstruck, losing herself in thought as she pondered Christ's death. From there she mused about her own husband's death, and the death of their life together. As Calvin continued his sermon, she drifted further into her own world of introspection. Her life in Amber Leaf was swiftly coming to an end with a new life about to begin. She glanced about and memorized the sounds and smells and sights she never wanted to forget. The robust pipes of the organ that vibrated the pews. That nostalgic hint of musty wood and burnt candle wax permeating the sanctuary. Specks of dust dancing on the sun's rays pouring through the tall and narrow stained-glass windows. Will she find a church in New York City anywhere near as quaint as this one? She only hoped as much.

At the end of his sermon, Calvin lifted his hand and recited a closing blessing over the congregation. Jo then turned to Brue and quickly swept her away by the shoulder, out the door and down the narrow sidewalk. This was not a day for making small talk. They needed to get home. She had a phone call to make.

CHAPTER FOUR

B ye, Mom."

Brue marched off to her last day at Ramsey School look-ing the way Jo felt—apprehensive to leave the warmth of the familiar, and at the same time excited to experience the wonders of a brand new world.

Jo got a call in the early afternoon and strolled over to the O.M. Harrington to pick up her final paycheck. She dawdled beneath the blotchy shade of leafing maples, elms, and oaks peppering Harrington Park. Too bad the sun didn't shine brightly enough to burn off her jitters.

She crossed River Lane then continued on along a path that cut through a well-manicured lawn and perfectly trimmed hedges. Pausing for a moment, she stared up at the grand O.M. Harrington House peer-ing back at her. How she would miss this place. The replica of a posh Victorian-style farmhouse, it had imposing white columns, balustrades, cupolas, and multi-paned windows, with a wide wooden porch wrap-ping around its front and sides. The porch was trimmed with hanging flower baskets and potted plants, and was furnished with rocking chairs and a swing just large enough for two. Feeling an unmistakable nip of sorrow, Jo drew in a dizzying breath of fresh spring air before opening its front door. She slipped inside and looked around. The great room was emptied of life. Quiet. No one in sight.

Dying embers in the fireplace. A magazine folded open on a settee with no one to read it. Two abandoned decks of cards and a cribbage board sitting askew on the game table in front of the bay window. How many times did Big Ole play cribbage there with his friends? She let out a slow sigh. Saying goodbye to him and to the O.M. Harrington ripped at her heart. What a shame the only direction from the absolute best is down. Those days in this place will never be recreated.

"Jo, is that you?"

Jo wheeled around toward the sound of the familiar feminine voice. "Sarah! I didn't see you when I came in."

"I was in the back room," Sarah Harrington replied, her smile as soft and pleasant as her deep Lauren Bacall voice. Her auburn hair bounced softly around her shoulders as she approached the registration desk. Her eyes, the color of blueberries and framed by sweeping lashes, exuded warmth.

"Where is everyone this afternoon?" Jo asked.

"Our chef hosted a gourmet cooking class over the noon hour. You know how it goes. Everyone ate too much. They're all probably sleeping it off."

"He does lay out a nice spread."

"I know. Too bad we're so low on coffee." Sarah smiled. "There's nothing like a strong dose of caffeine to keep everyone awake. So what brings you in today?"

"I'm here to pick up my paycheck," Jo said, a hard lump rising in her throat.

Sarah's countenance changed. "You'll find the bookkeeper in the back room," she said, emotion noticeably absent from her tone.

Jo glanced up at her for a disappointed moment, then slipped past the registration desk and opened the door of a room she never entered before. The instant the door swung open, a thunderous chorus of "Surprise!" flooded the great room as a crowd burst through the door and surrounded her.

And Jo burst into tears.

An hour later, she walked out with her paycheck in hand, an envelope stuffed thick with dollar bills from her friends at the O.M. Harrington, and thoroughly swollen eyes. Brue stopped home from school long enough to get her pajamas for one last sleepover with her friends, but Jo did not look up. She wasn't about to let her little girl see what the last minutes before moving had done to her. She fastened her attention on packing their suitcases and preparing the house for an extended absence as the hours too quickly passed by.

In the early evening, Jo jumped when she heard a familiar rat-a-tat-tat at her front door.

No. Not after all this time. Not him.

Apprehension clawed at the walls of her insides. She froze for a moment and gathered her senses, then quickly plunged her arms through the sleeves of her burgundy sweater. After a shallow attempt at a deep breath, she stepped out into the cold and dark of the front porch.

There he stood. Tryg Howland. With arms crossed over his tweed blazer, he appeared nonchalant leaning against the wooden railing. Gazing, no doubt, at the negligible ripples shimmering in the soft moonlight on Amber Leaf Lake.

Jo lifted her chin. "Hello."

Tryg straightened in slow motion and turned toward her. "Jo," he said, his tone sounding more like an acknowledgement than a greeting.

"You're welcome to come in if you'd like."

Although she held the door, he waited for her to go in first and then followed close behind. She led the way toward her small kitchen and, glancing back at him, said, "Your timing is pretty good. Brue and I are leaving for New York tomorrow."

"I know," he said matter-of-factly. "And I'm afraid my timing really isn't that great at all. I planned this visit."

"You did?"

"Yes, ma'am. By the look on your face, I get the impression that doesn't please you."

Jo said nothing.

"I was invited to your party," he continued, "but I decided I wanted to see you privately instead."

"I see. Would you care for anything? A cup of tea maybe? We're planning to make a quick trip back in a few months for a final yard sale, so I still have plenty of cups and saucers around."

He nodded, then eased a chair away from the table. While Jo fired up the stove, Tryg's intense eyes scanned the kitchen, everywhere from the ceiling to the chipped cupboards to the floral-papered walls and on to the well-worn linoleum. Looking every bit as uncomfortable as she felt, he didn't breathe a word. *Why did you bother to stop by if you aren't going to say anything?* Jo wondered. Fortunately, the teakettle whistled, bringing life to the awkward silence.

She emptied the spitting water into her teapot, then dangled a couple of teabags from the top to seep. "How strong do you like it?"

"Weak. That should do it for me."

Jo poured a cup and placed it on the table in front of him. "Careful. It's awfully hot."

He seized the handle, but rather than lifting it, he appeared to be entertaining himself by drawing circles on the surface of the table with the base of the porcelain cup, staring at the steam spiraling into oblivion.

Jo pulled a chair back at the head of the table. "Forgive me for saying this, but you look like you're someplace else...either that, or you'd like to be."

"No," he said softly, cutting a half smile, "not at all. I guess I'm feeling a little overwhelmed."

"Really? Why's that?"

"The last time I was here, so was Case."

The air whooshed out of Jo's lungs as she noticed the color had drained from Tryg's face. She then looked away, flashing on the night

Tryg and Case made plans to join the Airborne. Since that conversation started right here in this very room, she immediately changed the subject.

"So you were invited to my party, huh?" she said, a tremble splintering her voice.

"That's right, I was." Tryg lifted his cup, swirling the hot liquid for a moment. "What's in New York, Jo?"

"Case's dream," she said, suddenly noticing that she'd just done it again—she didn't say *my* dream or *our* dream. She removed the bags from the teapot and absently set them on her saucer. "I've saved enough to cover our expenses for a few months. If I decide I don't care for my new job or if Brue and I find we're not happy in New York, we can always move back to Amber Leaf."

"Well, if you run into any problems," he said, and then he stopped and broke into an impish grin, "or if you find yourself needing a good lawyer—you know I'm just a telegram away. And let me know if you run into any unexpected financial troubles."

Jo was taken aback. "No, I—"

"If you need anything at all, I'm here for you. I'm adamant about that."

The strength in his voice told Jo that fighting him would be a losing battle.

Tryg stayed long enough to finish his tea. The moment the screen door squeaked closed behind him, Jo went to the living room window, where she pulled back the drape to watch him drive away. But he did not drive. He was walking up the gravel road. Then Jo remembered. No wonder. He hadn't driven since the accident.

When she returned to the kitchen to wash the cups, a white envelope sitting on the table with her name handwritten in perfect penmanship drew her attention. *How did he slip that here without my noticing?* she wondered. She picked it up and slowly sliced it open.

Inside she found a hundred-dollar bill with a simple note that read *Compliments of T. W. "Tryg" Howland, III, Attorney-at-Law.*

"Oh, Tryg. What are trying to do to me?"

CHAPTER FIVE

P lease tell me you're having second thoughts," Evelyn Tomlinson said. "It's not too late to change your mind, you know."

Jo's best friend was older than her by a good ten years. She was slim with short, curly hair the shade of burnt toast. Through Evelyn's wire-rimmed glasses, Jo saw that her eyelids were swollen from her earlier rush of tears; the redness still markedly present around her olive green eyes. At least the dear woman wasn't crying anymore.

"No second thoughts. Not anymore. Feels kind of exciting. Like the first day of school. I don't know about Brue, though." Jo gave her daughter a hasty glance and lightly tousled her hair. "She's been moving around pretty slowly this morning. Haven't you, sweetheart?"

Brue nodded without looking up.

"I don't think she got enough sleep last night," Jo said. "Her slumber party must have done her in."

Jo's life in Amber Leaf now behind her, she was the last to step out onto the front stoop. She pulled the door closed, purposely not looking up at it. She slipped the skeleton key into the keyhole, turned it, then pulled it out, not bothering to look past it. She listened to her footsteps pounding down the hollow wooden stairs one last time, but readily dismissed it.

She pivoted into the uncharacteristically warm April morning sun.

It bathed her cheeks as she and Evelyn hoisted the two heavy suitcases, first one and then the other, into the trunk of Evelyn's Hudson.

Brue climbed onto the running board and crawled into the back seat. Jo got in front, anxious to have the Amber Leaf chapter of her life well behind her.

"Are you sure you have everything?" Evelyn asked.

"I hope so. I got up in the middle of the night and checked and rechecked to make sure I packed all the clothes and toiletries we'll be needing for the next few months. Did some serious thinking, too."

"What about?"

"Big Ole's words."

"Big Ole's words?" Evelyn repeated.

"Yes, ma'am. He asked me the other day if I was running to New York or away from Amber Leaf. At first I wondered how I or anyone else for that matter possibly knows if they are running to or running from anything. And if I were running away, what's wrong with that? If a barking hound ran toward me, I'd hightail it out of there."

"Any sane person would, Jo. "

"I know. Crazed animals can be rabid. No. Brue and I are doing the right thing. It's taken a while, but I'm sure of myself now."

"Really?"

"Yes, really. Don't you believe me?"

"I'm not sure. Do you realize that you haven't so much as given your house one last look?"

"So that's it," Jo said, feeling more defensive than she cared to admit. "It's not like there isn't any pain associated with that house."

Evelyn flashed Jo a hard look. "Yes, but you certainly had your share of good memories there, too."

Jo offered a labored smile. "You're right." She swiveled around and glanced at the aging house behind them that cozied up against the gravel road. There had been many good memories there. Maybe too many. She glanced back at the park and then at the O.M. Harrington as they motored on. "Big Ole's been awfully good to me these past months," she said, craning her neck for a final look at the boarding house. "I feel kind of bad about leaving him in a lurch."

"You haven't left them in a lurch."

"I haven't?"

"Oh my, no," Evelyn answered far too brightly. "He turned your work over to some guy's laundry outfit uptown. I think the man's name is Ernie Pritchard."

Jo gasped. "He what?"

"I said—"

"I heard what you said. Boy, and to think the bed sheets haven't even cooled yet."

"You wouldn't be having hurt feelings now, would you?" Evelyn asked with a chuckle and a sniff. "After all, you're the one leaving us, remember?"

"You're right. I'm sorry. I guess maybe I am being a little silly. It's just that—"

"I know." Evelyn's tone turned serious. "Jo? What if you don't like New York? I mean, what if you're miserable there?"

"Then my whole world will come crashing in on me," Jo stated matter-of-factly. "It's not like that hasn't happened before."

"But at least here you had your friends to help you through it."

"Evelyn, I know you mean well, but what can I do? Brue and I have little to no life here without Case. Look at me. I've been taking in laundry while Tryg is—" Jo caught herself, wishing she hadn't said that.

"Tryg is what?" Looking straight ahead, Evelyn nervously massaged the steering wheel. "Doing great with his new law practice? Near as I can tell that isn't cutting it for him."

"What do you mean? Why not?"

"Come on, Jo," Evelyn fired back. "Does he look like a happy man to you? I'm surprised his lady friend hasn't been able to bring back a brighter spark."

"His lady friend?"

"Yup." Evelyn glanced at Jo, surprised. "You didn't know about her? She's someone he met some time back at a—"

Jo watched as Evelyn's lips moved, but did not hear the words coming through them. Tryg had a flourishing new law practice, the warmth of companionship, and the excitement of a budding relationship that was undoubtedly serious. He never was one to do things halfheartedly.

Evelyn cranked down her window and rested her elbow on the window frame. "What a beautiful day for a train ride."

"The day is gorgeous," Jo conceded. Fruit trees frosted with white and pink blossoms; a dry, sweet, and gentle breeze; the bright sun floating above the heavens on a cloudless blue sky. No more sooty patches of ice. Lawns filled in nicely with delicate blades of young tender grass. Yes, a beautiful day for a train ride, but a day for traveling to, not from.

Evelyn turned right on Broadway, crossed the railroad tracks, then made a quick left onto a small dirt road and into the parking lot adjacent to the tracks. "We're here," she announced, her voice cracking something awful. "I m-miss you already and you aren't even g-gone."

Jo succumbed to silence as she slipped out of the car. She swallowed against a lump the size of a golf ball pushing up into her throat. Why did Evelyn insist on making this so difficult?

They entered the crush of people inside the depot, Evelyn and Jo each lugging a suitcase with Brue lagging a good distance behind. Jo plunked her luggage on the floor, double-checked her tickets, and then glanced at Evelyn. "You really don't need to wait with us if you don't want. This is going to take a while. Why make this any harder than it needs to be?"

"I have to wait. You haven't forgotten that servicemen get priority, have you? You may not even get on this train." Evelyn glanced around the station. "Why don't we wait over there by that far wall?"

Jo and Evelyn hauled the luggage to the bench with Brue again lagging behind. "Okay. I'll get our tickets." Jo glanced at the long line at the ticket counter. She patted Brue lightly on her shoulder and said distract-edly, and again without taking a good look at her, "Brue, you wait with Evelyn. I'll be back before too long."

When Jo returned with their tickets in hand, she sandwiched her-self on the bench between Evelyn and Brue. Brue immediately cuddled up to her, burying her head deep into Jo's shoulder. Something did not feel right. Jo finally took a serious look at her daughter. "Lift your face, sweetie." It was then that she noticed Brue's watery eyes and hot pink cheeks. She lightly pressed her hand against Brue's forehead, realization descending on her like a scourge.

Before Jo cried, *she has a fever*, Evelyn crouched down in front of Brue. "Oh dear, I hope she isn't coming down with the measles." Evelyn stroked the back of her fingers lightly against Brue's cheek. "Maybe the rumor I heard is true."

"What rumor?"

"They're having a measles outbreak at school," Evelyn said, stone-faced.

"Oh no!" Jo cradled Brue lovingly in her arms, touching her cheek against Brue's blond hair. "Now what are we going to do?"

"What can you do?" Evelyn asked.

"Well, we certainly won't be making a trip to New York today," Jo said, alarm emanating through her voice. She asked a sympathetic-look-ing stranger to keep an eye on her suitcase and then half walked and half carried little Brue back through the depot's front door. After getting Brue situated in the backseat of the Hudson, Jo quickly returned to the station. She retrieved her suitcase, then took her place at the end of the ticket line eight people long, her insides writhing with consternation.

CHAPTER SIX

M om?" Brue asked through a tired and worn-down cough.

"Yes, dear?"

"Would you mind opening the shade for a minute? I wanna see what measles look like."

After three days in a darkened back room with shade and drapes drawn, sponge baths too numerous to count, and plenty of fluids, a rash set in on Brue with a vengeance. Weary from her vigil yet relieved that Brue entered the second phase of the measles quickly, Jo let out a ragged breath. The measles setback sent her into a tailspin fighting hard against time. They needed to get to New York.

"Curiosity's gotten the best of you, has it?" Jo worked her way around the foot of the double bed. "If I were you, I think I'd want to take a peek at them, too. You might want to close your eyes, though. It's going to be awfully bright after being in a dark room so long."

Jo gently drew back the drapes and rolled the shade a quarter of the way up the window, subtly brightening the room. Brue recoiled and quickly turned away from the harsh light.

"Whoa! It's even too bright for me," Jo said incredulously.

The instant Brue's eyes adjusted, she pulled herself up in bed and twisted and turned her arms and legs, thoroughly inspecting them from every angle imaginable.

"Look," she said, lifting her pajamas for a good gander at her stomach. "It looks like someone splattered a bucket of pink paint all over me." She quivered as she touched it. "It kinda itches, Mom."

"I know, sweetheart, but try not to scratch it. I don't want you breaking your skin and getting scars. You need to be careful."

Brue nestled back under the covers. "Mom?"

"Yes, dear?"

"Are we still gonna go to New York?"

"Do you still want to go?"

Brue nodded.

"Good. You bet we will. Just as soon as you get better. Maybe we can take off sometime later next week." Jo felt a smile blossom as she folded Brue's covers gently under her chin and smoothed her cheek with the back of her hand. "Are you hungry? Want anything?"

"Hunh-uh."

"Okay. If it's all right with you then, I better get back to work."

"What kind of work?"

"I've got to finish getting things ready for a rummage sale. We're not going to have much time when we come back to sell the house and all of the stuff left in it."

Closing Brue's door quietly behind her, Jo pulled an empty box up to the cupboards and went to work packing the last of the bowls, pots, and pans. Although her back needed a healthy dose of liniment from hauling a stream of heavy boxes to the back porch, she didn't care. She was too busy daydreaming about what life was going to be like in the big city. Spurred on by her happy pursuit, she kept right on working.

In the early afternoon, Jo tripped over a crate box trying to get to the phone before it stopped ringing.

"I'm calling for a Mrs. Jo Bremley," the woman said, her voice highly professional.

"This is Jo."

"Mrs. Bremley, I'm Mrs. Masters calling from JD Barrister's in New York."

Jo's heart fluttered as she grinned into the phone. "How nice to meet you over the wires, Mrs. Masters. Brue and I are really looking forward to our move. We can't wait to get there. Her fever's broken now, so it looks like we should be able to catch a train sometime later next week."

"That's what I'm calling you about," Mrs. Masters said in a regret-filled voice. "You see, we really did need the help immediately. I'm sorry, but one of our other employees is doing such a wonderful job of filling in and just yesterday she requested…"

Jo stumbled back. Dizzied by the awful news, she caught her weight against the wall. Now what was she going to do?

She stuffed her hands into her apron pockets, sauntered to the kitchen window, and stared broodingly out toward Amber Leaf Lake. The sunless sky was as dull and gray and undefined as her unhopeful mood. She rested her forehead against the pane. She thought about Case, closed her eyes and hugged herself. How she needed him. If only he were here. How many countless times had he stepped up behind her right here in this very spot? Slipping his arms around her waist. His chin on her shoulder as together they soaked in the beautiful view of the lake. She gazed at the slim three-wire fence stretching across the perimeter of the backyard, slicing a thin barrier between the yard and the wheat-colored marsh, and then at the clusters of cattails poking up here and there like dandelions sprouting on a neglected lawn. She shook her head. At least she would not be losing this view now.

Jo retreated to Brue's bedroom where she reluctantly delivered the unfavorable news. Bless Brue's heart. She reached for Jo's hand, playing lightly with Jo's fingers. "Are you gonna go back to work at the O.M. Harrington House then, Mom?"

"I'm not sure what I'm going to do yet. But I don't want you worrying your pretty little head about it. You just get better, okay? Everything is going to be just fine."

But Jo was worried—worried sick.

She thought about Ernie Pritchard and how, according to Evelyn, he was doing a fabulous job for the O.M. Harrington. That man must have started the rumor himself, Jo decided. After all, he only did the work for a little over a week, for crying out loud.

Come on, Jo. That isn't kind. You were the one who decided to quit.

Now what, though? Try to get a job at Mr. Pritchard's laundry outfit? Be away from home? And at even less pay than before?

How about going down to Des Moines? Getting a job making munitions at that Iowa Ordnance Plant? But the war might be ending soon. Then what?

Every day she needed to comb the help-wanted ads, but it was going to be next to impossible to find a position for someone with her glaring lack of skills. If push came to shove, she might get a job cleaning or helping out in a nursing facility. But that would keep her away from home and the pay would be minimal.

She drew the drapes, kissed Brue on her forehead, and lovingly tapped her nose. "Time for you to get more rest."

Stepping out of Brue's bedroom, Jo rested her hand on the doorknob for a moment, thinking. As soon as Brue was well enough to go back to school, Jo needed to devote greater than full time to finding the best position available. At the moment, with little control over finding a job, she needed to assess her staples.

She descended the steps into the cold, dank, dimly-lit root cellar and took a look around. The musty odor of moist air gone bad assaulted her nostrils as she dug her way through the potatoes. They were definitely getting low. She counted the Mason jars of canned fruits and vegetables. Seven jars of peaches, six of plums, two of rhubarb, twelve of applesauce, eight of tomatoes, and only three of string beans. Barely enough to last through the spring. At least her three jars of peach and two jars of straw-berry jam would last a while. But what was she going to do during the early days of summer before her victory garden had a chance to grow?

She plodded back up the basement stairs and riffled through the pantry. Unfortunately, the canned goods were running low, especially soup. She needed more flour, too.

She then went to her bedroom and recounted her money. Knowing to the penny how much she had, she counted it one more time just to ease her troubled mind. Setting aside the hundred-dollar bill that needed to go back to Tryg now that they weren't making the move, she sighed. If nothing unforeseen happened, she might have enough cash to last until summer, but that would be a stretch.

As Jo sat on her bed considering her plight, Brue's faint cough car-ried from the back room. Jo buried her head in her hands, torn between fretting over the health of her young daughter and cursing the inoppor-tune time to be chained to the house. Jo wanted a job. She wanted hard cash. But for now her fatherless little girl was terribly sick and needed her desperately.

Jo tucked her money away in the far back corner of her empty bot-tom dresser drawer. She thought about that trip to New York, griev-ing over how long it would take to save up enough money now. When the war was over and Shirley's husband came home, Jo and Brue would no longer be able to stay with them. Their apartment was too small. Besides, they needed their privacy. Jo would need to find a place of her own. She thought about Brue's nod when Jo asked if she still wanted to go to New York. And she thought about fulfilling Case's dream, which during this past week had finally grown into her dream as well. Then she looked at the empty bottom drawer and remembered the boxes stashed away on the back porch.

Time to unpack.

CHAPTER SEVEN

Rain pelted hard against the living room windows as if knocking to come in. Jo shivered and reached for her crocheted shoulderette. In the early evening darkness, the wind gained strength, blowing stronger now. But not strong enough to make a loud racket. She listened closer, suddenly recognizing the familiar rat-a-tat-tatting on the screen door that once again rattled her insides.

She cracked open the door to the front porch and in a strong voice warned, "I'm sorry, but Brue has the measles, and we're still in the infectious period. I'm afraid you're not going to want to come in."

Tryg threw open the door and barged in, dripping wet. "That's not a problem. I'm immune. Had the measles when I was a kid, too."

Jo didn't need to invite him in. He was already there. What was he thinking? She wasn't presentable. The last time she ran a comb through her hair was early this morning. Not a hint of makeup on. Her apron still smelled of mildew from the cellar. Why on earth would she want uninvited company? *But what can I do?* she wondered as his assuming demeanor got the best of her.

"Brrr! It sure is chilly out there." He slipped off his raincoat and galoshes. "I'll leave these here in the porch if that's okay with you. How about offering me something hot to warm my innards?"

Jo backed into the living room reluctantly.

He stole past her and led the way into the kitchen at a strong clip. "Sure smells good in here."

A hint of vanilla and cinnamon from her bread pudding still lingered in the air. All day long it had been cold and gray with a steady and even drizzling of rain—an ideal day for lighting up the oven. It wouldn't take long now for the warm weather to settle in. With it would come suffocating humidity, fierce thunderstorms and tornadoes, and, living near the lake, the usual invasion of pesky mosquitoes. Not good days to heat up an oven. For supper, Jo prepared Brue's favorite meal—scalloped potato soup and bread pudding. She finished the dishes then wiped her hands on her apron. She checked in on Brue and retreated to the living room. The night was ideal for cozying up with a good magazine. Not ideal for sharing a hot cup of anything with Tryg Howland.

"Can I help you fire up the stove?" he asked.

What happened to this man all of a sudden? He wasn't this assertive the last time he stepped inside her home. Nowhere near it. Whatever was going on, Jo felt restless. Pent up. Stuck. Longing to just be alone. "That's all right. I can get it. Would you prefer tea this late in the evening?"

"Tea would be fine."

Tea would be fine. Tea would be fine.

Tryg helped himself to a chair by the kitchen table. "How's Brue doing?" he asked, looking as though he cared deeply.

"The rash set in yesterday. It's pretty bad." Jo lifted the lid from the kettle to check the water level. Not only was the water still warm, there should be plenty to fill a teapot. As she lowered the lid, the air in her lungs stopped moving. This was the second time in a short window of time that she was lighting up the stove for Tryg. The feeling was too familiar, too much like all of those nights when she fired up the stove for Case. Jo quickly shook off the thought. "Brue feels miserable, and I'm afraid it's going to last awhile. I hate seeing her like this."

"You're right. I remember those days only too well. It does feel miserable." He leaned back in his chair and softened his voice. "And how about you? How are you doing?"

Jo turned the knob on the stove, but nothing happened. "Pilot light's out." She lit a match and held flame to the burner until it caught fire. Turning the knob to the high setting, she stopped. "Wait just a minute. Back up. How did you know about Brue? And how did you know we'd still be here?"

"Oh, that," he said indifferently. "I ran into Calvin Doherty up at The Copper Kettle earlier today. He heard all about it from Big Ole who heard all about it from Evelyn Tomlinson, who I understand has been shuffling her work schedule around to help you out."

A painful lump seized Jo's throat and she turned away. Of course. Evelyn. That made sense. She cared. Everyone cared.

"How about you?" Jo asked. "How are you doing? How's the business going?"

"That's why I'm here."

Jo's back wrenched straight. Why did he say that? She glanced at him then looked away equally as fast. The teakettle whistled giving her a chance to quickly regain control of her dubious thoughts. She lifted the kettle and made her way to the table. "What do you mean?"

"You need a job."

Jo nearly dropped the teakettle. For a moment her thinking froze. Of course she needed a job. Still holding the steaming kettle, she lifted the lid off the pot.

"I heard Big Ole signed a contract with Ernie Pritchard," Tryg said, thrumming his fingers against her table, "so it looks like you won't get your old job back. Ernie might hire you, but why would you want to do that?" Tryg hesitated, and then in a no-nonsense manner, he said, "Look at me, Jo."

The air seizing her lungs, she reluctantly turned to meet his gaze.

"I want you to come and work for me," he said. "Business has been picking up lately, so I'm looking for extra help."

Jo stared at him, numb, watching his lips move while the beating of her heart accelerated.

"You'll be doing the bookkeeping, interacting with vendors, that sort of thing," he said, his smile sober, his tone authoritative, as if she'd already said yes. That bothered her. Felt a bit too presumptuous on his part.

"The day Brue goes back to school," he continued, "you show up at my office. We work nine to five. No breaks. An hour at noon for a bite to eat. Take your time thinking about it. No need to get back to me. Just be there when it's convenient."

Tryg stood. "I guess I'm not all that up for tea after all," he said, his chair scraping loudly against the linoleum. "Sorry to have put you to the trouble."

"Let me—"

"No need to see me to the door," he said. But the smile on his lips fell short of his eyes. "Look forward to seeing you soon." He left, leaving Jo standing in the kitchen in a daze.

She reached for the back of her chair, holding it. Something did not feel right. Why would Tryg want to hire her? Someone with no office experience whatsoever? If it was pity he felt, he needed to get past that himself. She wanted no part of it. If he felt responsible for her wellbeing, he needed to get past that, too. But what if it was to pacify his guilt over Case? Now that would be something entirely different. That would not be right. He had everything except a thriving sense of peace—peace about Case and the life Tryg ripped away from him. And undoubtedly all Tryg needed to achieve that peace would be for Jo to willingly place herself under his rule. He takes care of her, his conscience is cleared, and he has it all.

She clutched her stomach, her heartfelt compassion for him suddenly in serious decay. *No. He can't have it all. It would be a blistering hot day in Antarctica before I'd ever consider working for that man. And even then there's no way I can possibly say anything other than a gut-wrenching no. I can't do that to Case. I just can't.*

CHAPTER EIGHT

Jo arrived early, pulling up to the curb opposite the uptown law office on East William at ten minutes before nine. She straightened the seams in her rayon hose, took a nervous glance at her hair and lipstick in her rearview mirror, and then considered for a long-passing moment the possibility of one more drive around the block. Anything to eat up a few more skittish minutes.

Still reeling from last night's onerous decision, she glanced across the road. The shingle reading *T. W. "Tryg" Howland, III, Attorney-at-Law* looked eerily dark in the shadows, inundating her with a sense of uneasiness.

Tryg.

Jo sat in the early-morning cold, trying to make peace with unsettling questions and unconvincing motives. Was she deceiving herself? Was she making a mistake by caving in and accepting Tryg's job offer? Every day this past week she checked the want ads. Every day she found no jobs available for someone with her utter and complete lack of skills. And every day she made enough phone calls to businesses from the east side of town to the west to make the Operator wheeze at the sound of her voice. The only place Jo did not call was Wilson's. Touring it once left little question that working in a meat packing plant was not her life's calling. No, she hadn't made a mistake. Absolutely not. Not only was this the only job available to her, it also offered her the fastest path out of Amber Leaf. She needed to concentrate on being grateful to finally get a job. And it promised to be a good paying one at that. But yet the maddening question remained. By deciding to work for Tryg, was she compromising her loyalty to, and love for, Case?

Enough of that thinking.

She gave her watch another cursory glance. Three minutes before nine. She shivered in the confines of her car, her breath a light mist in the chilly morning shade. While she had been awake for hours antici-pating how this day might play out, the small Upper Midwestern town was only beginning to awaken. The sun peeking over the roofs of the two- and three-storied red, brown, and tan brick buildings had yet to bring warmth to the town's bustling sidewalks and streets.

At one minute before nine, a dark-haired woman unlocked the door to the pristine three-room office suite. Jo waited a courteous five extra minutes, then took a long and apprehensive walk across the forbidding street. The glass door beneath the shingle pushed open hard.

Once inside, Jo lifted her shoulders, pasted on a manufactured smile, then extended her hand and said, "Hello. I'm Mrs. Bremley. I'm here to see Mr. Howland."

"How nice to finally meet you. I'm Ardena," the unusually pleasant lady with maraschino cherry lipstick said. "Mr. Howland said you would be joining us."

He did?

"Please have a seat. He should be here any minute now."

Jo settled in a chair in the reception area feeling forlorn, more like a traitor than a new hire. She picked a copy of *The Saturday Evening Post* from the table beside her and fumbled through a few pages before dis-creetly stealing a peek at Ardena. She was definitely the young woman who poked her nose into The Copper Kettle last Christmas Eve day when Jo and Tryg had their first meeting since the accident. Ardena looked considerably older up close. Early-to-mid 40s, maybe. Quite attractive.

Warm. Friendly. Her square-shouldered burnt umber jacket, matching skirt, and ivory blouse beautifully offset her kind coffee-colored eyes.

And she worked for Tryg.

Jo shifted in her chair in a feeble attempt to make herself feel less on edge. She crossed her arms. She crossed her legs. She looked around the office. It looked and felt as sterile and cold as the last time she stopped by. Over time, a colored painting here and a potted plant there, though, might easily add a reasonable measure of warmth.

Ardena got up. "I'll be right back. Thought I'd get a fresh cup of Folgers from the back room. Would you care for some? It should be done perking by now."

"No, I'm fine, thank you," Jo said, then quickly reconsidered. "On second thought, that would be great."

Several minutes and a couple of sips later, the door swung open and Jo's coffee nearly launched from the pit of her stomach. Although Tryg walked past her unknowingly, Ardena caught his eye. He turned toward Jo, looking strangely taken aback.

That was odd.

Jo took a quick and long slide from feeling guilty for accepting the job to feeling embarrassed for doing the same. She recalled the night last week when Tryg stopped by and made the offer. Now that she thought about it, he left her home faster than he entered it. Maybe Jo misread him. Maybe he only made the offer because he felt it was the right thing to do.

"Morning," he said as he carefully hooked his coat on the clothes tree. "You've met Ardena, I take it?"

Jo nodded.

"Please. Come into my office."

Clearly Jo misread him. Not only did he adamantly refuse to take back the hundred-dollar bill he gave her as a going-away gift, by ten o'clock, she was sitting at her new desk poring through ledgers as though she'd been working at the law firm for months. And at one-thirty in the afternoon, she greeted her first new client when a wide-girthed Mrs. Henrietta Braddingly hobbled in on thick ankles. Her demeanor was as coarse as her salt and pepper hair. Plump jowls squared her deeply lined face, which only added to the harshness of her appearance. Jo quickly pulled out a chair on the far side of her desk to limit the distance the poor woman would have to walk. "Please, have a seat."

"I can get the chair myself," Mrs. Braddingly snapped.

"I'm sorry." Jo slowly drew back. "I didn't mean to—"

"Is Mr. Howland ready for me?"

Jo glanced up at the clock. "I'm sure he will be in just a few minutes."

"Well, I certainly hope so," she said with a scowl. "The last time I was in an attorney's office, I sat around and waited for half an hour before I even got in to see the man. You'd think I had all the time in the world."

Jo felt at a loss as to how to respond. But then the words, "You know, ma'am, your hair is the most beautiful shade of gray I've ever seen," rolled off her lips, and smoothly and easily at that. "And the texture. My! How fortunate you are to have such a healthy mane."

Mrs. Braddingly lifted her chin and, with the innocence of a child, she said, "Do you really think so?"

Jo smiled warmly. "Yes, I really do."

The woman's hardened eyes warmed and sparkled, her smile giving her cheeks a pleasant lift. "Thank you, young lady. How kind of you. I used to get compliments on my hair all the time, you know. Why, yours is the first I've gotten in ages."

Just then, Tryg's door swung open.

"Mrs. Braddingly," Jo said, "here's Mr. Howland now."

"Please, dear, feel free to call me Henrietta." She stood and doddered along with Tryg into his office.

The instant his door closed, Ardena said, "Oh my! You certainly handled that woman well."

"She isn't exactly the gentle type, is she?"

Ardena shook her head and grinned. "Not exactly. I noticed that too. I don't think I've ever seen anyone's demeanor change that fast. Didn't know it was possible."

"I got lucky. She's like a compliment-starved little girl."

"That was no luck," Ardena countered. "You knew what you were doing and you were sincere. You sanded her rough edges beautifully with just a few kind words. Too bad Tryg didn't get a chance to witness the transition."

Jo shook her head. "People do things because of who they are, Ardena, not because of who we are. She didn't show her stripes when she walked through the door; her stripes led the way, and she proudly waved them. It'll only be a matter of time before they show up again."

"She's an interesting study, isn't she?" Ardena said.

"Very. Interesting and enjoyable over the short term and at a distance. But over the long term and up close? I don't know." Jo returned to her work.

Much to her surprise, her first day on the job flew by quickly, and went far better than she hoped. Ardena appeared to be a wonderful office companion—helpful, warm, and kind, with a good sense of humor. Jo had familiarized herself with the company books, actually completed some of the billing, and gotten a good idea of what Tryg expected of her. After Mrs. Braddingly's meeting with him, even she chirped a cheery goodbye.

When the clock struck five, though, Tryg breezed out the door with a lively spring in his limping step and whistled a pleasant tune.

The same pleasant tune Case whistled during his happiest moments.

And Jo balked at her swiftly melting heart.

CHAPTER NINE

A few minutes before noon, Jo glanced out the window and up into a vast sea of gray.

"What do you say, Jo?" Ardena asked as if she read Jo's thoughts. "How about lunch at The Copper Kettle? We'll celebrate your new job. The office picks up the tab on this one."

Jo considered Ardena's request, albeit reluctantly. The rain piddling down all morning long only gnawed at her spirits, while a sinking feeling she made a slip-up by joining Tryg's firm weighed her down. Maybe lunch at The Copper Kettle would be exactly what she needed for an emotional lift—warm and pleasant ambience; polished oak counters, wooden tables and chairs, and small clusters of booths at its center; pleasant tunes resonating from its jukebox at the far wall. Just then the noon whistle blew signaling to the factory town that it was twelve o'clock straight up. Jo nodded. "Let's do it."

They grabbed their handbags and headed next door. A pack of lunchtime regulars pressed in hard behind them, nudging Jo and Ardena deep into the café. Jo didn't mind. The Copper Kettle offered a cozy refuge from the drizzle, and with the pleasant aroma of grilled onions floating on the air, she was happy to move in closer. That is, until she met the guarded gaze of an unusually attractive woman in her mid-to-late sixties seated at a table near the entry.

The guarded gaze aside, when the woman dipped to meet her food, Jo was taken not so much by her meticulous brown and graying hair, but by how neatly it was wrapped in a circular fashion at the top of her head.

The crowd pushed in harder and someone accidentally bumped Jo. She, in turn, bumped the older woman's arm. The woman flinched at Jo's unintentional slight.

"Pardon me," Jo said, but when the woman failed to respond, Jo dusted off the thought and returned her attention to finding a place to sit down. The tables, booths, and barstools were filled to capacity. From the jukebox across the room, Bing Crosby crooned, "On the Atchison, Topeka and the Santa Fe," but with the patter of rain, loud clatter of dishes, and buzzing conversations all about her, Jo scarcely made out the melody.

Ted, the genial owner of The Copper Kettle, approached Jo and Ardena with a quick smile, a preoccupied look, and two large menus. "Right this way, ladies." He led them toward the center of the restaurant. "You are very fortunate. You're hear in the nick of time. We only have one booth left." He placed the menus on the table and then backed away with an outstretched hand. "Your waitress will be with you shortly."

Rather than reading the menu, Ardena's eyes combed the restaurant as if she were looking for someone. "So what are we having for dinner?" she asked distractedly.

Jo scanned the menu, then set it aside. "I don't know about you, but I think I'm hungry for a bowl of vegetable beef soup and a side of coleslaw. Something warm to take off the chill."

"Hmm. That sounds good. I think I'll have the same."

"What are you looking at?" Jo asked.

Ardena nudged her menu toward the edge of the table as well. "Not what. Who. That Ted sure is a handsome guy, don't you think? Just look at him. Have you ever seen whiter, straighter teeth? A more masculine build? More gorgeous gray eyes? And his shirts are always snowy white and crisp."

Yes, as a matter of fact, I have, Jo thought. *On my husband.* "I guess I hadn't noticed. But isn't he a little on the young side?"

Ardena grinned. "For me, yes, but not for you."

Huh? "I don't think so," Jo said without hesitation. "I'm not interested in a relationship. Besides, he looked right past us anyway."

Ardena quickly craned her neck as though something or someone else caught her eye.

"Now what are you looking at?" Jo asked.

"Not what. Who."

Jo smiled to herself. *Not what. Who. Again.*

"There's a gentlemen a few tables away. I think he's trying to get your attention."

"My attention? Are you sure?" Jo turned to steal a quick look. "Well, for heaven's sake! It's Calvin Doherty."

A frazzled waitress appeared, blocking their nonverbal exchange. Jo felt tired just looking at her. The waitress plunked flatware, napkins, and two waters on their table. Drawing her pad from her apron pocket, she pulled a pencil from behind her ear, and every bit as quickly said, "What'll it be, ladies?"

"I'll have a bowl of your vegetable beef soup and a side of coleslaw," Jo said.

"Vegetable beef soup and side of coleslaw," the waitress repeated and then turned toward Ardena. "And how about you, ma'am?"

"I'll have the same, please."

As their waitress scrambled to the counter, Calvin Doherty stepped aside and let her pass before approaching Jo and Ardena's booth. He looked taller than his medium height. Sophisticated. Soft-spoken. Middle-aged with thinning dark hair flecked with gray at the temples.

"Afternoon!" he said.

"Afternoon," Jo echoed. "Seems strange seeing you here. Come to think of it, I don't think I've ever seen you anywhere besides the O.M. Harrington or Village Church."

"Change can be a good thing," he answered with a wry smile.

Jo glanced at Ardena and then back at Calvin. "Honestly! Where are my manners? Calvin, I'd like you to meet Ardena Okland. I work with her now in Tryg Howland's office. And, Ardena, this is Calvin Doherty, or should I say the *Reverend* Calvin Doherty. He recently took over the pastorate at Village Church."

"How nice to meet you." He hesitated, his dilated pupils exposing him. As he and Ardena tethered to one another's gazes, it was as though all of the sounds in the noisy restaurant quieted to the exaggerated thumping of their hearts.

"Nice to meet you, too," Ardena replied beneath her stolen breath.

Calvin quickly returned his attention to Jo. "I've got to get to visitation at the hospital. Just wanted to stop by and say hello on my way out. See you at church on Sunday, yes?"

"Absolutely. Brue and I wouldn't miss it."

He then turned to Ardena and smiled warmly. "Very nice meeting you."

After he was out of earshot, Jo grinned. "There was something uncharacteristically warm and receptive in the way he was responding to you," she said.

"You noticed that, too?"

"Absolutely."

"So what's his story? Is he married?"

"No, he's not. I used to work with him at the O.M. Harrington. He left there when he re-entered the ministry and assumed his new position at Village Church. I remember when I first met him. There was always a sadness about him."

"Any idea what that was all about? He looks fine now."

"Let's just say he spent a lot of years struggling with some personal issues that conflicted with his faith. He finally made peace with his Maker and now it's like he's a new person."

An unexpected and sudden upsurge of wind thrust the door open, drawing Jo's attention toward the entry. Tryg was hurrying in. A young man wearing an open-collared shirt and pleated pants followed at his heels. Something in the young man's troubled dark eyes did not feel right and much about him did not look right. Faded shirt with a large tear fraying near the shoulder. Wrinkles in his trousers more pronounced than the pleats. Clumps of dull brown hair sticking out every which way as if crying for a comb. Several days' growth of wiry whiskers. He looked uncomfortable and out of place and scanned The Copper Kettle as if he was looking for someone.

"Look at that," Ardena said.

"Look at what?"

"Do you see that attractive older lady, the one you bumped into earlier, the one whose hair looks like it's wrapped around a ring of summer sausage?"

"Ardena, that isn't kind," Jo said, unable to restrain a giggle.

"Neither is she. She just snubbed that poor guy who's pushing in behind Tryg."

Jo bit her lip, then leaned in with a grin and deliberately lowered her voice. "You wouldn't happen to be the kind of goody-goody who looks down on people who look down on people, now would you, Ardena?"

Ardena erupted with mirth until realization squeezed the life out of her laughter. Her face buckled. "Oh my. I guess I never thought about it in quite that way before."

"I'm sorry," Jo said apologetically. "But you are one of a large number. None of us ever think of it in quite that way, but all of us do it."

Ted approached Tryg with a menu in hand, turned, and searched the restaurant. *No room at the Inn.*

Ardena brightened. "Why don't we invite Tryg to join us?"

"Oh no." Jo forcefully pushed down a demanding gulp. "This booth is way too small," she said a bit too quickly. "Besides, it might be awkward, don't you think? I'm sure a table or a barstool will free up fast enough."

"You're probably right," Ardena said, sounding doubtful.

Jo ignored the pang of guilt tearing through her for her lack of generosity. After all, Tryg gave her a job. But she needed time. She needed to realign her feelings. She needed to pace herself.

"I wonder if Tryg will ever hook up with anyone," Ardena continued.

Jo's head snapped up. "I thought he was in a relationship."

"Not that I know of. He was, but that was some months ago. I haven't heard any more about it, so I assume they must have broken up."

Suddenly a shriek tore through the restaurant, silencing everyone and everything, including the clattering of dishes, until the panic seeped in. "Hey!" the lady with the meticulous brown and graying hair shouted. She leaped up and gaped at the door, vigorously shaking and pointing her finger. "He stole my handbag. That young man stole my handbag!"

The young man with the torn shirt and wrinkled trousers bolted past Tryg and out the door with the handbag clutched tightly beneath his arm.

Before the startled woman finished wailing, Tryg wheeled around and raced out onto East William. Through the window, the wind, and the piddling down rain, Jo watched him—a limping blur—sprinting after the thief.

A short while after Jo and Ardena got back to the office, Tryg drifted in. Not only did he let out an exhausted sigh, he was dripping wet and sporting a red and black and bluing eye coupled with a proud grin.

"What happened?" Jo blurted. "Sit down. Let me get some ice on that bruise before your eye swells."

Tryg pulled back, hand shooting up, palm flattened outward. "I'm okay, all right? Don't worry about it."

"Did you get the guy?" Ardena asked excitedly.

"Yeah, but not before he got in the first whack." Tryg's grin widened. "That was more fun than I've had in a long time. My military training finally came in good for something after all." He then swept his other hand from behind his back.

"You got the handbag, too!" Jo cried as he handed it to her.

"You wouldn't mind making sure it gets to its rightful owner, would you? I've carried that thing far enough." Tryg glanced at the clock. "I've got to get out of here. I'm running late and still need a bite to eat. I've got to get to the courthouse."

"But what about your eye?" Jo asked.

"It'll heal."

"Did you turn him into the police?" Ardena asked.

"I've got to get going."

"But did you turn him into the police?"

"No," he said matter-of-factly.

Ardena looked incredulous. "Why not?"

"I couldn't do that."

"But why not?" Ardena insisted.

"Because the poor guy was desperate for money to feed his hungry kids."

Jo listened to the clack of the closing door. Her lunch was threatening to back up on her. Playing hero was, without question, in Tryg's blood. It had always been in his blood. And he wore the role understatedly, the way Case wore it when they'd palled around together.

CHAPTER TEN

P lease tell me the flowers weren't stolen again," Ardena said as Jo hung her coat on the clothes tree.

"Again. From all eight pots."

"I can't imagine anybody stooping that low. Stealing flowers from a grave? That's unbelievable!"

Jo stopped at her desk, but remained standing. "I don't know either. This is the third time it's happened and it's only mid-April. Doesn't make any sense, does it?"

"No, it sure doesn't."

Jo picked up her pencil and mindlessly tapped its eraser against her desktop. She had a riddle to solve, but no idea where to begin. "Whoever is doing it is not consistent. Some of the geraniums are pulled out completely by the roots. Some lopped off at the stems."

"It's probably kids enjoying a prank."

"That's what I thought at first, but not anymore."

Ardena looked taken aback. "Really? Why not?"

"Because kids are careless. The petals would have spilled across the grass. I looked but there was no trace of the flowers anywhere."

A hint of aftershave swirling through the air announced Tryg's presence before he stepped into the outer office with a manila folder in hand. Why did he feel a need to scent up the place with the sweet aroma of spice? Jo wondered. But then again, why should she let it bother her? It was distracting, but it smelled awfully nice. Added something to the sterile surroundings.

"What's this about grave robbing?" he asked.

"Jo stopped by Case's grave over her lunch hour," Ardena offered.

Jo nodded. "Someone stole the geraniums from the wagon wheel again."

Tryg winced and then fumbled with the folder, accidentally spilling a half dozen or so papers across the marble floor.

Jo crouched down. "Let me help you."

"That's okay. I've got it," he insisted. As he knelt to pick up the papers, Jo leaned against her desk, scrutinizing his impeccable appearance— starched shirt, smart suspenders, shiny shoes, and pinstriped suit with a white satin handkerchief protruding neatly from his breast pocket. With the exception of a black and blue eye, he did not seem the sort of person that was easily ruffled, but by the haphazard way he shoveled the papers back into the file folder, he was definitely rattled.

"I'm sorry to hear about the thieves," he said. "What gets into people anyway?"

Why do you do that? Jo wondered. *Why do you have to look away just shy of making eye contact every time Case's name is mentioned?*

"Have you talked to the cemetery association?" he asked. "I'd be happy to give them a jingle if you'd like."

"Thanks, but that's not necessary. I can handle it."

Tryg cleared his throat, making it apparent he wanted to change the subject. How quickly he turned on his professional voice. "I'm expecting a couple to stop by tomorrow afternoon around three," he said. "That's their folder there that I just laid on your desk. They're having some issues with their neighbor. Sounds like it's getting serious. You might want to look through it to acquaint yourself with the case. I'm scheduled at the courthouse at one. If I run a little late, would you mind making them comfortable for a few minutes?"

"Be more than happy to."

As Tryg hovered over the file cabinet and riffled through the drawers, Ardena looked up. "Can I help you find anything?"

"No thanks. I've got it," he said as he extracted another file. "I'm on my way to the courthouse now. Should be back around four or so."

In the afternoon quiet, Jo and Ardena lost themselves in their work until the door opened and a lovely, familiar-looking older woman stepped in. Jo glanced up at the clock on the wall. It was a few minutes before three already.

"I'm Marianne Glanz," the woman said. "You haven't seen my husband, have you? He was supposed to meet me here."

Jo looked at Ardena and then back at Mrs. Glanz. "I'm sorry, but I'm afraid I haven't seen anyone."

"I haven't either," Ardena offered.

Why is this woman looking for her husband in Tryg's office? Jo wondered. She checked Tryg's calendar. No clients on today's schedule.

When Mrs. Glanz turned, her head swiveled back and forth as she took a thorough look through the front windows. Jo suddenly recognized her. "Say, aren't you the lady from The Copper Kettle? The lady whose handbag was stolen?"

CHAPTER ELEVEN

Tryg stopped by F.W. Woolworth's lunch counter for a quick egg salad sandwich and a Coke, eating the sandwich fast enough to initiate a mean bout of indigestion. He dropped a dollar on the counter. Still chewing a mouthful, he headed down Broadway at a fast clip, briefcase in hand.

Ray Miller, a local farmer to the north of Amber Leaf, and his son, Duane, stood passing the time of day in front of Spurgeon's, a local retail outfit in the heart of town. Ray, who was busily picking at his teeth with a toothpick, stepped forward and took a quick though penetrating look at Tryg's eye as he limped past.

"Say there, Mr. Howland, looks like that little lady friend of yours sure got the best of you," he teased, his grin cutting deep into his cheeks.

"That wouldn't be Miss Lauren Albrecht, now would it?" Duane chimed in with a gleam in his eyes. "She's got to be one awfully powerful little woman to inflict that kind of damage."

Tryg cut loose a prideful smile. "*He* got in the first blow, you good-for-nothing blowhards. I let him. We wouldn't want the poor guy feeling like less than a man after I got done pummeling him, now would we?"

Although Tryg did not have time to stop and catch up with his friends, he heard Ray and Duane's laughter for the better part of the next block. Tryg's smile felt wider than it had in quite some time.

He headed on to the courthouse. He was on a mission. The folder he gave to Jo was that of Del and Marianne Glanz. The Glanzes were very good people who happened to own a great deal of property spreading across four or five counties. Big Ole Harrington introduced Del to Tryg at the Hotel Albert one morning over breakfast and warbled Tryg's praises. That was all it took. Del quickly scheduled an appointment.

Although Tryg had done the bulk of his homework, he needed more information, needed to be fully prepared. The Glanz meeting was critical to the success of his practice. Not five minutes later, he breezed through the entrance of the Freeborn County Courthouse, an eighty-something-year-old red brick, sand-, and limestone building with five chimneys, four steeples, and a bell tower. Flames blazing in the fireplaces dominating the courthouse's larger rooms reflected off elaborate carved oak woodwork as Tryg passed through.

When he approached the counter at the Planning and Zoning Department at a fast clip, Barney Winters, with the face of a bulldog and the warmth of an Old English sheepdog, leaned far across the counter and gaped conspicuously at Tryg's black and blue eye. "Say, what happened to you? That's quite the shiner you've got there."

Rather enjoying the newfound attention, Tryg laughed. "I gave the guy a chance to get in the first punch. Figured he might need to save face. After that, it was my turn. I think I should take a picture of his craftsmanship for posterity, don't you?"

"Why not? I sure would." Barney lifted his chin, his keen gaze flowing down the bridge of his wide nose as he examined Tryg's eye a bit more closely. "I don't know, though," he said with the feigned tone of an expert. "You still have a little redness there. If I were you, I think I'd wait until it turns nice and black before I took any pictures. Then I'd hang it on my wall with the rest of my trophies. Too bad you can't get a taxidermist to do a little something special with it."

Tryg shook his head and grinned. "Now that's an idea. Do you know a good one?"

Barney let out a good-natured laugh, but then turned serious. "Say, did you hear what happened to that young man you took down?"

"No, I sure didn't. Why? What's up?"

"Word gets around. I understand the head honcho at Wilson's heard all about it. Sought the guy out. Gave him a job."

A wide grin cut across Tryg's face. "Is that right?"

Barney slapped both hands on the counter. "So what brings you in today?"

"I'd like to see the Project Planner. Is he around? I'm gathering some information for a meeting tomorrow afternoon, and I need to be well prepared."

"That's gonna be a tough one. He's on vacation this week. Anything I can do to help?"

Careful not to disclose too much information, Tryg said, "Well, maybe you can at that. I need a crash course about building permits and what have you."

"You've come to the right place anyway. So who's the lucky client?"

"Del and Marianne Glanz."

Barney's eyebrows shot up. "From just outside of town here?"

"Yes, sir. They're the ones."

"Ah! Good people. They'll keep you in the black for a while."

Barney slipped into a back room, leaving Tryg alone with his thoughts. *They'll keep you in the black for a while* had a nice sound to it. That's what Tryg hoped. Hiring Jo put a significant strain on his already overburdened office budget, but that was a risk he was willing to take. Securing an account with Del and Marianne would quickly put that concern to rest.

Barney returned several minutes later with a copy of the Notice of Application and plunked down a giant volume of the land use code. Tryg balked. "What are you trying to do to me, Barney? That monstrosity is going to take months to get through."

Barney laughed appreciably. "The Notice of Application is the important document. If you run out of time trying to find information from the City Code, you can always come back tomorrow. Sorry. I know I can trust you, but this is one of those volumes I can't let leave the courthouse."

"Thanks. Let's see how I do. I've got a sneaking feeling it'll be nearing sunup before I can slog my way through it, though."

As Tryg leafed through the pages, a gnawing feeling that something wasn't right nipped at him. He forgot something.

But what?

He pushed the thought aside and kept leafing through the pages, writing painstaking notes on his legal notepad about types and sizes of buildings, where they could be constructed, what needed permitting and what did not. Del expressed concern about a new neighbor named Jonathan Bellowitz who planned to build a tool shed uncomfortably close to their property line.

At ten minutes to four, an older woman walked past. The pleasant scent of her cologne distracted Tryg. He turned to take a better look at her. She looked familiar. Reminded him of someone. But who?

Marianne Glanz.

Del and Marianne Glanz!

That's what he forgot. Mrs. Glanz stopped him on the street about a week ago. Said they were going out of town. Asked to move their appointment ahead by a day or two. Tryg forgot to note the change on his calendar.

CHAPTER TWELVE

Mrs. Glanz sat across from Jo with her hands draped daintily over the black patent handbag she cradled on her lap. Under different circumstances, the older woman appeared surprisingly pleasant.

"I notice you received your handbag okay," Jo said, smiling.

"Yes, I certainly did." Mrs. Glanz gave her bag a light and appreciative pat. "I can't begin to tell you how grateful I am to get it back. I was afraid I'd never see it again. Our children gave it to me last year as a Christmas gift, you know."

"What a great present." Jo rested her elbow near the edge of her desk and inadvertently bumped the manila folder Tryg gave her earlier. With her gaze arrested on the folder, she fingered the button on the cuff of her blouse, buffed the crystal cover of her watch, and then finally reached forward and slid the folder to the side. She needed to get at it the instant Mrs. Glanz left.

"That's one of the reasons I'm here—to say thank you," Mrs. Glanz said, her emerald eyes sparkling. "The driver delivered it early on Friday morning. Around ten o'clock or so. And I'm pleased to tell you that thanks to your Mr. Howland, everything was still in there."

"That's great to hear. It's a shame he isn't here for you to thank, too."

Mrs. Glanz winced. "He isn't?" She sounded unmistakably disappointed.

"No, I'm afraid not. He's at an appointment this afternoon." When Mrs. Glanz's soft eyebrows raised in question, Jo added as an afterthought, "off-site."

Mrs. Glanz continued fidgeting with her handbag for a long moment and then swiveled around again, looking anxiously toward the front windows, undoubtedly still keeping an eye out for her husband. "Oh my," she said distractedly.

The woman already said thank you. Why is she still sticking around? Jo wondered. Why wait for her husband in Tryg's office? "It was awfully brave of Mr. Howland to go after that thief the way he did," Jo offered. "I thought I was seeing things when he tore off down the sidewalk through the drizzling rain, limp and all."

"That's a sight I'll sure never forget," Mrs. Glanz agreed. "And to think Mr. Howland got my handbag back with all my money still intact." But then her worried expression withered into a frown. "Why on earth would that young man do such a selfish thing? And in such a public place for heaven's sake! What was he thinking? He should have known we'd all be able to identify him."

"I understand he was desperate and desperate people don't think clearly," Jo said thoughtfully. "He had some hungry kids he needed to feed. It's too bad that doesn't make it right, isn't it?"

"Yes, it is. Too bad for him, too bad for his children, and too bad for me, too. I felt violated, but somehow I also felt guilty and sad." Mrs. Glanz wrapped her arms around her handbag, holding it tightly, protectively. She shook her head and then looked at Jo more closely, her troubled expression turning to one of sudden recognition. "Say, aren't you the young woman in The Copper Kettle that I was rude to just before the incident happened?"

Jo laughed uncomfortably. "I was the one who bumped into you, if that's what you're asking. There wasn't much standing room, I'm afraid."

"I'd like to apologize for my behavior. I really didn't mean to be unkind. It's just that my friend and I were deeply involved in a conversation about a neighbor of ours who is also selfish."

"I'm sorry to hear that."

"I'm sorry, too. We got a shocking Notice of Application last week. That horrible man is building a tool shed or a workshop or something of that nature, and he's purposely butting it right up against our property line. Bothers us no end." Mrs. Glanz twisted and pulled at the handle of her handbag and then hesitated as if her words got stuck.

But then the dam burst.

"We're at wits' end," she said. "We're not sure what to do. He's building it precisely ten feet and one inch away from our property line."

"Sounds like he's trying to make it legal to the letter of the law," Jo said.

"That's right. But who wants to live in the shadows of someone else's utilitarian tool shed? We sure don't. Aesthetically, it's going to be a real eyesore."

"Can't say as I blame you for being upset," Jo said. "I wouldn't care to live in the shadows of someone else's utilitarian structure either. You live out in the country, don't you? I noticed your address when we put in a request for the delivery of your handbag. It looked rural."

"Yes, we certainly do. Out east of town. We love it out there. Our parcel is pretty small. We only have about five acres or so."

Jo loved her view of Amber Leaf Lake, but living on a grassy rise overlooking the fields on the edge of town seemed idyllic. Seeing other farms off in the distance. Watching the corn grow. Watching storms come and go. Watching new falling snow quietly blanket the fields with pure white. "That's a nice little slice of land," she said finally. "Do you know your neighbors very well?"

"Oh heavens, no. And it's neighbor. Singular. We've never met the man. At this point, we're not sure we want to."

Jo flashed on Evelyn, the Wilders, and her friends at the O.M.

Harrington House, and realized how fortunate she and Brue were to be an integral part of their lives. It took a good deal of time, but eventually they became as close as family. What a shame the Glanzes didn't enjoy a similar experience.

"That Jonathan Bellowitz sure is one inconsiderate old coot," Mrs. Glanz continued.

Jo's forehead twitched involuntarily. "Jonathan Bellowitz? Not from the O.M. Harrington?"

Mrs. Glanz wriggled nervously on her chair. "You know him, then? All we know is that he moved in next door."

"I definitely know him. I'm surprised to hear you're having problems. He's really a great guy. Kind and decent."

Mrs. Glanz's eyes swelled. "I don't mean to be unkind here, but if he's as kind and decent as you say, he would not insist on building his tool shed so close to our property line."

Jo recalled Jonathan's going-away party and how excited he was to finally find a nice little place out in the country to build a small one-room shop. He wanted to build it under the shade of a weeping willow. Said he wanted the shop to look like a miniature home with a potbelly stove, French windows on all sides, and a wide front porch. Jo remembered because it reminded her of the O.M. Harrington House. Jonathan also wanted a swing on his porch to sway back and forth on while he whittled pipes and watched an occasional tractor poke along. "I knew he wanted to build a small one-room shop. It sounded so charming. But he never mentioned anything about a tool shed."

Jo glanced at Ardena who was being strangely quiet. Why not be thoughtful and help out by engaging in this conversation, too? Jo wondered.

"I'm sure it's a tool shed of some sort," Mrs. Glanz insisted. "That's what it said on that dreadful notice."

"Have you tried having a chat with him directly? There has to be some sort of misunderstanding here."

Ardena cleared her throat with unmistakable vigor. It startled Jo, and Mrs. Glanz, too, so much so that she turned and tossed Ardena a disapproving glance. "And how was that again, dear?" Mrs. Glanz asked, her gaze having yet to return to Jo.

"Meeting with Mr. Bellowitz face to face. Introducing yourselves and asking if he would consider moving the tool shed to a different place on his property."

"Oh no. Del's health is much too fragile. He's got to keep his blood pressure down. And I'm afraid I'm too nerved up about it myself. We'd feel awfully uncomfortable."

How sad, Jo thought—three wonderful people misunderstanding one another. "I see your point," she said. "Mr. Bellowitz hasn't lived next to you very long. About three or four months, isn't that about right?"

"That's right," Mrs. Glanz said, smiling reticently.

"I remember when he left the O.M. Harrington. We were all so sad to see him go."

"What a shame. And now we're so sad to see him come."

Jo was wading into something inappropriate and deep and needed to backtrack, but she wasn't sure how or why. Something about this conversation roused Ardena's interruption. But what?

Jo lightly rubbed the edge of her desk with the flat of her hand, wondering. Was Jonathan Bellowitz breaking any laws? Was he deliberately being selfish by building so close to the Glanz's property line? No. That wasn't like him. Must be because of that weeping willow. He must want to place his building under its shade.

Jo suddenly perked up. "Have you given any thought to planting trees? When I was a little girl, my grandfather lined our property with a row of trees so that any new neighbors moving in would get used to having their view obstructed if he decided to build more buildings."

Mrs. Glanz's eyes brightened. She quickly opened her handbag and rummaged through it. "Oh my. Wait, wait, wait. I'd like to jot down a few notes if you don't mind."

"Certainly. Take your time."

Ardena cleared her throat again then dropped her head into her hands, shaking it in defeat. Having this discussion within earshot of her compounded Jo's angst. *Honestly! Just a little while longer, Ardena. We're almost done here.*

As Mrs. Glanz drew out a small notepad, her ruby red pen fell to the floor.

Jo quickly scooped it up and handed it back. She found it difficult taking her eyes off of it. "What a beautiful pen. It's striking."

"It's a Parker," Mrs. Glanz said proudly. "I found it at the North Side Drug and Gift Shop about a month ago and knew I had to have it."

"It's the loveliest pen I've ever seen."

"Thank you. Now what was this about your grandfather planting trees along your property line?"

"He planted a row of poplar trees. I never understood why he didn't plant apple trees instead. We missed out on a lot of good pies and cider."

Mrs. Glanz's countenance lit up. "Apple trees! Why hadn't we thought of that before? We've wanted to plant an apple tree ever since I can remember. If we planted a couple of them we might not see as much of his awful building at all."

Jo leaned in closer and displayed a wily smile. "With five acres, I'm envisioning a small orchard planted ten feet and one inch away from your side of the fence that completely blocks the view of that offensive building."

Ardena coughed again, this time without muffling the sound, and then hammered away at the keys of her Corona.

Thinking how inappropriate, saying nothing about embarrassing, Jo glanced at Ardena, hoping this would not happen again, and then she continued. "I'll bet doing that might also increase the value of your property. If you've ever given any thought to engaging in a small business, you might set up a roadside stand and sell your apples there. Even bring a few bagfuls over to Mr. Bellowitz to show him some undeserved good will."

A smile rippled across Mrs. Glanz's cheeks, her eyes shining. "Oh my! Just think about all the apple pies I could bake for my husband—and applesauce, and apple butter, and even some nice ice-cold apple cider." Mrs. Glanz slapped her knee and laughed gleefully. "How my husband would love that. Thank you so much. And speaking of my husband," she said as she turned again and looked toward the window, "I can't imagine what's taking him so long. Wait a minute. Here he comes now."

She slipped her pad and pen back into her handbag and said, "You know, I never did get your name."

"It's Jo Bremley."

"Jo Bremley," Marianne Glanz repeated in her sweet older lady's voice. "What a nice name. Miss or Mrs.?"

"Mrs.," Jo said, a shot of pain nicking her heart.

"Well, Mrs. Bremley, we'll definitely give your idea a try."

Mrs. Glanz stood, then turned and as an afterthought, she said, "Say, how much do we owe you for your services? Or would you prefer sending us a bill?"

Jo smiled. "There's no charge for a chat."

"Are you sure? We'd be more than happy to pay you."

"I'm sure. Just enjoy your apple orchard."

The instant the door closed, Ardena turned on Jo. "Have you lost your ever-loving mind?" she said matter-of-factly.

"Wait, just a second." Jo shot up the flat of her hand to silence Ardena. "I want to see this."

Mrs. Glanz stepped out onto the sidewalk, and the well-dressed older gentleman with a stout cigar poking out the side of his mouth quickly approached her. They talked animatedly for a few minutes, Mrs. Glanz turning and pointing every now and then toward the office window. They then walked off arm in arm.

"Jo Bremley, do you have any idea what you just did?"

Did Ardena have any idea what she just did? Jo didn't particularly care for her tone. Jo also did not care for the feeling of impending doom rising from her middle. "What did I just do?"

"Oh, let's see. Hmm. Well, for beginners, you gave unauthorized legal advice. And did I say *for free*?"

"I did no such thing. Marianne Glanz stopped by to say thank you for returning her handbag. We were just having a polite conversation. I felt sorry for her, and I also felt protective of Jonathan Bellowitz. I know the guy. He was so excited about building his little one-room shop, and it sounded so adorable. I had to help."

"Didn't you hear Mrs. Glanz say, 'That's *one* of the reasons I'm here?'"

Jo's eyebrows floated involuntarily up toward her hairline as she raised her hand, stopping just shy of her mouth. "Come to think of it, she did say that, didn't she?"

"Yes, she did. And do you recall her saying that her husband was going to meet her here?"

Jo moaned.

"Wait," Ardena said. "This gets even better. Have you bothered to take a look at the name on that file folder Tryg placed on your desk before he left for the courthouse?"

A sick feeling tore at Jo's stomach as she reluctantly reached for the file, the file she had yet to take a look at. She slumped in her chair.

"You innocently talked the Glanzes out of pursuing any possible legal actions against their neighbor, let alone getting an opinion from Tryg. That's why I was trying so hard to get your attention."

"Oh no! What have I done? But she's such a nice person and so is Mr. Bellowitz."

"And so is Tryg. And he gave you your job."

"Ouch! I deserved that." Jo shook her head sheepishly. "I'm afraid I got so caught up wanting to help them both, and the idea of an apple orchard sounded so right."

"There's something else you might want to know," Ardena said.

"I'm not sure I want to know any more," she replied weakly. "I'm already feeling overwhelmed."

"Before you got in this morning, Tryg said that when he finishes with the Warner case, things will start to slow down. He's looking for business."

"Oh no. But I'm not sure what I might have done differently. I had no idea who Mrs. Glanz was, only that she was the lady with the stolen handbag. I wonder why she came in today. Tryg said their appointment wasn't until tomorrow afternoon."

"I know," Ardena replied. "That was strange. Maybe she's the forgetful type and just came in on the wrong day."

"Maybe."

"I'm not meaning to scare you, but what if Tryg blows his stack?"

"Boy, you sure don't mince words, do you?" Jo asked, her insides heaving.

"I'm sorry. I really don't mean to come on strong, it's just that—"

"He wouldn't fire me, would he?"

"Who knows? For both our sakes, I sure hope not. It's been nice having an office friend around for a change."

Jo stared at the folder then glanced up at the ticking clock, wishing Tryg wouldn't get back until after she'd left for the day. She needed time to decide when and how to approach him.

"Jo?"

"Yes?"

"Your idea about planting an apple orchard was brilliant."

"Thanks. I appreciate that. It's too bad Mr. Bellowitz didn't approach the Glanzes directly. I can't imagine getting a notice like that in the mail. It's too bad, too, that the Glanzes haven't given him a chance. I'm sure they might have struck up a great friendship, maybe even gotten some solid financial advice from the man. It's not like he wasn't one of the best investors to ever set foot on Wall Street." Jo shook her head emptily. "If nothing else, I hope my blunder has helped them sidestep regret."

"I'm sure it has." Ardena shoved her chair back and rested her arm on the edge of her desk. "So what are you going to tell Tryg?"

The air squeezed out of Jo's lungs in a rush. "The only thing I can tell him."

"Which is?"

"The truth."

Ardena chuckled. "Lots of luck with that one."

At five minutes after four, the door swung open and Tryg hurried in, gasping for air and looking upset. "Are the Glanzes here yet? They were supposed to come in today, not tomorrow. I can't believe I forgot to switch the date on my calendar."

CHAPTER THIRTEEN

I am so very, very sorry," Jo said. "There's no excuse for what I did. There's got to be something I can do to help make this right."

Tryg tried to suppress the whirlpool of vexation churning in the hollow of his stomach like an unhinged agitator wobbling loose at the bottom of a washing machine. He held the power to hire and fire and did not want to imagine how intimidating this was for Jo to find herself on the underside of that authority. But she was smart. Why hadn't she concerned herself with the toil demanded of him to make his business scrape along, saying nothing about making it thrive?

He calendared the Glanz appointment on the wrong day, but if Jo took even the hastiest glance at their file folder, the name Marianne Glanz should have sounded vaguely familiar.

Glanz was not exactly a common name.

Jo sat comfortably enough in the chair opposite his desk, looking every bit the consummate lady—hands folded loosely on her mint-green skirt, her chocolate hair flowing as freely about her thin shoulders as her words flowed freely and sincerely from her lips. And yet her eyes betrayed her, looking as though, in addition to losing her husband, another part of her peeled loose and perished as well.

She looked so vulnerable. Why?

And why didn't she comprehend of the gravity of her actions?

"I'd like you to run this whole encounter past me one more time," Tryg said, believing instead that this was no whole encounter; this was one whole *unbelievable* encounter.

Jo's posture stiffened the way one bristles when experiencing a verbal assault. Tryg needed to back off. Don't intimidate her, he told himself. Just gather information. Be gentle. Be straightforward. "Look, Jo. Let's make this easy for both of us, okay? Where, specifically, did we get off track here?"

"Where specifically?"

"Yes."

Jo looked down at her hands and fidgeted for a moment and then her pitiful gaze found his again. "The handbag."

"The handbag?"

She nodded. "Mrs. Glanz stopped by to thank you for returning it. She and I were enjoying a nice little chat. It never dawned on me that she and her husband had an appointment with you." A sudden look of remorse washed the innocence from her face. "You know, come to think of it, this wasn't a mistake. I really am guilty."

"Of what?"

"Mrs. Glanz," Jo said pensively. "When she came in, she asked if her husband was here yet. I remember thinking that was kind of strange. She also looked surprised when I told her you were off-site at an appointment. If I would have thought to question her on either of those things—"

"I understand. Continue."

"I wanted to get a few odds and ends out of the way before delving into the file folder you gave me. Thought it needed my undivided attention. I didn't bother to look at the name on it when I set it aside. I mean, I had no way of knowing that would be a problem. Between that and the theft of her handbag, the timing for her visit was pretty uncanny."

Tryg stared at his desk, not sure what to say or do. The timing of the visit was uncanny and there was no question his neglecting to change the appointment on his calendar contributed significantly to the situation. But there was a deeper problem at play here.

Jo's naiveté.

He looked at her, but did not say the words he was thinking. They were too harsh. *You work in a law office, Jo. My law office. Law offices handle, among other things, building disputes. You compromised my business. What are the chances you will do it again? I can't afford that kind of professional blunder, not again. No businessman can.* He tapped his desk lightly with his forefinger as if to tap down his angst. *You had no experience whatsoever when I offered you a position in my firm.* Why didn't I give this offer far deeper thought?

Jo leaned forward, breaking through the molasses-thick silence. "I understand the seriousness of what I've done, if that's what you're wondering."

He studied her, wanting to believe her. "Do you really, Jo?"

"Yes, sir. I really do. And I take full responsibility for my actions. It isn't possible for me to feel sorrier."

Between a tic in her forehead and the sincerity and brokenness in her voice, Tryg's insides turned squeamish. Only a scant handful of men excelled in handling upset women.

He was not one of them.

It appeared as though she was trying to hold back the tears that were gathering at the edges of her teal-blue eyes. *Please hold them back. I don't want to handle a weeping woman on top of everything else.* But then she suddenly caught him unawares.

"I know I haven't thought this through yet," she said, "but we both might want to rethink my position here. I'm sorry, but you need to know that I can't help being who I am, and I'm afraid I can't guarantee this sort of thing won't happen again."

Tryg's heart stuck in his throat at her anything but expected response. Her blatant honesty unnerved him. The poor woman had a child to raise for crying out loud.

"There's something I don't understand here. Why aren't you fighting to keep your job? How can you hold on to it so loosely?"

Suddenly the door burst open. Tryg looked up, startled by the interruption, yet pleased to buy a few minutes' time before speaking.

Ardena hurried in, her face ashen, her voice excited. "Forgive me for interrupting, but I was sure you'd want to hear the news."

"News?" Tryg said.

"Yes. President Roosevelt—he just died."

Stunned, Tryg's gaze fastened on Ardena. There was too much to digest in too little time.

"We can resume this conversation later, Jo," he said as a flutter of disappointment at what he was thinking wobbled his heart. Suddenly he felt too transparent, concerned she might be able to read his thoughts. His conscience was not about to let her go. He knew that. But if she had been someone else, anyone else, with a blunder as significant as the one she'd just made, he would not want to keep her.

CHAPTER FOURTEEN

C alvin stared into the dying embers. They reminded him only too well of his days working here at the O.M. Harrington House—days when his insides were withering. Nights in that single bed in his ten by twelve foot room behind the registration desk were lonely, too, with little to nothing to look forward to other than an occasional late-arriving guest.

He slipped another log on the fire, stoked it, and smiled when it burst into flames.

He enjoyed coming back to the boarding house for a visit every now and then, and far preferred the roaring fireplace here to the radiator and parched air back in his lackluster church office. But preaching, counseling, and visitations made getting up every day worthwhile.

"I appreciate your help," a soft voice said.

Calvin glanced back.

Sarah Harrington meandered toward the hearth wearing a charcoal slack suit that became her. Her hands enfolded a teacup, most likely to warm them.

"Old manly habits continue to die hard," Calvin said, breaking into a grin.

Just then the phone rang. "Be right back." She hurried to the registration desk and picked up the receiver. "O.M. Harrington, Sarah speaking." Her countenance darkened. "No. He isn't here. No. I'm not sure. I've given him your message. Yes. Yes, sir. I will remind him again."

Sarah hung up the phone and then settled in on the settee nearest the fire.

"Problems?" Calvin asked.

"I'm not sure. I don't know who that man is, but he's been calling Grandpa several times a day for the past week. Grandpa doesn't seem to want to talk to him."

"Whatever you do, don't worry about your grandfather. If anyone knows what he's doing, it's Big Ole Harrington."

Sarah nodded. "By the way, I've been meaning to tell you: you did quite an impressive job when you worked here. You left everything in unusually immaculate order."

"Military training will do that to you, I guess. Being Big Ole's grand-daughter, though, there's no question you can hold your own. But if you ever do need me for anything, I'm only a phone call away, and always happy to help."

"Thank you, Pastor Doherty."

"Calvin. Please call me Calvin." Sarah's ring finger caught his eye. "Say, I see you aren't married."

She hesitated then stared again into the fire. "I am...in my heart."

"In your heart?"

"We were married," she said, her voice barely audible, "it'll be five years ago next month. The seventeenth."

"I take it he's still back in California."

She shook her head in a long, drawn-out fashion. "He was part of a communications team in Operation Market Garden. I'm sure you understand a lot more about those sorts of things than I do. They were trying to secure the Rhine Bridgehead—road, rail, pontoon bridges— over the Lower Rhine at Arnhem." She hesitated and then her lips began to quiver. "I was told my name was the last word he ever..."

Calvin reached over and gently placed his hand on hers. "Forgive me. I had no idea."

"That's okay. The name Harrington threw you. I decided to start using it again. Too many people mispronounced my husband's last name, so it's easier this way."

"I intruded into your privacy."

She gazed at him with empty eyes. "You didn't know."

"Is that why you came here to Amber Leaf?"

"No." She placed her cup on the end table next to the settee, lounged back, and slipped her hands deep into the pockets of her slack suit. "I came here to help Grandpa."

"Really?" Calvin asked, surprised.

She glanced at him, looking as if she was trying diligently to hold back a grin. "He said I was the only one he knew of who was even remotely capable of stepping into your expert shoes."

Calvin burst into laughter. "I like your grandfather's dry sense of humor."

Sarah plucked her cup off the end table and lifted it, but before taking another small sip, she said, "So tell me about you. What is it like being a man of the cloth?"

"It's like nothing I've ever experienced before," Calvin replied without hesitation. "When you know it's your calling, you're miserable when you don't answer it and you're elated when you do. I love preaching. Counseling. Visitation. I think I can actually say this is the happiest I've been in my life...and I'm not all that young anymore."

"Grandpa says you were a chaplain in the Armed Services. What about then?"

"Now that's an entirely different story I think we'd better save for another time." Calvin took a quick peek at his watch and then stood. "And speaking of time, I need to get back to work. I do enjoy coming over here for an occasional visit, especially on cold April mornings like this one. There's nothing I like better than sitting in front of a warm fire. Thanks for joining me for a few minutes."

"The pleasure was mine."

Midmorning, Calvin fingered the dial on his office phone. He thought about Sarah losing her one true love and his heart went out to her. Yet he envied her—envied her for caring that much about someone, spending the best years of her life with him even though their time together got prematurely torn away.

He thought about his fleeting encounter with Ardena at The Copper Kettle and that tingling feeling he felt when he gazed briefly into her—a total stranger's—eyes. He found himself reliving that moment every hour on the hour throughout this past week. She felt it, too. Why else did she show up at church with Jo Bremley on Sunday morning? It wasn't just to hear his preaching.

He inhaled a deep breath. How long since a lady accompanied him for supper? His hands perspired at the thought. But dining with Ardena tempted him. He reached for the telephone book and looked up the number of Tryg Howland's law office, then sat back and tapped his finger lightly against his lower lip. A smile formed. He picked up the phone and started to dial the number.

"Pastor Doherty—"

Startled, Calvin's head snapped up as he peered at the equally startled yet innocent eyes staring back at him, and then he quickly cradled the phone. "Yes?"

"I'm sorry. I didn't mean to interrupt you," the woman said.

Calvin laughed. "You're fine, Mrs. Williams. Don't give it another thought. You're done with the cleaning then?"

"Yes, Pastor. That's what I came to tell you."

"Fine. Thank you. You know, you're a great asset to this church. We're thrilled with your work."

The grin on her face and the spring in her step as she walked away told Calvin he just made Mrs. Williams' day.

He glanced up at the clock. Ten-thirty. He got up, closed his door, and reached for the phone again.

Ardena picked up after the first ring. "Mr. Howland's office," she said. After re-introducing himself, he heard an unmistakable gulp at the other end of the line and went momentarily airborne before shifting around in his chair. She was as nervous as he was.

"Yes. Yes, of course, I remember you," she said. "No. I'm sorry. I'm afraid I have plans this Saturday evening. Yes. A week from Saturday night will be perfect. It's Franklin seven-seven-four-nine. I look forward to seeing you then."

Calvin hung up the phone and repeated, "Franklin seven-seven-four-nine." He looked down and smiled at the goose bumps prickling his skin. She was interested. He sensed it. What a shame that a week from Saturday night felt like it was years away.

CHAPTER FIFTEEN

J o smoothed her fingertips along the edges of her pencil and stared in a trancelike state at Tryg's door. Nothing on his calendar. No good reason to close it. Yet he had.

And of all mornings, why did Ardena choose this one to be late?

Jo's personality did not blend well with being a novice, but learning how to handle delicate office crises effectively was not about to happen overnight.

Maybe Tryg was composing a letter of recommendation for her imminent firing. No. Letters of recommendation are written after a three-month probationary period. She was nowhere near that yet. *Yet.* Jo shook her head. What a hopeful word.

Maybe he needed to concentrate on his work without interruption.

Or maybe he did not want to see or face Jo.

No. Enough of this kind of thinking. It isn't right.

She opened Del and Marianne Glanz's file. Because of Jo's blunder, the Glanzes sidestepped a lawsuit, at least for now anyway. They stood a good chance of living peaceably with their neighbor, too, and might be planting as much as an orchard of apple trees. So why was it necessary to seek legal counsel or engage in a fight in the first place when it was so easy to solve their conflict amicably? How does anyone win if angry feelings go unchecked and are allowed to kick up like dust on a wild wind?

At ten minutes past nine, Ardena finally arrived.

"Sorry I'm late," she said, but when she glanced at Jo, her face clouded. "Whoa! Looks like someone didn't get a whole lot of sleep last night."

"Oh, I may have dozed off for a minute or two," Jo said beneath her breath.

Ardena dropped a newspaper on her desk then hung her coat on the clothes tree, all the while watching Jo with no small amount of concern. "You never did tell me how the confession went yesterday afternoon."

"Not well, I'm afraid. Your announcement about President Roosevelt's death certainly put an abrupt end to it. Maybe that was for the best."

"So what's his mood like this morning?"

"I don't know yet."

"He is in, isn't he?"

"I think so. Looks like he's in hiding." Jo looked at Ardena thoughtfully. "I really blew it. I know that. Tryg needs people working for him he knows he can trust. Trouble is, if I can't trust myself, how can he possibly trust me?"

"What do you mean by that?"

"What do I mean by what?"

"'If I can't trust myself'?"

"Oh, that," Jo said resignedly. "I can trust myself to do things my way, but I can't necessarily trust myself to do things his way."

"I understand," Ardena said. "So what will you do if he fires you?"

"Fires me? Do you have to use such strong words?"

"I'm sorry. It's just that you need a job."

"I know. I did offer to quit, though," Jo said softly.

Ardena stepped clumsily to Jo's desk, as if her feet were shackled. "You did what?"

Jo slumped in her chair and peered into the sympathetic eyes of her new office friend. "Don't worry about it. I'll be all right. If everything heads toward the equator on me, I can always find someplace where I can at least scrub bathrooms."

At precisely a quarter past ten, the mailman came in to drop off his midmorning delivery. Stopping by Jo's desk, he held out a package. "I understand this is for you."

"What?" Jo asked, surprised.

"This is for you," he repeated. "A well-dressed older gentleman hailed me down a few blocks from here. Said he was in a hurry and asked if I would mind making the delivery. He said the package was from his missus."

The mailman then lowered his heavy shoulder bag onto the floor, slipped his hands into his pockets, and rocked on his heels looking as if he intended to stay a while.

Ardena glanced at the mailman and then at Jo with a questioning look.

"By the way," the mailman said, "How's Mr. Howland doing?"

"He's fine," Jo said, but something about his tone piqued her curiosity. "Is there any particular reason why you're asking?"

The mailman blinked noticeably several times. "I saw him in action the other day."

Ardena immediately swiveled toward him. "You mean with that handbag thief?"

"You bet. I saw Mr. Howland take him down. That sure was something. I saw the whole thing."

"I'm afraid he came away with a lot more than he bargained for," Jo said. "He got both the handbag and a shiner."

The mailman lifted his hat and lightly scratched his head. "I'm not at all surprised. But I just can't for the life of me figure out the likes of Mr. Howland."

Jo and Ardena exchanged a puzzled glance.

"Why would you say that?" Ardena asked.

"Well, by cracky, it just doesn't figure. Mr. Howland slammed that crook up against that brick building with a force like I've never seen before. I wouldn't want to be on the receiving end of his fist, I can tell you that for sure. He could have taken that thief out in a heartbeat. But like I said, it just doesn't figure."

"What doesn't figure?" Jo asked.

The mailman smoothed the top of his thinning hair with the palm of his hand then thoughtfully ran his fingers across the nape of his neck. "Why would a man with as much grit as Mr. Howland has pay a mugger for a handbag the guy stole?"

"What do you mean, 'pay a mugger?'" Jo asked, incredulous.

Ardena parked her hands on her hips. "Yeah, what do you mean?"

"Well, I was too far away to hear what was said, but I saw their mouths moving. Mr. Howland looked real mad and that young man looked scared to death. Next thing I know, Mr. Howland reaches into his own pocket, pulls out a fistful of bills, and folds the money into the guy's hand. Then, with a smile as wide as the Mississippi, Mr. Howland turns on his heel and struts away toting a woman's handbag, and the thief just stands there with his jaw flapping loose. It was the craziest thing I ever saw."

Jo and Ardena stared at one another, dumbfounded.

Meanwhile, the mailman slipped his hat back on, picked up his heavy mailbag, and said with a nod, "Guess I'd better be getting on my way. This mail won't get delivered by itself. A good rest of the morning to you, ladies."

He left, but his words lingered. How like Tryg not to bother to tell Jo and Ardena he gave the thief money to buy food for his kids.

Jo turned her attention to the package sitting on her desk then looked up to see an anxious Ardena hovering over it. "What is it? Who's it from?" she asked excitedly.

"I have no idea." Jo glanced at the return address. "It's from Marianne Glanz."

"Hurry! Open it!"

"I am, I am." Jo ripped off the outer paper and lifted the lid off the box. "It's the Parker pen! She went out and bought me one exactly like hers. Same color and everything. Isn't it gorgeous?"

"It is. It's absolutely gorgeous," Ardena agreed.

The muted sound of footsteps caught Jo's ear. Suddenly her heart thudded against her ribcage. She held up a hand to quiet Ardena.

Tryg's door swung open. He looked past Jo and directly at Ardena, his voice controlled. "Did you get a copy of *The New York Times* yet?"

Jo refused to recoil. She glanced from Tryg to Ardena. At least he wasn't scowling at her. Not wanting to feel like a victim, she needed to find a natural way to engage him, but how?

"Yes, sir," Ardena said. "I picked up a copy on my way to the office this morning. The obituary is right here. It's by Arthur Krock." She tapped it with her fingers and began reading. "'*Special to The New York Times. Washington, April 12 – Franklin Delano Roosevelt, War President of the United States and the only Chief Executive in history who was chosen for more than two terms, died suddenly and unexpectedly at 4:35 P.M. today at Warm Springs, Ga., and the White House announced his death at 5:48 o'clock. He was 63.*'" Ardena looked up. "Want me to go on?"

"No, that's okay," Tryg said. "I can read the rest later."

He snatched the paper and then glanced at Jo without expression. As he was about to disappear into his office, Jo said understatedly, "I wonder how Truman's going to fare. That's quite a freight load of coal that was dumped on him."

Jo sensed a surprised look as Tryg's head snapped back, but she kept her attention riveted on her work.

Five minutes later, Ardena got up and went to the back room. She stopped at Jo's desk and asked, "What's that faraway look in your eyes all about?"

"Marianne Glanz's pen."

Ardena rested her hand lightly on Jo's desk. "What about it?"

"I'm giving it to Tryg."

"Why on earth for?"

"Payment. After all, this is his business."

Ardena nodded. "You're right. That really is the right thing to do."

Tryg poked his head out his door. "What's going on out here?"

Ardena grinned. "Jo has a present for you."

Tryg gave Jo a puzzled glance, so much so that it caught a good share of her breath. She stood and extended her hand to him. "Here. Marianne Glanz had this delivered to us—a beautiful Parker pen."

He looked at it from afar. "It's very nice."

"It's yours," Jo insisted. "This is your business. After my mess up, I don't feel right about accepting it."

Tryg shook his head, refusing the pen, and disappeared into this office. Something about it appeared to bother him. Jo then heard nothing, nor did he step out again until noon. He wrestled his suit coat over his shoulders on his way through the office and said, "I've got a luncheon appointment next door. Be back in an hour or so." He headed out the door and did not look back.

The moment he was out of sight, Jo said, "What do you think?"

"What do I think about what?" Ardena asked, spinning her chair toward Jo. "You mean about the tension in the air?"

"No, silly."

"You're up to something, aren't you?"

Jo held Mrs. Glanz's pen high enough for Ardena to take a good look.

"The pen?" Ardena said. "What about it?"

"It belongs to Tryg." Jo busily got to work wrapping it neatly in a tissue. "His pride was on the line with both of us here," she continued nonchalantly. "He was being a gentleman. It really does belong to him."

She then wrote a note that said, "*This belongs to you, compliments of Marianne Glanz*" and taped the note on the tissue paper.

Ardena folded her arms and raised her chin. "I understand what you're saying, but I get the strong impression he does not want it."

"Look, I don't like being a victim. I don't care if he is the boss. The pen belongs to him."

"You don't want to overplay your hand, Jo," Ardena warned. "Why don't you just leave well enough alone?"

Jo thought about that for a moment. But then she thought about the wall between her and Tryg, a wall that needed a little help breaking down. To Jo's way of thinking, the pen represented their problem, their unhealthy communication, and they needed to face it. "Because I can't."

"I sure hope you know what you're doing."

"You're right. You're absolutely right," Jo conceded as she got up from her desk.

"So what are you doing? Where are you going?"

"Just watch," Jo said, glancing back. "It isn't right for us to take each other so seriously over one little mishap. Well, maybe the mishap wasn't so little. But I'd rather get fired and get it over with than walk around feeling guilty and unwanted."

She marched into Tryg's office and placed the Parker in his center desk drawer.

When she returned to her desk, Ardena leaned back in her chair. Her forehead creased as she asked, "But what if he gets mad?"

"What if he doesn't?"

CHAPTER SIXTEEN

L ook out! Look out!"

Tryg stomped his feet on the floorboard, working them hard—right foot, left foot, right foot, left foot. But there was no resistance.

Suddenly, an uncontrolled sliding sensation overwhelmed him and the ground underneath him disappeared. Like soaring through a cloud, he saw nothing. Only white. He shot out his right arm as though he needed to protect a child, but no one was there.

"No!" he yelled. "No!"

After a fierce jolt and a violent lunging back and forth, he glimpsed out the car window to his left where a deer scampered off through the blinding blizzard. His head throbbed, the pain crushing. But as he turned back to his right, he awakened as he always did—sitting ramrod straight in bed, gasping wildly for air, heart pounding noticeably, his top sheet and blankets piled in a heap at the foot of his bed, and his body drenched in his own sweat.

He stared at the clock. Six-thirty. The nightmares were coming more frequently lately. They seemed to pick up immediately after Jo started working at the firm. That was something not easily overlooked. Frankly, he wasn't sure how much more of this he could take. What triggered it this time? Marianne Glanz? Finding her ruby red Parker pen in his center desk drawer compliments of one Jo Bremley? If only he could get a handle on the nightmares. Gain some control. At least this time the night terror came in the later hours of the early morning. He clocked in some good sleeping time anyway.

He lobbed his legs over the side of his bed. After dropping his head in his hands for a moment, he raked his fingers through his hair. Might as well get up. Go catch a quick breakfast somewhere. He needed to shake this nonsense loose from his head again.

Half an hour later, he limped up the sidewalk. Must have slept wrong. What a tough morning. Now his bum leg was giving him fits. Every now and then his muscles seized up on him. Cramping. Making it next to impossible to take a few steps without flailing all over the place like he'd been squeezed out of the birth canal with one too many loose joints in one too many places. Oh well. At least there were signs of Saturday morning life out here—the sun doing its job, people beginning to poke their noses out of their front doors and scrambling for their early morning papers.

Where to go, where to go? he wondered to the uneven stride of his footsteps. *I know. Hotel Albert.* There was always someone there at the most unusual times of day or night, with a cigar poking out of his mouth or a pipe clenched between his teeth. The men residing at the hotel loved to pontificate about world news over a heaping plate of pancakes, ham and eggs, and a side of toast. And if no one was around, which he doubted, the day's paper always made great company.

Tryg climbed the few steps of the upscale hotel's impressive entry. He fancied its marble floors, grand staircase, elegant dining room, and the coffee shop located near its registration desk. He'd met a good number of interesting travelers here, many of whom were salesmen, who stayed or dined at the hotel before heading out for worlds unknown.

His shoes clicked and scraped along the marble floor as he passed the mahogany-walled registration area, waved to the attendant manning the desk, and continued on, sniffing the thick odor of stale cigar smoke lingering in the air.

He glanced first at the coffee shop and then at the dining room. Deciding he needed more than a stiff cup of coffee, he headed on into the formal dining room where he stopped and smiled at a familiar face. "Why if it isn't the great O.M. Harrington."

"It's Mr. Harrington to you," the old man said nonchalantly, correcting Tryg before lifting a brow. "What brings you out and about so early on a Saturday morning? I thought you young'ns liked to sleep in. Please," he said with a flap of his hand, "have a seat. A little company might be nice, even if it is from someone still wet behind the intellectual ears."

Tryg pulled out a chair and restrained a breaking grin. Big Ole was precisely what he needed this morning. "I think a better question is what are you doing hanging out in an outhouse like this? Food not good enough at your own boarding house these days?"

"The food at my place is the best in town and a far cry better than anything you could ever concoct. And I'm here at this palace, not that it's any of your business," Ole said with emphasis, "because I figure a man could use a little variety."

"You mean you're not checking out the competition then?"

"Respect your elders, son," Big Ole said, not missing a beat. "Respect your elders."

Tryg leaned back and exploded with laughter.

After Tryg placed his order for an order of pancakes and a side of bacon, Ole dabbed at his chin with his cloth napkin and said, "Say, I hear you hired the young Bremley widow."

"You heard right."

After a long pause, Ole shoved his plate aside and drew his cup closer. "You know, Calvin Doherty and Jo Bremley were the two best workers who ever darkened the doors at my boarding house. Now we've lost both of them. I'm afraid they left a hole in the place that can never be filled. Calvin had complete control. Paid attention to every minute detail. And that little lady you hired consistently did twice the amount of work we required of her, and did it twice as fast and twice as well as the best of the best. I'm afraid our loss is your gain. You're very lucky to have her."

"Thanks," Tryg said, hoping he didn't sound as half-hearted as he felt. "I appreciate that."

"So how's that leg treating you? Is it getting any better?"

"Oh, sometimes it gives me a little trouble. But mostly I ignore it. Thanks for asking."

Ole nodded slowly. "It's pretty tough times we're living in yet. You see this morning's paper? Looks like we're cleaning up pretty well in Europe. I wonder how much longer the unscrupulous Herr Hitler can hang on."

"I think we're doing a pretty decent job of closing in on him," Tryg said. "He can't have too much life left in him. Kind of makes you wonder how it's all going to end, doesn't it?"

"That it does," Ole replied with a shake of his head. He gazed around the dining room as if his thoughts were far away. "I don't want to imagine what it's like having to live there. Blackout regulations. Jumping to the blare of air raid sirens. Always on the alert. Dodging bombs twenty-four hours of every single day. Cleaning up the rubble. Must be a real nightmare."

Tryg tried to hide a flinch at the word, but he was too late. Big Ole noticed. He was consistently a full step ahead of everyone's game.

"Having nightmares, are you, son?"

Not that I care to talk about. "On occasion, I guess."

"Don't worry about it," Ole said in passing. "They'll go away with time. They always do."

Tryg's gaze dropped to the floor.

Not this one.

CHAPTER SEVENTEEN

In the early morning quiet, Jo glanced at Tryg's empty office. She then arranged and rearranged her workload, heavily distracted by the deafening sound of nothing. There's something about the silence, she lamented. It's not so much what is said, it's what is not said that has the power to carve a cavernous hole into the depths of one's soul. Monday passed. Tuesday passed. No unpleasant looks, but no pleasant looks either. No comment about the pen. No unkind words. But then again, very few words were spoken at all.

No resolution to the war of no words.

Ardena arrived at nine o'clock sharp. "Is Tryg in yet?"

"Good morning back to you," Jo said understatedly. "And in answer to your question, no. He's not in yet."

"That's what I was hoping to hear. Let me settle in first. I think it's time for you and me to have a little girl-to-girl chat."

Ardena slipped into the back room while Jo waited patiently, listening with rapt attention to all of the familiar start of the day sounds—the clinking of the cup, the free flow of coffee, the scraping of the pot onto the warmer, and finally, the clicking of Ardena's wedged heels as she made her way back to her desk. She lowered her small frame onto her chair and very daintily crossed her legs, her camel-colored cup blending beautifully with the ruffles fringing her ivory blouse. She finally sat back and said, "I've been giving a lot of thought to the problems plaguing us here lately."

Just then the door opened with its usual light thrust, and Tryg limped in. "Morning," he said to no one in particular. He hung his coat and hat on the clothes tree and disappeared into his office, leaving the air behind him leaden.

As soon as his door clicked shut, Jo repeated, "The problems we've been having?"

"Yes, ma'am." Ardena indicated Tryg with a brief nod toward his office. "It can't be comfortable for you to endure that man's indifference. It's not comfortable for me, either, and I'm not the one on the receiving end."

Jo let out a sigh that could have been heard miles past the outskirts of Amber Leaf. "I'm really sorry, but what can I do besides wait him out? He's the boss."

"There's got to be something you can do, Jo. You're a smart woman. Maybe there's a way to prime the pump."

"But how can you prime a pump when the well's gone dry? It's got to have water in it."

"You're never going to know if you don't give it a try. You have way too much on the line here, way too much to lose."

Jo sighed. "You're right. Let me think on it."

"Jo?"

"Hmm?"

"I'm crossing my delicate little fingers for you."

Jo smiled and then returned to a draft of a letter she'd been working on, but the words sitting on the surface of the paper also sat on the surface of her mind and refused to sink in. She glanced at Ardena, who was already making notations on a document of some kind.

"Ardena?"

"Hmm?"

"Thanks for crossing your delicate little fingers for me."

After tens of minutes of switching aimlessly from project to project, Jo pulled her document closer to help her concentrate, but only succeeded in helping her see the words better. She looked up. "Ardena?"

"Hmm?"

"About what you said…"

"You mean about priming the pump?"

Jo nodded.

"What about it?"

"If I did give it a try, do you really think I'll find any water at the bottom of the well?"

Ardena grinned. "I don't think so, I know so."

Jo glanced at the clock and got up. "Okay then," she said with a fair measure of staged confidence.

Ardena spun her chair around, looking stunned. "What are you doing? Where are you going?"

"I'm doing precisely what you told me to do."

"Which is?"

"I'm going to prime the pump, silly."

"You wh—"

Jo lifted her chin and knocked on Tryg's door—a serious knock.

"Come in," she heard him say.

She lifted her shoulders and walked in with no small sense of purpose. "I understand you wanted to have an audience with me."

Tryg tossed his pen aside, his eyes growing wide. "I did? Who in the world told you that?"

Jo shot him an I-have-nothing-more-to-lose-because-I've-lost-it-all-anyway look. "I did."

"*You* did." It took a moment for Jo's words to register, but then Tryg flopped back in his chair, lost himself in nervous laughter, and shook his head. "Maybe that's not such a bad idea after all."

CHAPTER EIGHTEEN

Tryg snatched Marianne Glanz's pen out of his desk drawer. "This isn't fair, Jo," he muttered to himself.

Where daylight ends and evening begins can be hard to decipher, especially in the Upper Midwest, where thick and formless clouds have been known to blanket the sky for days on end. Tryg's day had been like that. Gray without form. He'd spent hours in the office fretting about his dwindling workload. Fretting about Jo. He rolled the pen slowly through his fingers, and stared out across the room. Unable to see clearly about how to proceed with his workload, Jo, or the pen, he slipped the Parker into his coat pocket and headed out the door.

Tonight will be different.

He knocked on Lauren Albrecht's door at six o'clock straight up. The engine of his taxi rumbled loudly at the end of her sidewalk as he waited. The instant Lauren opened her door, Tryg's heart fluttered. They kissed one another lightly on the cheek, and when they headed down the sidewalk and she draped her hand over his arm, Tryg whispered in her ear, "You are, without a doubt, the most beautiful creature within a one hundred mile radius of Amber Leaf."

Lauren laughed appreciatively. "What did I ever do to deserve you?"

"I don't know," Tryg said, folding his hand over hers, "but if we keep this up, I'm going to look strange wearing my wading boots."

As Tryg helped Lauren into the cab, the driver rotated toward them. "Where to?"

"How does Chinese sound, Lauren?"

"Sounds great."

"To the Canton Café, please."

The taxi rolled along the tree-lined streets of Shoreland Heights, around Fountain Lake, and headed down Broadway, Tryg all the while holding Lauren's hand and drinking in the rapidly changing scenery. He loved the nightlife. Loved great food at nice restaurants. Loved going to picture shows. Loved the bright lights of Broadway. And he loved spending time with Lauren. But when he recalled his comment to her about her beauty and how warmly she'd responded, he also recalled a fleeting thought he'd had about Jo, a thought he unhesitatingly brushed aside. Jo was every bit as lovely. But she was not an issue. Nor would she be. Nor could she be. Ever.

Halfway through supper, Lauren said, "Something isn't quite right with you tonight, Tryg. What is it?"

"Now why would you ask a question like that?"

"You seem distracted, like something's bothering you. That's why."

Tryg grinned awkwardly. "I'm that easy to read?"

She nodded and said in passing, "When you're ready to talk, I'm here for you." She then craned her neck, looking toward the far windows, and changed the subject, as if trying to draw him out. "So tell me, then," she said sweetly. "Do you plan on buying your own car someday? Yellow Cab is getting rich off of you."

He ignored her question, but a pull in his stomach didn't, especially when she reached across the booth and tenderly stroked his cheek with the back of her fingers as if to say all was okay. He picked up his chopsticks and rhythmically tapped them together as if they were drumsticks and he the drummer. "I'm having a few challenges with one of my employees," he finally admitted, albeit uncomfortably.

"Ardena? You can't be serious. I thought you said she was a fantastic worker and so easy to get along with."

"They're both excellent. And, no, it isn't Ardena."

"Jo?" asked Lauren, looking astounded. "How could you possibly be having problems with her? She just started working for you."

Tryg trusted Lauren. Needing a confidant, he shared the details of Jo's misstep with Marianne Glanz, how much it cost him, and how heavily he was relying on that possible new flow of income.

Lauren reached for his hand and held it lightly from across the table. At least he didn't feel that strange pull in his stomach this time.

"This must be very difficult for you," she said.

He nodded. "We need the business, Lauren. Badly."

"And? You look as if you might have more to say."

Tryg hesitated and then said pensively, "She owned what she did like a real lady. I was proud of her and thought for a moment there we were back on track. But it's what she said afterward that has me concerned."

Worry lines formed across Lauren's forehead. "What did she say?"

"She said she couldn't guarantee it wouldn't happen again."

Lauren gasped. "That *is* serious. What are you going to do about it? You can't have one of your employees undermining you."

Tryg shrugged.

After supper, they strolled across the street to the Rivoli Theatre. A picture show Lauren had been looking forward to seeing—*Having Wonderful Crime*, starring Carole Landis—was playing. As they stood on the sidewalk in the sizable ticket line, Lauren asked with no small amount of concern, "Are you going to let her go?"

"Let who go?"

"Jo, silly."

"Oh. We're still on that conversation, are we?" Tryg shook his head. "No, I can't do that. I'm not sure what I'm going to do, though. Wait it out, I guess. Hope it doesn't happen again."

Later that evening, Tryg walked Lauren to her door and helped her unlock it. After a meaningful embrace and a warm kiss good night, he began whistling Bing Crosby's *I'll Be Seeing You*, but his whistling faded well before he reached his waiting cab.

As the taxi retraced the streets toward home, Tryg stared out the window and watched the houses roll by. Two things happened over the course of the evening that he hadn't anticipated, two things that left him wondering.

The car. Lauren asked if he planned on one day buying his own car. When his mind emptied at the thought, she reached across the booth and tenderly stroked his cheek with the back of her fingers as if to say all was okay. Although he cared for her deeply, he flinched at her touch, but did not know why. Lauren noticed.

Then there was the Rivoli Theatre. When they no more than took their seats and the lights in the theatre dimmed, he panicked for a moment and poked through the pockets of his blazer. He feared that he left Marianne Glanz's Parker pen in the Canton Café. When he located it in an inside pocket, Lauren asked him why he reacted so strongly to the possible loss of an insignificant little pen. A pang of guilt tore through him like a charge of electricity from an electrical socket. He found himself stammering when he answered, but again he did not know why. And Lauren noticed his stammering, too.

Hours later, he lay in bed, staring at the ceiling, listening to an occasional car drive past, listening to the sporadic creaks of the house settling, and the constant tick, tick, tick of the clock on his night table. But mostly he heard Lauren's question turning over repeatedly in his mind—her question about the car. 'Do you plan on buying your own car someday?' she asked innocently. At first, he cringed at her question. It triggered the recollection of his all-too-frequent nightmares. Maybe it was wrong to give in to them. Why give them undue importance? But he felt at a loss as to how to stop them, so he switched his focus to far more pleasant things.

He forced himself to concentrate on the good things a new car offered, rather than its danger—like the purr of its engine. He thought about the appealing smell of new leather. He thought about the gentle list of a heavy piece of metal motoring down curvy tree-lined roads. New car production would resume again after the war was over. Maybe he would be ready by then. Maybe he could handle buying a car if he only drove it around town.

The last time he'd looked at the clock, it was three in the morning. He rubbed his eyes and looked again. It was nine o'clock already.

He rolled out of bed, smiling.

CHAPTER NINETEEN

T ryg's words backed up on Jo. 'Don't worry about the Glanz blunder,' he had said. How she wished she could erase the memory and Del and Marianne Glanz's file folder would magically disappear.

Blunder.

The mere memory of hearing that word gave her a good case of the chills all over again.

Tryg also reassured her. Said he was confident that an incident like that wouldn't happen again. Although that was generous of him, his tone carried the ring of a warning. Jo knew better than to feel confident. Heeding those words wasn't easy.

She pulled open the dreaded file drawer marked "G" and quickly slipped the folder into its final resting place then turned her back on it and made her way toward her desk.

To Tryg's credit, the past few days had gone quite well, so much so that by Friday the tension in the office dwindled to nonexistence.

At three o'clock, Ardena said, "Would you mind holding down the fort, Jo? I'm helping throw a surprise party tonight, so I'd like to leave a little early."

"Go ahead. We'll be fine."

Tryg and Jo were alone.

The next time she glanced up at the clock, she smiled. Half past four already. Now that she and Tryg were at peace, she was able to see how fascinated she was with her work, finding herself increasingly oblivious to time. A whole new behind-the-scenes world opened up to her in just a few short weeks—learning and understanding legal rights and responsibilities, actively interacting with vendors, assisting with various types of research, helping Ardena with Tryg's calendar, and greeting clients. Her job offered more remarkable opportunities than she'd hoped. At this point, she treasured it too much to compromise it or in any way give it up.

A few minutes before five, Tryg's shoes clicked across the marble as he sauntered to the file drawers to retrieve another folder. He looked dog-tired, hair disheveled, sleeves rolled halfway up his forearms, tie askew, and yet he kept pushing.

"Are you staying late again tonight?" Jo asked.

"Don't have much choice. I still haven't prepared my opening remarks for Monday morning's hearing."

"Need any help?"

"No," he said, his smile appearing appreciative yet fatigued. "I'll be fine. Besides, you've got to get home. Brue needs you. But thanks anyway."

Kneeling, Tryg riffled through the bottom drawer. "Say, you wouldn't happen to know where the Berger file is, would you? I can't seem to find it here."

Jo swiveled around in her chair, facing him. "I have it. I've been holding it for the end of the month billing. It's somewhere in this stack at the corner of my desk."

Tryg got up and stretched back his shoulders. "Mind if I steal it for a few days?"

"Not at all."

Jo reached for the stack of folders, but before she had a chance to retrieve the file, Tryg leaned across her desk, also reaching. He touched her lightly at the shoulder, undoubtedly to keep his balance and leaned too far into her personal space.

Way too far.

One whiff of his manly scent and her nostrils flared. Her heart hammered savagely. The air caught in her lungs. She found it hard to breathe. Her head felt woozy and her cheeks burned. Feeling the panic rising, she recoiled.

Tryg quickly backed away. "Are you okay? You look flushed."

"I'm fine," Jo lied. But what else could she say?

Tryg retrieved the file, and as she watched him disappear into his office, an unwelcome realization crawled over her. What had she done? What had she been thinking? Why did she accept his offer in the first place? Although the job paid well and was timely, that didn't make it right. Tryg was every bit as appealing as Case. How could she be so naïve?

She needed to get home. Fast.

Still shaken by her ridiculous overreaction, Jo wrung the steering wheel anxiously as she powered down the streets of town, aging brick buildings passing by in a blur.

Everything about Tryg reminded her of Case—hardworking, Ivy League good looks, highly responsible, serious, reserved, mature, kind, generous, keenly aware of everything that happened in his surroundings. What would Case have thought had he known about her sudden unwanted attraction to, of all people, Tryg Howland? It rushed in from out of nowhere. She needed to control her infatuation, but how when she had a hole in her heart the size of the Grand Canyon, a hole that ached to be filled?

Jo headed down the brick-paved hill on Newton. In the distance, the whistle of the five-fifteen blared. She engaged the clutch and downshifted, crossing the railroad tracks well ahead of the slow-moving train.

She pulled into her driveway and turned off the engine. Sitting quietly for a few minutes to clear her thoughts, she listened as a distant train chugged down the tracks. Had Brue not come down with the measles, they would be in New York now and the unwelcome incident with Tryg would never have happened.

She glanced up at her dilapidated house and sighed. In a few minutes she would walk across her living room, with its sparse furnishings and worn linoleum flooring, her footsteps sounding as hollow as she felt. What was she going to do now with this realization that she despised?

She jumped at a sudden knocking. Brue stood with her nose pressed against the window. "Hi, Mom. What are you doing in there?"

Jo crawled out of the car and drew Brue into a warm and welcoming embrace. "Hi, sweetie. I was resting for a minute. How was school?" she asked, engaging Brue at her own eye level.

"It was good. And d'you know what?"

"What?"

"We had a spelling bee, and I won!"

Jo gave Brue another tight squeeze. "I'm so proud of you."

Brue pulled back, her eyes widening. "Mrs. Wilder made homemade bread today."

"She did?"

"Uh-huh, and she gave us a loaf. I put it on the kitchen table a little while ago. It's still warm."

The moment they stepped into the house, Jo glanced at the bread cooling on the table and thought of all the loaves of bread she'd baked over the past few years. How she longed to have those days back.

Hearthside days.

Days without T.W. "Tryg" Howland, III, Attorney-at-Law.

CHAPTER TWENTY

T ryg was exhausted; he was exhilarated. He scratched out the final words of Monday morning's opening remarks and read them one last time. He stood a good chance of winning this case. He felt it in his innards. Smiling at the thick sheaf of papers, he tossed his pen aside. With the burdensome weight lifted, he felt better than he had in months.

And all it took to lift it was exceedingly tedious brainpower and formidably hard work.

Automobile lights streamed past his windows. An occasional impatient driver honked in the distance. Dads late for supper. Farmers pouring into town for a little Friday evening shopping. Hungry families searching for a good place to eat supper. He glanced at his watch— Lauren Albrecht waiting for him.

Lauren.

Just then the phone rang and he picked up the receiver. "Tryg Howland."

The soothing sound of Lauren's feminine voice immediately reduced him from a confident and highly successful professional to a love-starved adolescent surging with goose bumps. He smiled to himself. The warm feelings were back.

"I was hoping it was you," he cooed. "Looks like I let the time get away from me again. What? When?" Tryg glanced at his calendar and grinned. "This is the sixth consecutive month you have my weekend calendar packed, you know. You are definitely broadening me socially. Between political activities, social clubs, dinners, and concerts, I don't think it's possible to have more opportunities for expanding my business. What? You're right, it will take time for the seeds to germinate, but at least they're being planted." He smiled and sighed and lightly ruffled his hair. "I've been getting some bites the past few days. It's looking as if our hard efforts are finally paying off despite Jo's losing that Glanz account. What? Don't be silly. You don't need to worry about her. How about if I head up your way in a couple of minutes? You must be starving by now."

He cradled the phone, called a cab, and then pulled open his desk drawer, but not before a hurts-so-good smile slithered across his face. He plucked Marianne Glanz's ruby red pen from his drawer and tapped it lightly and repeatedly against the palm of his hand.

Tryg had refused the pen. Jo gave it back. And with a note nonetheless saying it belonged to him.

The pen reminded Tryg of an old, used-up baseball. He'd found it on his family's lawn one day when he was a little shaver. He tossed it over the fence. His neighbor tossed it back. He slung it over again only to watch it come hurtling back. After several more volleys, Tryg waited until after dark that night and lobbed it over one more time. The baseball had been barely reduced to a memory when one spring day it showed up at the bottom of a wicker basket decorated like an Easter egg. At Christmastime that same year, he returned it in a handsomely wrapped gift box, not that a boy that age could wrap a gift well. And on and on the exchange continued, Tryg and his neighbor always upstaging one another with their creative abilities. He had not seen that old baseball for a couple of years now. His former neighbor probably lost it. How Tryg missed those days.

He rolled the Parker thoughtfully between his fingers.

And then he remembered Lauren's distress when he feared he'd accidentally left the pen at the Canton Café. Her overreaction was beyond him, but he was sure of one thing. His relationship with Lauren was the most serious one he'd had in quite some time, and he didn't care to trifle with it. If he returned the pen to Jo, he wouldn't have to worry about Lauren getting agitated again if she ever laid eyes on it. Besides, Jo worked hard enough for two people, and Mrs. Glanz did give the pen to her, not him, so Jo was its rightful owner.

He placed it back in his drawer and closed it and then made a mental note to find a convincing way to return it, an inoffensive way that Jo could easily accept.

On his way toward the clothes tree, he glanced at her desk, but then stopped and thoughtfully jingled his change.

Why was she so upset when he retrieved that file folder from her desk? That didn't make any sense. Maybe she was embarrassed about not having placed a checkout card in the file drawer. That had to be it. He needed to have a chat with her. It wasn't necessary for her to take filing so seriously. After all, it was just filing.

Or was she still reeling over the Marianne Glanz misstep? Maybe that was it. That was a problem, though. Jo needed time to simmer down and feel comfortable again. Maybe he overreacted. He wasn't expecting too much of her, was he? After all, she was new on the office scene. He needed to back off. Besides, chances were slim she would duplicate that situation again.

There had to be a way to put Jo at ease.

He headed toward the door and stopped again.

Hmm! The pen.

Tryg slipped back into his office, retrieved the ruby red pen, and scribbled a note that read, "*Tag, you're it, Jo.*" He placed the pen along with the note in Jo's center desk drawer. Despite the troubles he'd experienced recently with his newest employee, knowing Jo, the to-and-fro of the pen could become a fun and amusing pastime—just like the to-and-fro of the baseball.

Pleased with himself, he grabbed his briefcase and headed out to East William with a spring in his step, a cab blaring its horn, and his lovely lady friend waiting.

CHAPTER TWENTY-ONE

Jo's supper did not settle well. She stood at the kitchen counter and watched Brue drop two Alka-Seltzer tablets in a glass of water and stare, mesmerized, until they finished fizzing.

Brue handed the glass to Jo. "Here you go, Mom," she said. "Now I get to take care of you just like you take care of me when I'm sick. Do you want to go into the living room? You always seem to feel better after you do a little mending."

Jo gulped down the bubbling potion. "You want to take care of me, huh?"

"Yup!"

"Okay." Jo grinned. "But don't worry about me too much. My indigestion isn't that bad."

Settling in on the sofa, Brue buried her nose in a book. She looked as if she did not have a care in the world. Meanwhile, Jo sat next to her, admiring the care Brue so easily hurled to the wind.

Jo rummaged through her mending basket, plucked out a sock, and busied herself with darning.

Several minutes later, Brue looked up. "Is your stomach feeling any better yet?"

Jo smiled. "Maybe a little. The Alka-Seltzer probably needs a few more minutes to work, though."

But much like her stomach that even Alka-Seltzer did not easily soothe, Jo's thoughts were hard to tame. She mused about her significant increase in income and how much she needed it. She recalled those heavy baskets of laundry at her old job and how relieved she was that she no longer had to lift them. She considered the interesting new challenges she was facing, the people she had the privilege of meeting, and the joy of making a great new office friend.

But then there were those opposing thoughts that niggled at her.

Did Tryg really forgive her for her misstep with the Glanzes or did he tell her what she wanted to hear? Did he find her inexperience too burdensome? Would he feel relieved if she left his law practice? She forced down a flutter of rejection accompanying that dreadful thought. What bothered her most was Tryg himself. How could she possibly hold her feelings for him in check day after day for the rest of her working life? She stopped stitching and stared at the sock she held with both hands. *Day after day for the rest of my working life? Now that's presumptuous.*

With every stitch she pulled up, Jo's appreciation for her job intensified. With every stitch she pushed back down, fears about losing it and her thoughts about Tryg grew stronger.

Jo folded the sock on her lap and gently smoothed it with the tips of her fingers, and gazed at Brue. "Sweetie?"

"Hmm?"

"I was just thinking. You remind me of when I was about your age. I don't think I ever told you, but I used to love sitting at my grandmother's knee. Those days bring back such warm and happy memories."

"Did your grandma darn socks, too?" Brue asked.

"She sure did. I remember loving it when she stopped every now and then and mussed with my hair."

"She sounds nice."

"She was."

"What was your grandpa like?"

"He was great. Completely devoted to his family. He was an avid reader, too. Used to read by lamplight."

"What kind of stuff did he read?"

"He read the newspaper mostly." Jo smiled. "Reminds me a little of you."

"Why?"

"Because he loved reading books. He had a library full of them. He also read a passage from the Bible every day. I can still hear his voice. It was so reverent and mellow."

"Why are you smiling, Mom?"

"Oh, I was just thinking, I guess. I still remember his favorite passage of scripture. He quoted it all the time. It was from the Book of Romans... *'And we know that all things work together for good to them that love God, to them who are the called according to His purpose.'*"

Brue wrinkled her nose. "You mean good things even come out of bad things?"

"That's right. They can."

"Hunh!"

Jo reflected on her trials with Tryg and looked up. *All things?* How could anything good possibly come out of that?

Sorry, Granddad. Wrong scripture; wrong time.

Later, after tucking Brue into bed, Jo went to bed, too, but was still too worked up to sleep. Life in the office was growing increasingly worrisome. Her feelings toward Tryg violated Case's memory. Accepting his job offer was a huge mistake. Without thinking, she willingly opened a door that needed to stay closed. But what could she do about it now? She needed a job, but not at the expense of trespassing against her husband or, for that matter, trespassing against herself. She punched her pillow, whipped around like a dog chasing its tail, pulled up the covers, and started all over again.

Anyone but Tryg.

In the wee hours of the morning, she gave up her idea of getting any more sleep, pulled herself out of bed, slipped on her pink robe and matching slippers, and wandered from window to window, staring out into the night as though it might be possible to find Case out there. She stopped when she reached the kitchen window and rested her fingers lightly on the sill, her forehead cooling against the pane. *Why did you have to die Case? Why? We had each other. We had a future. We had harmony in our home. Together we had everything.*

But nothing could undo his death.

She continued staring out the window for the longest while, contemplating her options, which were few.

Finding a new job was a possibility, but where? She'd already found out how few jobs were available to someone with her glaring lack of skills.

Like Tryg, she might consider indulging in a new relationship, but looking for a relationship wasn't her style. Besides, that needed to happen naturally, fall into place easily, and she was anything but interested anyway.

Like it or not, it all simmered down to finding a new job or finding a new relationship, and fast. "But I don't want either one," she whispered to herself. And either one would be a challenge.

Then, like a boat that finds its way back to harbor, her granddad's favorite scripture returned, setting her to wonder. *'And we know that all things work together for good to them that love God, to them who are the called according to His purpose.'* This time, she tucked those words away in her heart, determined to look for a way out of her dilemma while at the same time looking for the good in her sad and broken-down world, even if that meant nothing more than putting a smile on God's face. That thought alone meant everything.

CHAPTER TWENTY-TWO

J o! How nice to see you," Sarah said, but the reticent look in her blue-
berry eyes seemed to mock the cheerfulness in her voice. "You're
back again so soon?"

Jo smiled to herself. *Yes. I'm helping all things work together for good,
thank you very much.*

"And so early on a Saturday morning?"

The second question caught. Jo unthinkingly wheeled her gaze back
toward the entry. What if she'd made a mistake by coming here? Too
late to worry about that now. "Yes, ma'am. I hope it's okay to stop in
again unannounced."

"Of course it is." Sarah looked at Jo warily. "Say, is everything okay
with you?"

"Not yet." Jo forced a confident smile. "But it will be, I hope. I'd just
like to have a few minutes with your grandfather, if that's possible. Has
he finished eating breakfast yet?"

"Just finished. Your timing is great. Go right on back."

Jo hesitated. A handful of footsteps later, she knocked lightly on
Big Ole's door. "Good morning! I was wondering if I might have a word
with you."

Ole looked up from his massive desk, his chunky cheeks bunching
up at the sight of her. "Certainly. Come in."

"No need to get up," Jo insisted.

Ole stood briefly just the same. "Jo Bremley, you're a sight for old and dimming eyes. Please. Have a seat. And tell me, what brings you back again? And so soon?"

Jo lowered into the black leather chair, not ready to answer. "I still miss seeing Calvin Doherty and the rest of the men here," she said, making a weak attempt to set the stage for her request. "It's so good to still find you around."

"Well, I continue to be happy to be here," he said, his smirk as charming as his voice was strong. "And it's wonderful that you stopped by. But I'm far more interested in learning about the law office. How are things up town these days?"

"Oh, they're doing fine."

Ole twisted in his chair. "Fine, you say?"

"That's right. Tryg's making some pretty good headway. He's quite the up-and-coming professional."

Ole sat back and lightly rubbed his ample chin. A raised brow erased a few wrinkles around his gray eyes, softened others. "We shared breakfast together not all that long ago," he said. "If you'll indulge me...I'd be happy to let you in on what I said to him. That is, if he didn't already tell you."

"I'm afraid he didn't mention anything about it."

"He didn't want you to get a fat head." Big Ole released a sizable laugh, but then he winked. "Not that you ever would, of course."

Jo smiled weakly. She wasn't here to talk about Tryg. She came hoping to get away from him.

Big Ole rested his elbows on the arms of his chair and intermittently pressed his steepled fingers together, his expression sincere, his tone thoughtful. "Let's just say that I let him know in no uncertain terms that our loss was definitely his gain."

Jo's cheeks grew warm. "Thank you. That's awfully kind."

"So what brings you to the boarding house? Or is this just a social visit?"

Jo drew in a deep breath.

"Oh my. Is it that bad?" he asked, his voice filled with concern.

She rubbed her palms against the arms of her chair. Her nagging feeling that she might be making a mistake by darkening the doors of the O.M. Harrington promptly gained strength. "Look, I know I can't have my old job back and that things are going well with you and Ernie Pritchard...which is great," she added quickly. "But I was wondering if you might have any other positions available. It would be temporary, of course, until I can get enough money together. I'd like to make another try at that move to New York. I'm happy to do just about anything— cleaning, cooking, whatever."

Ole leaned back in his chair and clasped his hands over his generous midsection, looking uncharacteristically apprehensive. "So that's the reason for your surprise visit today, is it?"

"Yes, sir. Over the greater scheme of things, I know my problems are golden. But I fear I made a mistake when I agreed to work for Tryg."

Ole interlaced his fingers and slowly began rocking. "Really? Now that surprises me. I thought you'd be very happy there. Tryg never mentioned a thing about any problems between the two of you."

"Oh, I am happy there. It's just that—"

He stopped rocking and looked strangely amused. "It's just that what?"

"Let's just say there are other things in life that are far more important than money."

"Such as?"

"Doing things for all the right reasons," Jo replied, her heart in her throat. She wanted to wriggle into a hole and take cover. "Peace of mind. Please don't ask me to explain."

Ole swiveled around in his oversized chair and gazed out the French windows lining the far wall. He rocked slowly for about a minute or so, undoubtedly collecting his thoughts. When he turned back, he said, "If you don't mind my asking, how old are you, Jo? Late twenties, maybe?"

She nodded.

"I see." He hesitated then twiddled his thumbs. "You know, you're about my granddaughter's age. You remind me a lot of her. The two of you could nearly be sisters."

"Thank you, sir. I consider that quite a compliment."

"And if you were my granddaughter, too," he continued, "do you have any idea what I would say?"

Jo shook her head, but expecting nothing less than a positive response, she felt a smile stretch throughout her insides. She'd worked exceptionally hard while at the boarding house. She knew he wouldn't let her down. Not Big Ole. They were bonded like family.

"I would say no."

Jo nearly fell off her chair. "No?"

"That's right. *No*. Absolutely not."

He turned on Jo! And so cruelly. "But why not?" she asked, her words breathy and too quickly spoken.

"Because you're running away from something," he said equally as fast, but then his tone softened, as if he downshifted emotionally. "What has you so afraid?"

This man could see right through her and, what was worse, she felt powerless to do anything about it. "I'd rather not say."

"Tryg Howland?"

Jo's eyebrows snapped together. She looked down at her wringing hands. "Why are you asking that?"

"Doesn't take much thought. That's where you're working, isn't it? At his law office? Now why would anyone want to leave an excellent and, I'm sure, very well-paying job for no apparent reason? Doesn't make sense, does it?"

Jo didn't respond at first, but then said, "Forgive me, but I'm feeling uncomfortably transparent at the moment."

"Don't apologize, my dear. I think I understand more than you realize. Tryg Howland is a very handsome young man. He's available. And he was your husband's best friend, wasn't he?"

"You certainly don't mince words, do you?"

"As I recall, neither do you." Big Ole chuckled lightly. "So you're feeling uncomfortable and want to 'come home' so to speak."

"I guess you might say that."

Ole stood and walked slowly to the front of his desk. He crossed his arms and leaned back, half standing, half sitting against it. "Even if I chose to help, which I would love to do, aiding you in running away from Tryg wouldn't help you at all, now would it?"

Jo eyed Ole. He had a reasonable point. She reluctantly shook her head, her eyes drifting toward the windows, wishing she could crawl through them. "Life sure doesn't get any easier, does it?"

"No, that it doesn't," he replied thoughtfully. "And what I'm about to say to you, I'm saying as if I were speaking to my own granddaughter."

"Do I really want to hear this?"

"No, but you need to."

"Okay," she said softly.

"I don't care if you go charging off to New York or to Paris or to London for that matter. You're never going to get a handle on life if you keep choosing to run away."

As Jo made a beeline for the door, Sarah was on the phone. She looked up and motioned for Jo to wait. "I told you he will call you back," she said into the phone. Her voice had an edge. "I know I told you that the last time you called and the time before that. He needs time. Yes. Thank you," she said.

After hanging up the receiver, she lowered her voice. "Do you have a minute, Jo?"

"Sure. Is everything okay?"

"I'm not sure. Grandpa refuses to talk to that man and yet he keeps calling. I'm worried about Grandpa. He doesn't need that kind of harassment."

"Has he told you what's going on?"

"No. Refuses to."

"Have you thought about involving the police or isn't it bad enough?"

"Not yet. I'm not sure how to handle this."

"You could always talk to Tryg. I'm sure he'd be happy to offer his two cents."

"Let me think about it, okay?"

CHAPTER TWENTY-THREE

J o wasn't in a partying mood. Not today. But she'd committed. Besides, thoughts of the aging farmhouse sitting on that small sliver of land immediately to the north of Hollandale and thoughts about Bill and Arendine warmed her insides. When she was in their presence, all seemed right with her world.

She and Brue arrived at one o'clock. A train of cars already lined the gravel roads sandwiching the country home to the south and east. Through its open windows and doors, an outpouring of music sung a cappella by a men's quartet from the Reformed Church drifted on soft air currents all the way down to the farthest end of the road. Card tables spread with white tablecloths checkered the yard along with semicircles of folding chairs, disheveled by the large number of guests settling in.

From a distance, the movement of an unusually attractive, middle-aged woman caught Jo's attention. Strangely well dressed for the casual occasion, she weaved effortlessly through the tables and chairs sprinkled across the farmyard. A sea of eyes followed her as she climbed the stairs of the tidy two-story home.

Must be new to the area, Jo decided.

Wearing a stylish off-white silk blouse and black skirt descending to mid-calf, the woman cradled a large handbag under her thin arm. Her auburn hair, brushed with golden highlights in the warm spring sun, was combed into an elegant upsweep.

Who is that woman anyway?

Jo and Brue said their usual pleasantries as they, too, weaved through the crowd and on up the front porch. Once inside, Arendine greeted Jo and Brue with warm hugs, then quickly readied a place on the tables for Jo to squeeze in her applesauce spice cake. Two tables butted together in the small dining room were filled to overflowing with potluck dishes—goulash, corned beef hash, scalloped corn, pot roast, mashed potatoes and gravy, pickled beets, string beans, peas, Jell-O, fruit salad, warm bread, and sweet-smelling cakes and cookies of all kinds.

"Thanks for your help," Jo said as she lightly patted Arendine's arm and looked around. "Sure is a wonderful turn out you always have."

Arendine's clear cocoa eyes gleamed, a grin further plumping her round cheeks. "We always seem to get a nice crowd when we open our doors. Seems people need people, don't we?"

Jo smiled and was about to respond when she noticed the lovely, beautifully coiffed woman with the large handbag passing by. "Who's that?"

Arendine glanced back, looking from side to side. "Her? Why, she's one of the Christiansen sisters, the one who lives in New York. She came home to spend a month or so with her parents." Arendine shook her head, the light in her eyes quickly dimming. "Bad time for the family, her brother getting buried overseas and all."

Jo recognized the familiar look of loss pervading the woman's eyes and slowly shook her head. "I heard about that. So that was her brother. What an awful shame."

"It sure is. You might want to have a chat with her," Arendine said. "She's a widow, too. She could probably use a friend while she's here."

After helping fill a plate for Brue and then herself, Jo and Brue headed outside to find a table.

"Jo!" someone cried out. "Over here."

Alice Ravenhorst stood in the shade of a large elm, waving them to her table. Alice's husband, Hank, was well-read and discerning. Jo found his views on local and world affairs fascinating, these days even more so with all the talk about war. As Jo and Brue seated themselves, Hank, who was sitting with his back to the picnic table, leaned forward, his thick forearms resting on his muscular thighs, sun-baked hands folded, deeply lost in conversation with Jack Muilenburg. But not too lost to give Jo a welcoming nod.

Holding a glass of lemonade in midair, Jack leaned toward him with his foot propped against the table's wooden seat. He nodded warmly at Jo, too, and then quickly returned his attention to Hank. "It's a rotten shame that Operation Market Garden got to be such a mess, but now that the Allies finally took over Arnhem, I say it's only a matter of time before the rest of the German forces surrender."

Jo lifted her fork. The men already gripped her attention—her hope surging for a swift end to that dreadful war.

"Can't happen soon enough as far as I'm concerned," Hank said, his voice straining. "Our boys took quite a beating over there."

Jack's thick eyebrows raised a good inch. "Hear anything more from Cousin Arend?"

"Sure have. Just the other day." Hank hesitated. A wily smile wriggled across his lips, and with a tilt of his head and no small amount of pride, he said, "He's got mettle, Jack. That boy's sure got mettle."

As if he sensed Jo's need to know, Hank offered by way of explanation, "Arend's our cousin. Lives in Arnhem. Right in the middle of this whole mess."

Jo shuddered at the thought. As she listened intently, she visualized what life must be like at the other side of the world. When Hank told how his cousin had been hauled off to a work camp, Jack said, "No!" then set his lemonade on the table hard and fast, spilling it over the top of his glass.

Jo quickly reached across the table and wiped up the spill. But as she did, she flashed on Tryg, what he endured, and the significance of what he had been fighting for. She felt drawn to him harder than ever and wished for a moment that she could wipe clean her random thoughts of him as easily as the spill.

"Oh yes, and you know Arend," Hank said. "He always did know his own mind. He has no intention of helping out the Germans."

"But what did he do?" Jack asked.

"They forced him to dig trenches. Imagine that! He wasn't about to cooperate any longer than he had to. Not for the Krauts. He said that before he found a way to get out of there, the Allies flew overhead and unloaded a few bombs. There Arend stood with a shovel in his hands and nowhere to run. Some men just up the trench from him got buried. That was a little too close."

Jack choked down a man-sized bite of cake and quickly chased it with a swig of lemonade. "When you say Allies, you're including the Americans, too, right?"

"No. The Allies and Americans split their missions. Allies fly by day, Americans by night. That way they stay out of each other's flight patterns. I think I have that right, anyway." Hank stopped long enough to look around at the interested faces at the table and then continued. "Arend waited it out. He knew the Black Forest like the back of his hand, so as soon as he got a chance, he hightailed it out of there. Slipped into the woods and doubled back home."

"That sure took grit."

"It gets better. He said he ran into another group of workers on his way out. An officer saw him and confronted him. Asked him what he was doing. Told Arend to get in line with the rest of the workers. Arend didn't flinch. He had his fill of helping out the Nazis."

"What did he do?"

"Told the guy he was carrying a message to a German commandant farther up the line." Hank shook his head, but not without a cheering grin.

"Let me guess," Jack said. "That gullible officer let him go."

"That's right."

"Unbelievable." Jack balanced another forkful of cake in midair. "Where'd he get that kind of courage?"

"Probably from us."

"Why do you say that?" Jo asked incredulously.

"He believes in us. Said there was no way the Americans would ever bow down to Hitler." Hank shook his head. "He said he watched a train blow up, too. The train must have been hauling munitions. All he commented on was the fire and how huge and bright it was. Said he'd never seen anything like it."

As Jo considered the trains chugging so freely and deeply into the Netherlands, something made no sense. "Why don't the Dutch blow up the tracks?" she asked. "That would block the flow of Hitler's supply lines, wouldn't it?"

"They would if they could," Hank said without hesitation, "but I'm afraid it's not that easy."

"Why not?" Jo asked. "The Dutch are principled people."

"What we Americans have difficulty comprehending is how controlled and afraid everyone is over there. Even though the Dutch don't want any part of helping Hitler, they're forced to guard a mile of track. If anything happens during their watch, they get killed. Simple as that. And it's the old German men who are forced to oversee them. Arend says a lot of those guys are good men, really good men. They don't want the war any more than the rest of us."

"But what about us and the Allies?" Jo asked. "Why aren't we blowing up the tracks?"

"We do. Every chance we get. I understand there's a place in Arnhem where the tracks intersect. Gets blown up all the time."

As the afternoon progressed, the more people ate and drank coffee, the warmer their smiles and the louder their chatter. And still Jo listened, absorbed, as Hank and Jack chatted on about the fate and deteriorating power of Adolph Hitler, Roosevelt's sudden death, and the mountain of headaches Harry Truman got saddled with.

Jo became concerned, however, when she noticed the attractive and impeccably coiffed Christiansen sister slipping in and out of the old farmhouse increasingly often. Feeling a need to make her feel comfortable and at home, Jo politely excused herself from those gathered at their table and ascended the porch steps.

"Excuse me, but I've been wanting to meet you. My name is Jo Bremley," she said with an outstretched hand.

"Nice meeting you," the stranger said. "I'm Rainy."

"Rainy? What an unusual name. I like it very much. Actually, I have heard it before, but only once. Calvin Do—" Jo stopped speaking when Rainy flinched. "Don't tell me!"

Rainy clutched her purse tighter beneath her arm. "You know him, then?"

"I know him very well," Jo said. "He's a wonderful, wonderful man."

Staring off toward a grove of trees in a neighboring field, Rainy appeared to disengage. "How's he doing? Married? Children?" she asked softly, sounding as though she wasn't sure she wanted to hear the answer.

"No, I'm afraid not. He's still single. And he's the new pastor at Village Church now."

"I guess that doesn't surprise me." Rainy refocused her attention on Jo, but only briefly. "Nice meeting you," she said in passing, then slipped down the stairs a little too quickly and rejoined her family.

Finding her guardedly friendly, Jo didn't know what to think. But she did know how she felt—brushed off. An hour later, however, things started to make sense when Jo sought out Arendine and asked, "Have you seen Brue? The rubber on my tires isn't that good anymore. I think we'd better get home before it starts to get dark."

Arendine glanced around thoughtfully. "The back bedroom. She's probably there with some of her little friends."

Three doors cut into the narrow hallway, one on the left and two on the right. The first door on the right was barely ajar, but open enough that Jo caught a glimpse of something she felt anything but comfortable seeing. A woman was gulping amber liquid from a small glass receptacle, the liquid no doubt far stronger than water. Not wanting to make her feel uncomfortable, Jo quietly tiptoed back a few steps, called Brue's name, and then headed purposefully back down the hallway, careful not to look again through the slightly opened door.

The woman was Rainy.

CHAPTER TWENTY-FOUR

T he sun piercing through Jo's window prodded her eyes open, but failed to brighten her mood. She pulled herself up and perched on the side of her bed, where she lingered, swinging her legs slowly back and forth, staring at her slippers.

Big Ole Harrington.

What was she thinking? Why didn't she know better? The sting of the old man's words two short days ago still had the uncanny effect of reducing her to feeling like a small child—a dishonorable child at that. His counsel about running away was wrong, though. If a shoe doesn't feel comfortable, why wear it?

Exhaling a weighty sigh, she shuffled to Brue's bedroom and peered in. "Time to get up, sweetie."

An hour later, Jo kissed a cleaned, dressed, and well-fed Brue on the forehead, then with a loving pat on her backside, Jo stood on the sun porch and watched her march off to school.

A Canadian goose squawked excitedly near the shore of the sun-streaked lake. Jo turned and gazed at the commotion, stunned by a breathtaking palette of pastels, which brushed the entire eastern sky with wide, brilliant strokes. Under the circumstances, walking to work in the crisp morning air might do her a world of good, she decided. Besides, this would be a good time to pull herself up by the bootstraps.

She donned her flats and cardigan, grabbed her handbag, and trekked up the gravel road at a brisk pace.

She glanced cattycorner across the park at the O.M. Harrington, where Big Ole stood in the window lifting a cup to his lips while looking out toward the lake. Her unpleasant feelings flooded back. Fortunately, he didn't appear to notice her. How she regretted humbling herself only to get rebuffed. Big Ole's words were easy for him to say, but seemingly impossible for her to achieve. What if working for Tryg took her one stop sign too far? She needed to get away from him and stay away if she ever intended to shake off her infatuation.

At the corner of Charles Street and River Lane, the gravel road turned into a paved sidewalk. As Jo climbed the small hill, she exchanged a quick wave and hello with the milkman, who was hauling empty bottles away from the Engebretsons' front steps. Jo descended the hill, turned right on Newton, crossed the railroad tracks, and trudged up a far steeper hill toward town. At the halfway point, she paused to catch her breath.

Three blue jays soared above in the ice-blue sky. They split off, two flying to the east, one to the south. As she watched them, her mind yawned open. Suddenly, she understood.

Tryg served as an ever-present reminder of Case.

She was inadvertently projecting Case's attributes onto Tryg. Although they had been best friends, they were nothing at all alike. Case had blond hair and blue eyes; Tryg's hair was dark, his eyes brown. Case carried himself well with a smooth gait; Tryg acquired a limp that would never go away. Case had been approachable, warm, and kind, while Tryg was aloof and hard to read, especially when he wanted to be. No. They were nothing alike. Nothing at all.

She turned left by the county jail where a few men peered through iron bars and called out to her from the jailhouse windows. She smiled pleasantly and waved. She turned right onto Broadway, walked up several blocks, and then rounded the corner on East William. A few doors later, she gazed at the *T. W. "Tryg" Howland, III, Attorney-at-Law* shingle and smiled, not only at the shingle, but at her own silly deceit.

Ardena said a perfunctory good morning, commented about Jo's looking especially fresh and happy, and mentioned that Jo must have had a good weekend.

"It wasn't too bad," Jo replied.

Ardena gave Jo a more discriminating look. "Wasn't too bad? That's not what your smile is saying."

Jo grinned at Ardena's remark and tucked her handbag into the bottom drawer of her desk, then switched into her heels. A moment later, she opened her middle desk drawer and gasped.

Ardena gaped at her. "What's the matter?"

"'Tag, you're it, Jo'?"

"What are you talking about?"

"Look! It's the pen," Jo said incredulously. "Tryg gave it back to me."

"What's wrong with that? That's a good thing, isn't it?"

Friday afternoon's uncomfortable emotions gushed out faster and stronger than Old Faithful. Jo determined not to say anything to Ardena about the file folder incident. She had enough difficulty admitting her embarrassing feelings to herself. But to her misfortune, her early morning revelation was wrong. Case and Tryg had been very much alike. What was worse, she realized she couldn't wait to see Tryg come walking through the door. This was not good. Their relationship needed to stay professional. They had too much history behind them. Now the murky waters were turning to mud.

Ardena's rosy fingernail tapped Jo's desk. "Why do you have a problem with Tryg giving the pen back to you? And with a cute note? I think it's kind of sweet."

Jo didn't want this conversation to get any deeper, so she backed down. "You're right. I am being silly. It is. It's awfully sweet."

While Ardena returned to her desk looking anything but convinced,

Jo slipped the pen into her handbag. She needed to find a place to bury it. Somewhere at home.

"Tag, you're it, Jo"? I don't think so. This cat-and-mouse game needs to come to an abrupt end.

CHAPTER TWENTY-FIVE

"You certainly are at odds with your work today," Ardena said. Within the space of an hour, Jo successfully broke the lead on three pencils before trying again to lose herself in another day's work. But as she worked, Big Ole's words niggled at her. *How do I not run away?* she wondered. There has to be a way to do that effectively. Maybe he said that to punish her for leaving the O.M. Harrington in a lurch. No. He was too straightforward. It wasn't like him to play that game. But what earthly good could possibly come from sitting around and enduring Tryg Howland's presence? That had to be an exercise in willpower and nothing more.

Ardena sashayed to the supply room. On her way back, she stopped at Jo's desk and grinned. "We have more pencils in the back. I'd be happy to get some for you, if you'd like."

"I'm okay," Jo insisted. "This pen works fine."

"Everything's okay at home?"

"Everything's fine."

"Anything you want to talk about?"

"No!"

"I see," Ardena said. "Oh," she caught herself, "I forgot to tell you. Tryg called a few minutes before you got in this morning. Said he won't be in until closer to noon. He has some business to attend to at the courthouse."

Terrific! Had Jo known that earlier, she would not have broken the lead on three perfectly good pencils.

At a quarter to twelve, the door swung open and five feet, four inches of eau de cologne breezed into the office suite with the fresh feel of spring. "Hello. I'm Lauren Albrecht, here to see Mr. Howland," she announced. A gorgeous young woman with chestnut hair, hazel eyes, and long and sweeping eyelashes worth coveting, Miss Albrecht's voice was every bit as genteel as her presence. So much so that Jo found it difficult taking her eyes off of her. Rarely did such femininity, confidence, and poise come all wrapped together in the same package.

"He's running late," Ardena said. "You're welcome to have a chair in the waiting area if you'd like."

Ardena and Jo glanced at one another curiously, yet something about Miss Albrecht's presence said everything they needed to know and then some.

When Tryg strolled in a few minutes later, Miss Albrecht quickly met him at the door and lightly pecked him on the cheek. "I hope you don't mind my meeting you at your office," she said sweetly. "My appointment this morning didn't last as long as I thought it would."

"No. Not at all." He swept her gently forward by the small of her back. "Have you had a chance to meet Ardena and Jo?"

"I'm afraid not really," she answered with a demure smile.

Tryg led Miss Albrecht to Ardena's desk first. As he made a proper introduction, Jo burned with embarrassment and, if she were honest, disappointment. Trying to distract herself until they approached her next, she quickly riffled through a stack of papers, only to notice her polished nails had one too many chips. Normally something so insignificant wouldn't bother her, but right now she wanted to sit on her hands.

It didn't take long for the sound of footsteps on marble to hammer in her ears. "Jo, I'd like you to meet Miss Lauren Albrecht," Tryg said respectfully.

Jo stood and reached for Lauren's hand. "How nice to meet you," she said. But she noticed that something felt amiss. Lauren's handshake felt limp and her penetrating look cold.

Tryg seized Lauren's hand and said, "I'll be back in a couple of hours."

Jo felt a strange tightening inside as she watched them walk away. She took a healthy breath and steadied herself before saying, "She must be—"

"Tryg's lady friend," Ardena said, finishing Jo's sentence. "What do you know about that! Guess I was wrong about his dating status. They must have been seeing each other all along."

"Good for them," Jo said as nonchalantly as possible. "Do you know her then?"

"Sure do. She's an Albrecht. Comes from big money."

"My, she's absolutely lovely."

"She is, isn't she? But then, so are you," Ardena teased.

"Any idea how long they've been seeing each other?"

"I'll bet it's been at least five or six months now. Tryg's private about his personal life, and I sure haven't known him to be one for surprises."

"She looks like a class act," Jo said. "It must be awfully serious for her to feel comfortable showing up here at the office unannounced."

"That's what I was thinking. Tryg definitely looks happy with her."

But she did look a bit snooty, Jo mused. And frigid. *What on earth is the matter with me? Why am I being so petty?* "Think I'll get my brown bag."

Ardena looked up. "Say, are you okay?"

"Of course," Jo said, her words tasting too much like paste. "Why wouldn't I be?"

Jo lingered in the backroom. Big Ole's words resurfaced, striking her with the force of a flying brick. He was right about not running away after all. And, unfortunately, she just learned swiftly and in the most embarrassing way possible what earthly good can come from sitting around and enduring Tryg Howland's presence.

"What did Tryg's note say again?"

Jo jumped.

"I'm sorry," Ardena said, peering around the doorway. "I didn't mean to frighten you."

"I'm okay. What note? You mean the one with the pen?"

"That's right."

"It said *'Tag, you're it, Jo.'* Why are you asking?"

"I don't know. I was just thinking about it, I guess. Something doesn't make sense. Tryg is a good guy. He isn't cruel. But he has a lady friend. If he doesn't want the pen, why doesn't he give it to her?"

"I don't know."

His motives aside, Jo felt presumptuous and small. Suddenly, she just wanted to go home.

CHAPTER TWENTY-SIX

T ryg hurried across the office, a string of puddles trailing his footsteps. "That's quite some storm out there," he said as he tore off his galoshes. "It's pouring so hard, I swear the water splashed as high as my knees."

Jo glanced out the window where mist rose from the sidewalks in the battering torrent of rain. Lightning bolts sawed the sky, illuminating the office with a series of brilliant flashes followed by a deafening crack of thunder. The floor vibrated. The lights flickered. She gazed at Tryg and smiled at herself for thinking how good he looked even when he was wet. But then she caught herself. *Honestly! This is inappropriate. Get past it, Jo.*

"It'll move through fast," Ardena offered. "These storms always do."

Tryg draped his slicker over a hook on the coat tree and carefully balanced his umbrella on the floor beside it. "You're right about that."

Jo glanced at his calendar as he passed by, but then did a quick double take. "Ardena?"

Ardena's eyes remained transfixed on the sheet of paper she was rolling into her typewriter. "Hmm?"

"I see Sarah Harrington's name is penciled in on Tryg's calendar. Is that your writing or Tryg's?"

Ardena looked up and glanced at Jo curiously. "It's mine, why?"

"Sarah Harrington, as in Big Ole Harrington's granddaughter?"

"I think so."

"Did she say why she wants to meet with him?"

"No, she sure didn't," Ardena said, returning her attention once again to adjusting the paper in her roller. "She called over the lunch hour a couple of days ago. Asked if she could have a meeting with him. When I asked what it was regarding, she said it was personal and didn't seem to want to give out any more information, so I didn't press her."

"Something's going on with her grandfather. It must have gotten worse."

"What's going on?"

"I have no idea. She mentioned something about it the last time I was at the O.M. Harrington. I told her she might want to have a chat with Tryg."

The thunderstorm passed through quickly, but not without leaving the air oppressively heavy, gray, and damp. By midday, the sun broke through the cloud cover, but the air still felt close and moist.

Sarah arrived at half past one. She stepped up to Jo's desk and looked at her sheepishly, yet said nothing other than, "I decided to see Mr. Howland after all."

Jo nodded and offered Sarah a welcoming smile. "Yes, of course. I'll see if he's ready for you."

Not five seconds later, Tryg headed across the room with his hand extended. "Hi, I'm Tryg Howland."

Sarah smiled warmly. "Nice to meet you. I'm Sarah. Sarah Harrington."

"Please, come with me."

As they disappeared into Tryg's office, Ardena gaped at his closing door and shook her head. "She certainly is attractive. Another real beauty and in such a short window of time. Has a quality about her, too, just like her grandfather."

"She does at that."

A half hour later, Tryg's door grated open. "Jo, would you mind joining us for a few minutes, please?"

Jo casually slipped into his office. Judging by the tone of his voice, she was curious to learn what was happening with Big Ole yet not sure she wanted to know.

"I'm afraid we have a rather delicate situation here," Tryg said.

Jo directed her response at Sarah. "We do?"

"What you are about to hear is not to leave this room," Tryg continued. "Is that understood?"

"Understood," Jo said, her insides growing squeamish.

Tryg cleared his throat. "We have reason to believe our friend, Mr. O.M. Harrington, is being blackmailed."

Jo's eyebrows snapped together. "He what?"

"That's right. You might want to have a chair, Jo. Sarah can fill you in on the details."

Sarah shifted nervously in her chair then said, "Early last week, my grandfather was expecting some special guests, so I took it upon myself to tidy up his office. There were some ratty-looking notes that I stacked into a neat pile. I thought I'd slip them into his upper desk drawer until the meeting was over. When I opened his drawer, I couldn't help noticing a handwritten letter with large handwriting. The penmanship was unusual, not familiar at all. My curiosity was piqued so I unthinkingly started reading. You know how that goes. You get started and can't stop. I'm afraid I read the whole thing," she said, eyes cast down, cheeks flushed pink.

"Do you have the note with you?" Tryg asked. "It might be better if you read it to us."

Sarah looked upset. "I'm sorry. I wouldn't dare to take the note out of Grandpa's desk drawer again. But it did warn him against involving the police or any of the attorneys in town unless he didn't mind seeing his name plastered in the headlines of the daily paper. There was also a request for an unspecified amount of money. It said something about 'the same amount as before would be acceptable,' but didn't disclose the amount. It was signed by a man named Howard Rasmussen."

"Howard Rasmussen?" Jo repeated.

Sarah nodded pensively. "The man also gave my grandfather a time limit. That's why I came to see Mr. Howland, here."

"Do you have any idea what he could possibly have on your grandfather?" Jo asked.

"None whatsoever."

"Doesn't make any sense, does it, Jo?" Tryg said. "I can't imagine Big Ole Harrington ever doing anything he needed to hide. That's not consistent with his character and, knowing him, he would never have jeopardized his position as circuit judge."

"Sarah, have you talked to your grandfather about this?" Jo asked.

"Yes, I have. And as you can imagine, he's furious with me. He said I had no right to clean up his desk, let alone snoop around inside it. He warned me never to do that again and refused to say anything more." Sarah looked down, cradled her handbag tightly in her lap as if that gave her comfort, and then looked pleadingly at Tryg. "Howard Rasmussen has been calling a couple of times a day every day for the past week. I have no idea what the calls are about, but I do know they're taking their toll on my grandfather. He's been pretty subdued."

"Have you called the police?" Tryg asked. "Anonymously, I mean. Tried to feel them out to get a little direction?"

"No. I didn't want to take any chances. I need to keep this quiet for my grandfather's sake." Sarah turned halfway toward at Jo. "I know I can trust you," she said softly and then her gaze shifted again toward Tryg, "and I've heard only good things about you and your practice. I was hoping you might do some discreet checking around behind the scenes."

"I can't tell you how much I resent anyone being blackmailed, let alone your grandfather," Tryg said.

"What are you going to do now, Tryg?" Jo asked.

He gave his hair a quick comb with his fingers. "Sarah, why don't you give us a few days to do a little research? You have my word we'll be careful. Unfortunately, I can't promise we'll be much help, but we'll certainly give it a try."

Sarah's eyes narrowed. "You have to help," she said. "There's no one else I can turn to. My grandfather is getting up in years, and I'm worried he's more vulnerable than he would ever admit."

"Like I said, we'll look into it." Tryg glanced at his watch. "I'd like to take you next door for a cup of coffee to discuss this further, but, unfortunately, I'm waiting for an important call."

"If you go to The Copper Kettle," Jo quickly interjected, "I'll be happy to come and get you when the call comes in."

Was that irritation Jo noticed in Tryg's brown eyes?

To Jo's surprise, precisely one-half hour later, she heard Tryg and Sarah before she saw them. They giggled like a couple of school kids when they returned to the office. Tryg hadn't looked that carefree since his days before the war.

Ardena looked up from her typewriter. "What are Jo and I missing out on, if I may be so brazen as to ask?"

"Sarah here just told me some unbelievable stories about her grandfather," Tryg said. "He's one amazing man."

Sarah took a step toward Tryg and extended her hand. "I'd better get back to the boarding house. Thank you so much for taking the time to see me. I'll look forward to hearing from you when you have some information."

The instant the door closed behind Sarah, Tryg turned to Jo. "I want you to find out all you can about our friend, Howard. Make it a priority, okay?"

Jo pulled a thin manila folder out of the file drawer, titled Howard Rasmussen. She quickly leafed through the onionskin copies, reading them word for word, but found the information far too scant.

"Ardena, I need to run to the courthouse to do a little research," she said as she reached into her bottom drawer for her handbag. "Would you mind catching my calls? I'll probably head straight home from there."

"Be happy to. But what's going on? Dare I ask?"

"I've been advised not to say anything. I'm sorry, but I know you'll find out soon enough."

The hands on the clock on the courthouse tower were positioned at half past three. Jo had her work cut out for her. Once inside, she headed toward the staircase, the oak floor creaking beneath her heels. This was her first trip to the Clerk's Office; hopefully, the first of few in the Rasmussen quest.

Jo found a lady at the counter who bore a remarkable resemblance to Myrna Loy and exhibited a warm, efficient demeanor. When Jo asked for Howard Rasmussen's old records, the clerk returned a few minutes later with three manila folders, all thick.

"All of these are for Howard Rasmussen?" Jo asked.

"Yes, ma'am. You can use that corner table," she said with a point of her finger. "If you can't thumb through them before closing time, you're welcome to check them out, if you'd like."

"Thanks. Let me take a look first."

The wooden chair scraped loudly against the hardwood as Jo pulled up to the less than ample table in the furthermost corner of the file room. She realized she was in for a long haul when she stumbled across the name Butch Rasmussen, Howard's son.

Jo then asked for Butch's files. He had four, which were all thicker than his father's. Feeling she was undoubtedly wasting valuable time, Jo quickly riffled through them, scanning the pertinent information at the beginning of each document. About halfway through the second folder, however, she stopped and drew a deep breath. Big Ole Harrington had been named as a witness, but a witness to what?

Butch Rasmussen was a convicted felon.

CHAPTER TWENTY-SEVEN

J o glanced at her watch. I can't stop now.

The reprehensible information on the onionskin paper drew her in deeper than a prospector into an intriguing mine. Yet as she swiftly skimmed the pages, she sensed the courthouse growing eerily quiet. Just a few more minutes, a few more pages, a few more words. She glanced at her watch again. Nearing five already.

The kind clerk eyed Jo anxiously for the second time as she switched off the first set of lights. "Excuse me, ma'am, but we really do need to close."

"I'm terribly sorry." Jo gathered the thick manila folders and shot up a bit too fast, her nylon catching on a rough surface on the side of her chair. She hastily assessed the damage and moaned. Another nylon to mend. She needed to pay closer attention. New nylons were hard to come by these days.

"Would you mind setting these folders aside for me?" Jo lifted the heavy stack of files and shoved them across the clerk's counter. "I'd like to come back first thing in the morning and continue where I left off."

Jo returned to her car, trying to brush off a nagging sense of trepidation. She feared she might be on the verge of finding out something else she didn't particularly care to know. And yet, she found Butch's peculiar world intriguing—a normal person living a seemingly normal life who, for some strange reason, decided to blatantly exercise his right to live carefree and above it all. Unfortunately, he stumbled and fell over a jagged edge and headlong into a world that imprisoned him. Why would he willfully jeopardize his freedom?

The next morning, Jo stopped in Tryg's office before returning to the courthouse. "Got a minute?"

"Sure thing. Come on in. Have a chair. How's the research on Rasmussen coming along?"

Jo sat in the chair nearest Tryg's desk. "That's what I wanted to talk to you about. I'm concerned."

"Why's that?"

"Did you know Howard Rasmussen has a son?"

"No," Tryg said, his tone indifferent. "Lots of people have sons."

"Not in prison, they don't."

Tryg's eyebrows hiked a good inch. "You aren't serious! What for? What did he do?"

"I'm not sure yet, but I flagged a page in one of his files. I've got a sickening feeling this is going to get worse."

"What do you mean?"

"Big Ole was named as a witness."

"Big Ole Harrington?" Tryg pulled back, rested an elbow on the arm of his chair and lightly smoothed his chin, as if that gesture increased his ability to think.

How I wish he wouldn't do that! "Yes, sir."

"Any idea why he was named as a witness, or why the Rasmussen kid is in prison?"

"Butch Rasmussen isn't exactly a kid anymore." Jo smiled at Tryg's innocence. "He's older than we are by a good twenty or twenty-five years."

Tryg swatted his forehead with the heel of his palm. "Of course. What was I thinking? But that makes this whole thing even stranger, doesn't it?"

"What do you mean by that?" Jo asked.

"Someone the age of the senior Rasmussen blackmailing another man who's well up in years, too? Why would he do something like that?"

"You're right," Jo said. "That doesn't make sense."

Tryg rocked back in his swivel chair. "What about Big Ole being named a witness?"

"I'm still keeping an eye out for his transcript. Haven't come across it yet."

"Any idea why Butch Rasmussen is behind bars?"

Jo shook her head. "Haven't found that out yet, either. Thought I'd go back to the courthouse this morning. If I can't get through all of his folders before noon, I can always check them out and bring them back here to the office."

They said nothing for the better part of a minute, both lost in their own thoughts until Tryg rested his gaze on Jo. "Are you okay? You look troubled. Is there something you haven't told me?"

When she looked back at him, her mind derailed, shifting maddeningly to feelings rather than facts. Not feelings about Butch or Howard or Big Ole. Those feelings were appropriate. Her mind shifted to her guilt about having feelings for Tryg. She felt it again as she gazed into his warm eyes. It was wrong to feel this way. In some respects she was no better than Butch. Her unwanted feelings violated Case, Tryg, Lauren, and herself. She needed to get past them and promised herself she would.

"I'm fine, really. It's just that this doesn't have a good feel to it."

"No, it doesn't," Tryg agreed.

"I get the impression that I've only scratched the surface," Jo continued, "that our friend, Butch, indulged in some pretty deviant behavior."

"Why would you say that, other than the fact that he got hauled off to prison?"

Jo picked at a fresh ink spot on her wheat-colored sweater set. "Because at first I was sure his transgressions were only financial, but I get the feeling this goes well beyond money. I read something about an assault against an older man. Now that's serious stuff."

"That is. Any idea what happened or why?"

"Not yet. Hopefully I can have better information for you by early this afternoon."

As Jo stood to leave, Tryg looked down at his calendar, the wheels spinning in his mind nearly visible.

"Sounds good," he said. "Maybe I'll give Sarah a call. See if she can stop by the office or meet with me at The Copper Kettle at noon. I'll ask her if her grandfather ever mentioned Rasmussen's name."

"That's a great idea. Tread carefully, though."

Tryg looked up. "Why'd you say that?"

"We both know Big Ole. We don't want to cross him. And it's not like we haven't already taken an immense step in that direction."

Tryg nodded. "I know. I've been thinking the same thing."

CHAPTER TWENTY-EIGHT

isregarding the soft voices and careful tiptoeing across the room, Jo studied Butch Rasmussen's files for the better part of the afternoon. When she finally gazed at the clock to give her strained eyes a well-needed rest, it was three minutes to four. She checked the files out of the courthouse and lugged them back to the office. She was still heavily engrossed in them when Tryg returned.

On his way back to his office, he stopped by Jo's desk and asked, "Can I have a word with you?"

Tryg closed his door behind them, requesting that she please have a seat. He rested back against the corner of his desk, a little too close to her chair for her to fully relax. He was deep-in-thought serious.

"I have the feeling we're wading knee-deep into something sinister here," he said.

Jo didn't feel comfortable with the tone of his words. "What do you mean?"

"While you were at the courthouse, I had that luncheon meeting with Sarah."

"Did you ask her about Butch or his dad?"

Tryg slipped his hands deep into his pockets and shook his head. He appeared doubtful. "I got the feeling that wouldn't be a very bright move."

"Why not?"

"Well, it was the oddest thing. I thought I'd ease into my questioning by going back in time, so I asked her about her parents."

"Sarah's parents," Jo said thoughtfully. "Now that you mention it...I never thought of it before now, but I've heard plenty about Ole's wife and his granddaughter, yet never a word about his children. Parents brag about their kids. They don't hide them as if they didn't exist unless they were somehow estranged. What did she say when you asked her?"

Tryg shrugged. "She recoiled."

"Any idea why?"

He nodded. "Said her mother died in childbirth."

"No wonder." Jo looked away. "How sad. I can't imagine what it must be like for a young girl to never get the chance to know her own mother."

"I thought she was just feeling apprehensive about that," Tryg said, "so I pushed further."

Jo's head snapped up.

"That wasn't the right thing to do," Tryg said.

Jo felt a brief tic as her forehead tightened. "Why not?"

"Because I embarrassed her."

"You embarrassed her? How could you possibly do that?"

Tryg lightly kicked at the floor with the heel of his shoe as if he were a small boy getting caught skimming frosting off a layer cake. "She doesn't know who her father is either."

"She what?" Jo asked, stunned.

"I'm serious. She said Big Ole and his wife raised her. Whenever she asked him about her father, Ole would only say that Sarah's mother never mentioned that much about him."

"Kind of makes you wonder why, doesn't it?"

"I'd say it means that Ole was telling the truth, or he didn't want to talk about it. Either that, or he didn't want to find himself getting caught telling a fairytale to appease her."

Jo stared at Tryg in disbelief. "That's not the O.M. Harrington I know."

"That's not the O.M. Harrington I know, either."

Neither of them said anything for a few moments. "What do we do now?" Jo asked finally.

"I don't know. I guess we're going to have to give this some healthy thought."

Jo pushed back in her chair. "Look, I don't mean to change the subject on you here, but I thought you'd want to know that while I was at the courthouse anyway, I took a few minutes to do a brief background check on Henrietta Braddingly. It appears that she—"

"We can go over that another time," Tryg said, cutting Jo off. "Right now I'm much more interested in finding out if you've learned anything more about Ole being subpoenaed to testify."

"No. I still haven't come across his transcript."

"I wouldn't be surprised if he got swindled by Butch somehow."

"That is a possibility," Jo said.

"Either that, or he might have witnessed that assault."

"You're right. I've thought about that, too."

Tryg straightened, stepped around his desk, and sat down. "Why don't you get back on it? Let me know the minute you find out anything."

Jo stopped on her way out. Resting her hand lightly on the doorknob, she turned back to Tryg, "But about Henrietta Braddingly—"

Just then his phone rang. He picked it up. "Tryg Howland," he said, listened for a brief moment, and then swiveled quickly away, waving Jo on without looking at her again.

CHAPTER TWENTY-NINE

C alvin fretted about this date, hoping beyond hope there would be no negative surprises. Although butterflies fluttered his insides, he restrained a smile as he strolled past the immaculately manicured hedges and up the narrow sidewalk. With its white-trimmed bay windows and receded double-door entry, he found the primrose house quite charming.

Having spent the bulk of the past couple of days rehearsing this evening in his mind, he felt as if he were back in high school again. He reached for the doorbell, recalling the moment he first laid eyes on Ardena in The Copper Kettle. His attraction to her was immediate. When she attended Village Church with Jo on Sunday morning, he knew he read her motives correctly. She was attracted to him, too. Besides, she didn't hesitate to give him her phone number when he took a chance and called her at Tryg Howland's law office to ask for it.

But she wasn't Rainy. There will never be another Rainy.

The instant Ardena opened her door, the cadence of Calvin's heart accelerated, vibrating softly like brushes on a snare drum. She looked strikingly beautiful in her cocoa-brown dress. As they strolled down the paved path toward his car, she holding lightly onto his arm and the faint scent of her perfume pervading the air, he felt a sprightliness in his step for the first time in years. How swell to have a woman at his side again. Why did he wait so long?

Ten wonderful minutes later, they pulled into the parking lot at Stables Supper Club, a rustic yet upscale restaurant forged from an old stable. Immediately inside the entry, candlelit round tables with white table linens and wooden chairs dotted the rough-hewn floor. *Twilight Time* drifted softly from the grand piano in the loft above. Calvin gazed at the spiral staircase with its wooden banister sprawling up toward the lounge. He'd never been in the loft before. Few ministers frequented those sorts of places. But he was curious just the same and wanted to give it the once-over someday.

Following the hostess to their table, Calvin smiled appreciably. Ardena, even with a few years behind her, still had the ability to rotate heads.

Their first topic of discussion over supper was the war. They discussed, in depth, where it waned and where it escalated. Calvin sat with rapt attention, fascinated by how effortlessly Ardena managed the ebb and flow of the conversation, speaking knowledgably about the atrocities carried out abroad as well as the military's strategy and might.

"You may think this strange," she confided, "but I do miss the front."

"You what?" Calvin asked, incredulous. "The front of what?"

Ardena giggled. "I was a nurse in the European Theatre."

"You were?"

"I see that surprises you."

"Yes, it does. I'm very surprised. But with all of your military knowledge, I should have known better. How'd you manage to get out? The war isn't over yet."

Ardena shook her head and said understatedly, "We don't generally think in terms of nurses receiving the Purple Heart, do we?"

Ardena appeared to balk at Calvin's light burst of laughter. "What's so funny?" she asked guardedly.

He reached across the table, and as he lightly touched her hand, he smiled at the butterfly wings fluttering again throughout his insides. "I'm sorry. I certainly didn't mean to come across as being a cad. It's just that we share something in common."

The waitress appeared and gathered their dishes. "Would you care for dessert?"

Calvin turned to Ardena. "Would you?"

"No," she said graciously. "I'm fine."

"I'll be right back with your bill, then."

Ardena watched as the waitress slipped away then said, "You mentioned that we share something in common?"

He nodded pensively. "I have a Purple Heart, too."

"Oh my. But then, that doesn't surprise me, really," she said with a generous measure of warmth. "I hope your wound wasn't too bad. Or should I say wounds?"

"A little shooting pain in the shoulder every now and then when I move the wrong way, and sometimes in my right leg, but nothing I could ever complain about."

"So after you healed, you returned stateside and took over the pastorate at Village Church, right?"

"That's not exactly the way it went," Calvin confided. He picked up his napkin and rearranged it neatly on his lap, diligently ironing out the folds with the flat of his hand as if he were ironing out his thoughts before speaking. "Let's just say that God and me, we weren't on the best of terms for quite some time."

Furrows of concern creased Ardena's forehead. "Oh dear. I'm sure whatever separated you must have been very painful."

"What separated us was my fault," he said, looking unwittingly and deeply into the warmest, kindest, and most accepting eyes he'd seen in his lifetime—with the exception of Rainy's. "If you want, I'll tell you all about it later. That aside, if I'm not being too inappropriate here, I'm curious. Why are you working at Tryg's law office instead of Naeve Hospital?"

Ardena shook her head, her smile reticent. "You're not being inappropriate at all. Actually, there were two things I wanted to be when I grew up—a nurse and a stenographer. Because of my injuries, it looks like I'll have some physical restrictions for the rest of my life. So when I found out Tryg was looking for a stenographer, I jumped on it. Fortunately, he hired me, and I'm pleased to say that I'm every bit as happy working for him as I was nursing. To be honest, though, after all of the stimulation and demands that come with working on the front with wounded soldiers, I think taking a position in any hospital would feel like a step down."

At the completion of one of the most delightful dinners he ever had the privilege of sharing, Calvin drove along the tree-lined avenues toward Fountain Street. He wasn't about to cut this night short. Welcome sensations he hadn't experienced since his youth were beckoning him—the stirring of a fresh spring breeze; the staggering glow the moon cast over the sizable rippling lake; and most importantly, the intoxicating feeling of sharing the close of day with someone who made him feel highly regarded...the intoxicating feeling of falling in love. He parked the car at the side of the road and invited Ardena out into the uncharacteristically warm April evening for a casual stroll along the shores of Fountain Lake.

"Listen," he said as they walked slowly arm-in-arm. "The waves lapping against the shoreline. I love that soothing and rhythmic sound. Always have."

As they meandered along, stopping briefly every now and then to gaze out across the lake and up into the star-studded sky, they shared their life's stories—where they grew up, how many brothers and sisters they each had, their favorite childhood memories, how much differently their lives unfolded than either of them anticipated. As it turned out, they had much in common.

A few strokes before midnight, Calvin reluctantly walked Ardena to her door. How sad the night had to end. He expressed the desire to see her again—soon. To which she answered an unequivocal yes.

But as he powered down the streets toward home, how quickly the warm glow of the evening faded when wonderful memories of Rainy, dammed up long ago, rushed back in a torrent and flooded his heart.

CHAPTER THIRTY

Mom, do woodpeckers get headaches?" Brue craned her neck. She was looking at a red-headed woodpecker noisily pecking away at a dying oak.

Surprised by the question, Jo laughed lightly. "I'm not sure. But if they do, they're in real trouble."

Wearing their Sunday best, Jo and Brue stepped across the gravel road and into Harrington Park. The cool morning sun glistened through its fledgling elms, casting mottled shadows along its paths like a dappled work of art. Steeple bells pealed in the distance.

But the beauty of the early April morning did little to assuage Jo's apprehension when she locked unusually brief eyes with Sarah Harrington, who also entered the park, but from the west side. She looked lovely, wearing an ivory square-shouldered knee-length suit and a pompadour hairstyle. Big Ole ambled close at her side, eyes fixed straight ahead. His blatant lack of acknowledgement coupled with Sarah's hesitant glance caused Jo no small amount of concern. Ole, in particular, was a friend far too valued to lose.

Wanting to give Sarah and Ole an ample opportunity to gain some distance between them, Jo stopped Brue for a moment and unnecessarily refastened her shoe. As she knelt at Brue's feet, a pang of guilt niggled at her as persistently as that woodpecker tapping at that old tree.

Delving into Big Ole's private life without his knowledge or permission may not have been right, even if it was for all the right reasons. But Jo and Tryg were stuck. Why allow a viper like Howard Rasmussen to, figuratively speaking, sneak through Big Ole's back door and do nothing to stop him?

"Good morning," Jo said when she and Brue met up with the Harringtons at the double door entry of the church.

Big Ole turned, albeit hesitantly, while Sarah's fair cheeks blossomed into a brilliant shade of pink. "Morning," they mumbled in unison before disappearing into the vestibule.

Jo's heart sank. Ole knew about Sarah's meetings with Tryg, and appeared anything but happy. Jo was sure of it. But why shun her? Sarah approached her then Tryg, not the other way around, Jo mused in an effort to justify her guilt. Unfortunately, she was stuck in a miserable place, a place where she made a compromised decision and hoped beyond hope that, in the end, she made the right call.

Jo and Brue assumed their usual seat in the fourth row, far right side. The bells in the belfry chimed one last time. The congregation immediately settled down when Big Ole led the singing of the Doxology. Then, following the announcements and hymns, Pastor Doherty approached the pulpit. "Let's begin this morning's sermon with a recitation of The Lord's Prayer." He paused briefly as he looked over the congregation, his expression sober. "Please stand."

Calvin tended toward being purposeful. This was the first time he'd asked the congregation to stand at the beginning of his sermon. This was the first time he'd asked the congregation to recite The Lord's Prayer. He didn't hesitate to be heavy-handed when he had a point to make from the behind the pulpit, which fascinated Jo. She wondered what he was up to now. The congregation rose. The moment they completed the words, "forgive us our trespasses as we forgive those who trespass against us," Calvin broke into the recitation, and the worshipers grew silent.

"Lord, forgive us our trespasses," he repeated thoughtfully, "as we forgive those who trespass against us." He paused again. "As we forgive those who trespass against us," he repeated hammering home the thought; and then, without completing the prayer, he asked everyone to be seated.

"I received word from a good friend in the Netherlands this past week," he said, "about the release of an elderly woman from Ravensbruck Concentration Camp just north of Berlin. The woman's name is Corrie ten Boom. She was a watchmaker there in Haarlem before her imprisonment. A watchmaker," he repeated. "She was just released.

"These past few months, we've heard an increasing number of stories unfolding about the presence of concentration camps in Europe. Unconscionable stories. As we can all imagine, living conditions in these camps were and continue to be subhuman." Calvin gripped the pulpit and rocked uncomfortably on his heels.

"While at Ravensbruck, Miss ten Boom's diet consisted of a potato and thin soup at noontime, but only because she was assigned to hard labor. She was given turnip soup and a slice of black bread in the evening. Not enough to keep a squirrel alive. Betsie, her sister, had actually been whipped for not working hard enough.

"Imagine, if you will, the conditions in these camps. Inmates sleeping on flea-infested straw mattresses. Mothers helplessly forced to endure watching their young children starve. Many of the inmates shot, strangled, gassed, buried alive, or worked to death." He gripped the sides of the pulpit tighter. "Ungodly, unconscionable, and inhumane treatment.

"I suppose you're curious as to why Miss ten Boom was imprisoned, as was I. As it turns out, she, her father, and sister were active in the Dutch Underground. Simply stated, they hid Jews from the Nazis. This brave and loving act cost her father and sister their lives, breathing their last breath in a vile concentration camp. Now that Miss ten Boom has been set free and the war in the European Theatre is nearing its profoundly needed end, she will have another battle to confront. This battle will be a personal one—whether or not to forgive her captors. I don't doubt for a moment that she will take this on. I can't imagine a woman with her kind of courage and solid sense of moral decency not having the will to fight that battle as well, and win.

"Which brings to mind the question—from where did she get her courage and sense of moral decency when so many around her have lost their moral compass? I've given that a lot of thought recently. Which brings me to the book of Deuteronomy, chapter five, verses nine and ten, *'for I the LORD thy God am a jealous God, visiting the iniquity of the fathers upon the children unto the third and fourth generation of them that hate me, And shewing mercy unto thousands of them that love me and keep my commandments.'*

"Miss ten Boom was privy to her father's generational example and learned from him. He paved the path so much so that his love of God's chosen people and his commitment to their safety cost him his life."

Calvin then personalized his sermon, addressing the individual battles his parishioners were confronting, asking them to bring to mind someone they were unable to forgive, someone who had inadvertently caused them so much pain that they felt compelled to push the memory aside.

Jo considered his request. She was no Corrie ten Boom. Her challenges were embarrassingly minuscule in comparison. She did, however, reflect on her own shortcomings, and her need to forgive herself. She thought about her struggle with Tryg, and how it evolved into an ongoing and murky process of forgiveness, resentment, attraction, and guilt. Where, when, and how would it all end? Then she thought about Big Ole. Sadness squeezed her like the talons of a hawk sweeping in on its prey. After the dust settled, would he give her a chance to explain? Would he have the heart to forgive her when he understood her motives? *Please, Lord, help him to forgive me.*

Jo looked up and away from her musings, listening intently as Calvin continued his sermon.

"If Corrie ten Boom does, in fact, choose to forgive her captors, who initiated the tragic passing of her father and sister, her captors who made her life in the concentration camps a living hell—and, yes, she was in more than one camp—can we have the courage and moral decency to forgive the trespasses of those who have hurt us? Let's think on this as we go to our separate homes this week."

As Calvin was about to close in prayer, Jo looked up and observed him. When he preached, he definitely knew how to make everyone squirm. He made people accountable for their thoughts and actions when they were in his office, too. Counsel with him was not for the fainthearted.

Jo then glanced across the aisle at Big Ole.

But he did not look back.

CHAPTER THIRTY-ONE

Watching Lauren lost in decorating and art was more beautiful and moving than any piece of fine art Tryg had ever seen. She looked especially lovely and feminine in her high-collared white cotton blouse, three-buttoned black and white striped vest, and black slacks. She was standing in the entry between Tryg's kitchen and dining room, admiring the print of a Picasso she'd bought. Twisting and turning the picture. Studying it from various angles.

A grin tugged at his cheeks. After a long moment, he shifted his attention to banging pots and pans as he worked on Sunday's dinner. Not much into cooking, this was a rare happening for him. He glanced at Lauren and asked, "Would you prefer your spaghetti with or without meatballs?"

"With, thank you," she said distractedly.

"French dressing okay?"

"Mm-hmm."

"Garlic toast broiled or fried?"

"Fried, please."

"Water or milk?"

"Hmm?"

"Water or milk?"

"Water."

"Liver on your ice cream or chocolate syrup?"

Lauren hesitated. But then her gaze rotated slowly toward him and she burst into laughter. "I'm sorry. What a poor guest I am. Too absorbed in the arts here. In answer to your question, chocolate syrup would be absolutely delicious."

Tryg restrained a smile. "Chocolate it is, then."

Lauren held the print out to him. "Do you like this?"

"Looks great."

"What about the plants? Do you like them?"

"Yes, ma'am. They look great, too."

"You're making this too easy," she said. "You'd say you loved a painting if a cat dipped its paws in buckets of paint and slid them around on a large piece of canvas."

Tryg shrugged. Although he would never admit it, she was right.

Her eyes scanned the kitchen and then she strolled into his living room, her voice fading as she asked, "Are you sure you don't mind my bringing in an interior decorator?"

"Do whatever you'd like, just as long as I don't have to sell my law practice to pay for his services."

Twenty minutes later, Tryg called Lauren to the table. Dinner was one of his best yet—he didn't burn a thing.

He basked in the reinvigoration and reflection of Sundays. No thoughts about caseloads or how to drum up business allowed. Just steaming coffee with the early morning paper. Calvin Doherty's sermon at Village Church. A slow and easy dinner. A leisurely walk around the lake. Or a ride out into the country to clear his head and appreciate a world much broader than his everyday going-to-work world. A world where his mind slowed and he viewed life through a pure and honest lens.

After dinner, he and Lauren strolled the perimeter of Fountain Lake, one of the state's famed ten thousand lakes. Sailboats glimmered in the mild afternoon sun. A rowboat here, a motorboat there, listing on the quiet, soft waves. Taut fishing lines pulled deep into the fresh water. The afternoon was pleasant. But the farther they walked along the shaded trail near the northern perimeter of the shoreline, the less Tryg found he had to say. That troubled him. A good attorney had an arsenal of words at his disposal at all times. Whether or not he chose to voice them was inconsequential.

"Minnesota sure is a haven, isn't it?" he asked awkwardly. "I mean especially for sportsmen. All they need to do to get in some good hunting and fishing is just take a stroll outside."

Lauren must have sensed his discomfort. She stopped and looked up at him, her gaze innocent as she swiftly redirected the conversation. "I have a present for you."

"You do?"

"That's right. It's back at your place."

He picked up a large stone from the side of the road and hurled it into the water, then watched its ripples expand. "What's the occasion?"

When he turned back to her, she gave him an affectionate nudge and looked deep into his eyes. "Us," she said warmly.

He slipped his arm around her waist and pulled her close. "Us. I like that. I like that very much."

The moment they returned to his home, Lauren snatched the gift from her handbag and held it out to him. "Here. This is it."

"Want me to open it now?"

"Absolutely!"

Tryg ripped the paper away and lifted the cover off the long and thin box. "A pen?"

"You look disappointed. Don't you like it?"

"Oh, of course, I do. Thank you." But as Tryg studied the pen for a moment, a curious uneasiness enveloped him. Whatever he was feeling, he needed to ignore it. It was ridiculous. He slipped the pen into his blazer pocket. "You can bet I'll get a lot of good use out of it," he said determinedly. "Lots of good use."

CHAPTER THIRTY-TWO

eanwhile, Jo held the screen door open for Evelyn and
Poke.

"Mom, do you care if Poke and I go to the park and
play ball for a while?"

"We've talked about this before, Brue. You're no match for those
boys."

"But Heath won't be playing with us this time. It'll just be Poke and
me, and we'll only hit balls to each other. We'll be careful. We promise.
Don't we, Poke?"

Jo turned to Poke. "Have you asked your mother yet?"

His eyes lit up. "Can we, Mom? Huh? Can we?"

Evelyn looked to Jo who gave a hesitant nod. "I guess so," she said.
"But don't you go playing rough now."

"Oh goody. We won't." As they marched down the steps, Poke
turned to Brue and scoffed. "You're not gonna go and play like a girl
again, are ya? That's embarrassing."

Hearing the amusing exchange, Jo quickly called after them. "Come
back in an hour or so if you want popcorn."

Jo and Evelyn retired to the kitchen. Seeing the chess set readied on
the table, Evelyn grinned confidently and pulled up a chair. "I'm ready
for you today. I've been practicing my moves."

"We'll see about that," Jo said. However, after seven ingenious moves and the aggressive loss of her queen, she changed her mind. "You really have been practicing, haven't you?"

"Yes, I've been practicing, but I'm not this good. Is it my imagination, or is your mind somewhere else?"

"I'm okay, Evelyn. Really I am." She looked at Evelyn and chuckled. "No, I'm not. Things are kind of a mess right now, but they'll straighten out in time. They always do."

"Do they?"

"Yes, Evelyn. They do."

"Problems at the office, huh?"

"I guess." Jo thought for a moment then said, "Lauren Albrecht stopped by the other day unannounced."

"Tryg's lady friend?"

"Yes, ma'am."

"Their relationship must be pretty serious then."

"Must be. What I don't understand is why he didn't bother to tell Ardena and me in advance that he was having lunch with her. I mean, why the mystery? Why introduce Lauren with an added element of surprise? And you know that pen we got from Marianne Glanz?"

"I remember your telling me about it, yes."

"He returned it again with a note saying '*Tag, you're it, Jo,*' as if it were some sort of children's game. I feel like he's toying with me."

Evelyn moved a bishop. "Try not to make too much of it. It's too easy to slide deep down a dark and inappropriate pathway. The Tryg we know is anything but childish. He doesn't have it in him to be deceitful, to cruelly set people up, or to trifle with anyone's emotions."

"I know. That's what I thought. It's just that things aren't making much sense thee days."

After several more moves, Evelyn said, "You've gotten awfully quiet."

Jo nodded. "I was thinking about Case, how he and Tryg used to compete in sports. They were both such gentlemen. It didn't matter who

won or who lost, the loser held out his hand and genuinely congratu-
lated the winner. Always. I remember when they crammed for exams.
They were untiring, always quizzing each other until they exhausted
their cache of questions. They used to talk for hours out on the front
porch, too, discussing the news of the day, sharing their dreams into the
wee hours of the morning. They never spoke unkindly of anyone.

A light switched on. Jo sat up straight. "You're right, Evelyn. Tryg
isn't childish or deceitful or trifling with me. If Case were alive, I wouldn't
give the playful exchange with him another thought. It doesn't mean a
thing. It's one friend enjoying with abandon the friendship of another.
Nothing more. Tryg obviously connected lines I never thought to connect before—a triangle of lines from him to Case to me and back again.
He considers me his friend." *Nothing more.*

Reaching for her rook, Jo's hand froze in midair when a spine-chill-
ing howl rang out from the direction of the park. Jo and Evelyn hopped
up and in an instant, they shot out the door.

Brue came running toward them. "It's Poke," she shrieked. "He fell
down and I can't get him to get back up."

Poke was still wailing when Evelyn and Jo reached him. They hurried him home, packed his arm in ice, and fashioned a makeshift sling
out of a dishtowel. Ten minutes later, they arrived at the emergency
room at the west end of Naeve Hospital. Poke moaned and cried the
entire time.

When they entered the examining room, Evelyn carefully removed
the sling and ice pack. Several minutes later, a concerned doctor entered.
"I understand we've had a little accident here," he said gently. "May I see
your arm, young man?"

Poke held out his arm. The doctor no more than lightly touched it
when Poke let out an ear-splitting shriek.

Brue shifted to the edge of her chair. "But that's the wrong arm," she
said.

The doctor glanced at Brue and then at Poke's other arm. "You're right about that. The other arm does look a little swollen," he said, a grin cutting deep into his lean cheeks.

After an x-ray revealed a hairline fracture, the doctor insisted Poke keep his arm in a sling while it healed. He then handed a wet-eyed Poke a cherry sucker and released him to his mother's care.

On Sunday evening, after tucking Brue under her covers, Jo sat at the far end of the sofa to unwind. The white marble lamp beside her cast a glow across a crocheted doily that draped the end table, exposing a few offending specks of dust, which Jo easily polished away with a quick wipe of her handkerchief.

The lamplight also shimmered on Marianne Glanz's ruby red pen. Jo picked it up. Smoothing it with her fingertips, she stared across the room at nothing in particular.

The afternoon's drama with Poke lay heavily on her mind. She relived the sight of the doctor's smirk when Poke wailed at the touch on his uninjured arm. He sounded unrelentingly tough when he trudged down the steps with Brue, telling her not to embarrass him by acting like a girl. But in the end, he was the embarrassment. Did his hairline fracture hurt? Sure it did. Did he need to be that dramatic? Absolutely not.

And then she thought of her reaction to Tryg and felt herself blush.

She switched off the lamp and headed to her bedroom, where she carefully wrapped the pen in a handkerchief and buried it deeply in the back of her bottom dresser drawer. She crawled into bed, burying her thoughts of Tryg as deeply as she buried the pen. That was, after all, the right thing to do.

Tomorrow would be Monday, and she would return to the office. She smiled a relieved smile as she drew her covers up past her shoulders then rolled over onto her side to nestle in for a good night's sleep.

She fluffed her pillows. Stared at the ceiling. Stared at the shadows on the walls. Rolled over again. Glanced at the clock only to realize that sleep wasn't about to come easily.

Lauren Albrecht. That look. That handshake. Something is very not right.

Jo glanced at the clock again. Five minutes past eleven. Ten hours to go. Why were Sunday nights so difficult?

CHAPTER THIRTY-THREE

B y sunup, her sheets and blankets were strewn across the foot of her bed, her sleepless head feeling as miserable as her disheveled bedding looked. After a quick breakfast with Brue before scooting her off to school, Jo hurried to town. Like entering a dark and abandoned house alone in the middle of the night and switching on a light, there was something about the sights and sounds and smells of an office that also had the power to mute a distressing reality.

When Jo arrived, however, Tryg was not only in his office, but behind closed doors as well.

She hung her coat on the clothes tree next to his and then slipped into the back room to percolate a pot of coffee. But it was already perked.

She poured a steaming cup and went back to her desk.

Ardena arrived a short while later. "You're here already?" she asked as she peeled off her gloves and hooked her coat on the clothes tree.

Jo nodded.

"Everything okay? You look a little under the weather."

Jo shrugged. "I'm fine. Problems sleeping, I guess."

Ardena's face clouded. "Again? Why? What's going on now?"

"Just a second," Jo said, looking curiously toward Tryg's door. "I don't know if it's my imagination or not, but I think I hear someone in there with him. I wonder who that is. There aren't any meetings on his calendar this morning."

"That is odd, isn't it?" Ardena lowered herself onto her secretarial chair. "We'll find out soon enough. So in answer to my question..."

"I just have a few things I'm trying to work through. Don't worry. I'll get a handle on it."

"I'm here for you if you need me," Ardena said reassuringly.

Jo jumped at a loud pounding sound that unexpectedly resonated from Tryg's office.

"What's going on in there?" Ardena asked, her eyebrows hugging each other. "Sounds like someone's hammering."

"I have no idea. I wonder if something happened over the weekend."

Jo listened intently, hearing soft voices again, one that of a woman, then more hammering, and then utter and complete quiet. Twenty minutes later, Tryg's door flew open and a cheery Miss Albrecht materialized. She trilled a warm, "good morning," sounding as if she was singing rather than exchanging a clichéd greeting as she breezed through the office and out onto the street.

As the minutes ticked by, curiosity about the hammering got the best of Jo, her eyes drifting every few minutes toward Tryg's door. It appeared from an occasional glance at Ardena that her curiosity was piqued, too.

Tryg emerged every now and then to refill his cup, grab a paperclip, or a file folder of some sort. But he said nothing about Lauren Albrecht or the hammering, and his silence invited no questions.

At five minutes to twelve, he fled the office, his mood still unreadable. "I'll be back in a couple of hours," was all he said.

As the door closed behind him, Jo thought about Tryg and the ever-present mystery surrounding him.

Ardena interrupted Jo's musing. "I don't know if I'll ever understand that man," she said.

"What do you mean?"

"His overt silence."

Jo sighed, relaxing in the solace of her office friend. "It can be loud at times, can't it?"

Ardena placed her pencil lightly on her desk and swiveled her chair toward Jo. "You know, when I was growing up, a wise old sage once told me that silence shouts without shouting, speaks without speaking, and whispers without whispering. I never forgot that. He warned me that I needed to be wise when I decided to use it. It draws attention. Sends messages the messenger doesn't necessarily wish to send."

How many countless times did Tryg blatantly exercise silence, drawing Jo's attention? And how often did he appear oblivious to what he was doing? "Who was the wise old sage, if you don't mind my asking?" Jo said.

"My grandfather. Tryg's silence intrigued me from the first day I started working for him. I've felt drawn to it. At times he's candid, but I'm usually left wondering what he's thinking and why he chooses to live so deep inside himself."

Jo fingered the corner of a manila folder. "I'm relieved to hear I'm not the only one who feels that way. I don't remember him being like that before he went overseas." But then a brief wave of emotional pain flowed through her. She moved the folder aside. "I'm sure it's the accident that's changed him. It's nearly impossible to not get caught up in it. And speaking of wondering about what he's thinking, curiosity's been pestering me all morning. Any chance you want to see what's he's been up to in there?"

"You bet."

"Since we're shamelessly invading his privacy, how about if we wait a few minutes to make sure he doesn't come back for something?"

"I've got a better idea." Ardena shielded herself near the window, peering out like a guilt-ridden kid. "He's standing out on the sidewalk waiting for someone. Wait a second. There's a car pulling up now. It's Lauren. I'll let you know when they take off."

Jo grinned as Ardena gave a blow-by-blow rundown of Tryg and Lauren's every move. "He's in her car now. Just closed his door. He's leaning over, giving her a quick peck on the cheek. Yup! That's what he's doing all right. She's rolling down her window. Shifting. Looking back. Signaling hand straight out. Oh my. There they go!"

Jo and Ardena rushed into Tryg's office like children set free for a long-overdue recess, Ardena grazing the side of the filing cabinet in her haste. They slipped inside and gaped around wonderingly, as if they were entering the Smithsonian for the very first time. Then Jo stopped abruptly. "Well, for heaven's sake," she said. "Would you take a look at that picture?"

"Isn't that a print of a Picasso?"

"Sure looks like it."

"Adds a little something to his room, doesn't it?" Ardena nudged forward, looking up, down, and all around. "And look at the healthy-looking plants in his bookcase."

"What about those handsome bookends?" Amazed, Jo stepped farther into the room. "Back-to-back sculptures of *The Thinker*," she said. "Those are the classiest bookends I've ever seen. Must have cost him a bundle."

Ardena touched her fingertips to her cheeks and slowly shook her head. "Looks as though Miss Lauren Albrecht is heavily into ambience. I'll bet her home is beautiful."

"I'll bet so, too." Jo's curiosity satisfied, she said, "Come on, Ardena. Let's get out of here. It's past noon. Time to eat."

Sitting at their respective desks, Jo realized that Ardena was strangely silent about her date with Calvin on Saturday night. The expression on her face was about as easy to read as a newspaper doused with a generous amount of black paint.

Jo drew a sandwich from her brown bag and painstakingly unwrapped the wax paper. "How'd your date go?" she asked understatedly. "You haven't mentioned a word about it. Did you and Calvin have a good time?"

Ardena lowered her sandwich, her eyes sparkling. "It was absolutely one of the most wonderful evenings I've ever had in my life."

Ardena had been holding back. It did go well. Jo sighed. "Why didn't you say something?"

Ardena shrugged.

"You have no idea how happy I am for you," Jo continued. "Calvin is by far one of the kindest and most honorable men I've ever known."

Suddenly a strange and sad look overshadowed Ardena's blissful smile. Not wanting to pry, Jo kept her questioning generalized. "So how was Stables Supper Club? Did you find lots to talk about? What did you do afterward?"

Ardena perked up again, but by the time she finished recapping the events of the evening, the light in her eyes had all but burned out.

"Okay. That's it," Jo said. "I wanted to be polite, but... There's something you're not telling me. Want to talk about it?"

Ardena gazed at Jo, her eyes revealing defeat. "When we were eating supper, he accidentally called me Rainy, and I swear I saw him blush. I can't seem to get it out of my mind. Who's Rainy?"

"Rainy?" Jo slowly shook her head and returned to her sandwich.

Rainy!

Jo and Ardena spent the remainder of their dinner hour lightly playing with their food, eating their meals in silence. With every bite she took, Jo would have preferred prodding Calvin Doherty with her fork instead of stabbing it into her salad. How could he carry Rainy in his heart while he was out on a date with Ardena? *How could he?*

Shortly after one o'clock, Tryg returned and called Jo into his office, said he wanted to plan ahead for the meeting they would be having with Sarah. Jo made sure he saw her gazing at the wall and bookcases when she entered. "Wow! What nice new plants you have here." She strolled up to the print and studied it. "And a Picasso, too? Nice. Very nice. Very, very nice."

She turned to see Tryg nodding briefly in acknowledgment. No eye contact. No words. Merely a slight and casual bob of his head.

CHAPTER THIRTY-FOUR

J o and Tryg were alone in his office, his door closed. He slipped his hand into the pants pocket of his navy pinstriped suit, revealing smart-looking navy blue suspenders with a burgundy stripe down the center, which set off beautifully his well-pressed snowy white shirt. His split-toe oxfords, the deep color of soot, were buffed to a high shine. One look at him and Jo feared she was going to have to make another trip to the cemetery to get her thoughts realigned. Her late husband was the only man she ever knew who had more appeal than T.W. "Tryg" Howland, III.

Rise above it, Jo. You're out of line again.

She waited patiently as he stepped behind his desk. Although he lowered slowly into his chair, she sensed his interest in an update on her research.

"You find out anything more about Butch?" he asked.

"Unfortunately, yes."

His eyebrow arched like the sliver of the moon. "Unfortunately?"

"It appears that he specialized in violating women."

"Is that a fact?"

"Rich women."

Jo waited for the shock to hit and Tryg's eyes to tether on hers. Didn't take long.

"So that's it," he said incredulously.

"So that's it," she concurred. "What are we going to do now? We can't say anything about this to Sarah."

Tryg tapped his finger lightly against his desk and stared mindlessly across the room. "But we don't know the truth yet. Maybe if we did more due diligence—"

"We're already in over our heads with Big Ole." Jo insisted. "I can't bring myself to go any further. Who knows what we'd find out? It wouldn't be right."

"But maybe Sarah's mother wasn't one of his victims. Have you given any thought to that?"

"How old is she?" Jo asked, having given the matter considerable thought. "Twenty-seven, right?"

"I don't really know, but that's got to be in the ballpark." Tryg hesitated, his analytical attorney mind appearing to kick into full gear. "Any idea when Butch went to trial?"

"Yes, sir. Try Nineteen Eighteen."

Tryg inhaled a roomful of breath before completely emptying his lungs of air. "Oh no!"

"Oh yes," Jo countered. "I still haven't found Big Ole's transcript, but it's not hard to calculate how those numbers add up."

After a long moment of silent distress, Tryg said, "I can't imagine the torment Ole must have gone through when he found out his only daughter was violated."

"And extorted," Jo added.

"And extorted," he repeated softly and then finger combed his hair, a habit he appeared to be unwittingly well into the process of developing lately. "Look, Jo. About my meeting with Sarah again later on in the week; Thursday, as I recall. I scheduled her at noon. Our meetings are short since she's usually breaking away during her noon hour. You wouldn't mind joining us, would you?"

"Be happy to."

"Great. I could use the support. I haven't felt good about this whole thing from the start, and won't feel good until we can get out from under it. But I'm afraid we're going to have to handle this very carefully."

"What are you going to tell her?" Jo asked.

"I'm not sure yet. How about a stunted version of the truth? We can't violate Big Ole's privacy any more than we already have."

"But if he's being blackmailed—"

"Think about it, Jo. If he's being blackmailed, he's a grown man. More so than most in every way imaginable. I'm sure he can handle the elder Rasmussen himself. It's more than clear that Ole's protecting Sarah."

"You're right," Jo said. "I'll be relieved when we can get out from under this, too."

Since she passed by the courthouse on her way home anyway, Jo left the office a few minutes early and stopped by the Clerk of Court's office to drop off the Rasmussen folders. Not five minutes later, she returned to her car and headed down the streets toward home. When her tires rolled off the asphalt and noisily crunched gravel on her short dead-end road on Charles Street, she turned and glanced into Harrington Park.

Big Ole was sitting alone on his usual bench in the middle of the park, mechanically tapping his cane against the concrete sidewalk. He looked deep in thought, troubled. She slowed down, hoping he would look up and wave as she motored past.

But he did not.

CHAPTER THIRTY-FIVE

Wanting to get a good booth for privacy, Jo and Tryg arrived at The Copper Kettle early. At twelve o'clock straight up, Tryg met a swift-moving Sarah at the door and escorted her to their table. Not only was her entrance timely, she attracted no small amount of attention in her stunning crimson dress with its square neckline, pleated skirt, and matching crimson gloves. The look in her eyes, though, was difficult to read.

As they settled in, Tryg, who apparently felt some unwarranted obligation to explain, said, "I asked Jo to join us. I hope you don't mind."

Jo reached for her arm, "Look, if you prefer that I leave—"

"No," Sarah said, shaking her head firmly. "I want you to stay."

The waitress appeared with menus wedged beneath her willowy arm, hurriedly plunked tableware and napkins on their table, and then placed menus at their individual settings, and said, "I'll be back in a minute. Take your time deciding what you'd like."

Tryg made small talk about the weather and a few benign local events. They ordered. Halfway into their meal, he reached for his napkin and dabbed an absence of food lightly away from the corners of his mouth. "Sarah, I'm afraid we don't have much time. Since we're here to talk about the case, I—"

Sarah raised her petite hand to stop Tryg, then blotted her mouth with her napkin as well. "We don't need to talk about it anymore."

Tryg's sidelong gaze cut toward Jo. "What? Why not?"

"Because my grandfather is furious with me."

Noticing how upset she appeared, Jo reached for Sarah's arm again, touching it lightly. "I can't tell you how sorry we are to hear that. Are you okay?"

"I'm fine. Sort of. I know I should have told you before now. That way you wouldn't be wasting an entire noon hour on me."

"You aren't wasting our time," Tryg insisted. "We all care about your grandfather very much."

As he looked to Jo, his eyes a silent plea for help, Sarah said, "I didn't know what to say or how to say it. The phone felt too impersonal. And I couldn't take a chance on the Operator listening in. Not that she would, of course."

"But what happened?" Jo asked. "That is, if you don't mind sharing with us."

"No. You deserve as much." Sarah inverted her napkin and slowly stirred it in a circular motion on the surface of the table, staring at it, looking as though she preferred crawling under it and hiding for the duration of their chat.

"When I got back from your office last week, Grandpa was waiting for me," Sarah said broodingly, a pained expression draining the youth out of her fair face. "Met me at the front door. Asked me where I'd been. It wasn't possible for me to feel guiltier."

Jo visualized Sarah's words as she voiced them. Big Ole's formidable presence standing at the door. Waiting. Glowering. It wasn't a visual she wanted to experience. And as for the guilt, Jo's culpability took on a life of its own, growing exponentially, making her insides feel as if they were in desperate need of a good washing down.

"He saw right through me," Sarah continued with a resigned sigh. "He's not the kind of man you want to play with. I learned that when

I was a kid. So when I told him I'd met with you, he led me down the hallway and into his office. He pulled his desk drawer out so hard that everything flew to the back. I nearly jumped out of my skin. Then he asked, 'Did you see them about this?' I didn't say anything. I didn't have to. I felt like a self-indulgent kid who can't keep her fingers out of a candy dish."

Tryg sat in rapt attention at the edge of his seat. "What happened then?"

"Let's just say he let me know in no uncertain terms I had no right meddling in his personal affairs. Said there are some things that are better left alone." Sarah picked up her napkin and carefully folded it, and then mindlessly folded it again. "So we've done enough. We don't need to intercede. He's walking into this mess with his eyes wide open."

"But what do we do now?" Jo asked. "I feel like I violated the poor man. And after all he's done for me." Immediately feeling guilty by her unchecked remark, Jo turned to Sarah. "I'm sorry. My comment has nothing to do with you. I really didn't mean to be insensitive."

"You didn't do anything wrong," Sarah insisted. "I came to you, and with what I thought was a very good reason."

"If I were you," Jo said, "I would have done precisely the same thing. It's just that somehow I feel like I need to make this right with him. What can I do? I feel stuck not being able to say anything. But professionally what *can* I say?"

"I've already handled that," Sarah said, her tone straightforward and confident. "I told him that I was the one who asked you to look into the blackmail, but that you hadn't accepted the case yet."

"What did he say to that?" Tryg interjected.

Sarah crushed the napkin. "I hate to tell you this, but he ordered me out of his office." She then shook her head and looked at Jo, hurt exuding from her eyes. "He's never been that mad at me before."

They sat in silence for several awkward minutes, then Jo looked to

Tryg. "I think it's time for me to get back to the office and leave the two of you alone."

"No." Sarah got up and gathered her handbag. "I'm the one who'd better leave. I've caused enough problems. I just wish for the life of me I knew why."

CHAPTER THIRTY-SIX

Tryg peeled a bill from his wallet, tossed it on the counter, and was limping toward the door of Hotel Albert's coffee shop when he stopped short, the sudden thump of his heart erratic. Big Ole Harrington was sitting by himself at another one of his legendary tables for two, party of one. Tryg restlessly stuffed a hand in his pants pocket, his gaze shifting toward the marble floor. O.M. Harrington. A great man. A great encourager. A trusting friend. Unworthy of being violated by anyone, let alone by Tryg. Not certain this was the right venue, but also not certain that it wasn't, he sidled up to Ole's table. "This seat taken?" he asked guardedly. "Sorry, but I didn't realize you were here until now."

"Help yourself." Ole pulled his silver pocket watch from an inside vest pocket and burrowed his gaze into it. "I'm not planning on staying long, though. I'm a very busy man, you know."

Tryg smiled inwardly at Ole's gesture as well as at his comment, but Tryg wasn't about to let the smile reach his face. "I'll only be a minute. Just came from the courthouse. Thought I'd stop by for a quick bite on my way back to the office."

Tryg glanced around the coffee shop while he gathered his thoughts. Where to begin with the man called Big Ole? He pulled a chair from the opposite side of Ole's table. It shrieked noticeably against the marble floor. In many respects, his timing was not too bad, Tryg decided as he sat down. The coffee shop had all but emptied. And not having an opportunity to think things through meant that he could speak off-the-cuff. From his heart. Big Ole deserved as much.

Tryg plucked a saltshaker from the side of the table and anxiously rolled it back and forth, eyeing it. "Done any fishing lately?"

"Fishing?" Ole asked flatly. He anchored his gaze on what little was left of his coffee and swirled it in his cup, playing with it the way he was undoubtedly playing with Tryg. "Is that what you stopped by to talk to me about, Mr. Howland? Fishing?"

Mr. Howland? "No." Tryg hesitated. "No. Not at all."

"That's good, because I'm getting a little low on exaggerated tales to tell."

Tryg smiled uncomfortably at the quick and dry comeback. "Look, I'll cut to the chase."

"See that you do. I respect a man who gets right down to business."

Tryg was anything but surprised to see that Big Ole, not to be bested, was in command of this conversation, not only by his tone, but also by his forthrightness. Justified vexation, however, did appear to add into the mix, making Tryg's task more formidable than it had to be.

"I'm sure you've heard all about our meetings with your granddaughter by now," Tryg said as he shifted uncomfortably in the silence.

Ole sat, poker-faced, no doubt void of audible words on purpose. That was fair. The man had been accused, convicted, and condemned, as they say. Accused of having been blackmailed, convicted of not having been able to handle his own affairs, and condemned to having those who cared about him most clambering around behind his back, invading his privacy.

"We met again yesterday over the noon hour," Tryg continued, "but then, you undoubtedly knew about that."

Big Ole didn't respond. His gaze rested idly on the cup he cradled in his large hands, as if he were ignoring Tryg's words as they passed by rather than allowing them to enter his made-up mind.

"Before we had a chance to tell Sarah we'd decided to withdraw from the case," Tryg said, "she informed us that our services were no longer needed."

Big Ole looked up and finally engaged. "The case you shouldn't have accepted in the first place? That case?"

Tryg didn't like the sourness roiling up from way down low in his own belly. But he'd earned that and more. He glanced around for a moment to gather his thoughts while wishing he could leave. In Big Ole Harrington he had definitely met a more than formidable contender. "We hadn't formally accepted the case," Tryg assured him. "It started out innocently enough, though. We were only hoping to help the grand-daughter of a friend."

"A *friend*, you say?"

Tryg nodded. "Yes. A friend. Suffice it to say, it didn't take long for us to find out more than we wanted or needed to know."

Big Ole slowly shook his head. A flicker of flame in his eyes indicated he understood much more than was stated. "If you'll excuse me," he said as he pulled out his silver chain once again, this time glaring at his pocket watch. "I believe it's time for me to head on home now."

"I'm sorry," Tryg said softly. "I'm truly, truly sorry."

When Tryg returned to the office, Jo looked up. Reading despair in his eyes, she noticed that he was about as talkative coming back as he'd been when he left.

"Before you go into your office," Ardena said to him, "I have a few documents that could use your signature. I'd like to get them out in the afternoon mail if that's at all possible."

"Let's see what you have here," he said. He reached inside his blazer for a pen and then quickly scanned the pages. "Everything seems to be in good order."

Ardena gaped at Tryg's new writing instrument and then up at him. "You've got a new pen?" she said incredulously.

Jo couldn't help overhearing—or seeing for that matter. Tryg certainly had gotten a shiny new black pen. But why would he buy a new one? Why not accept Marianne Glanz's pen? It was every bit as classy, if not more so.

"Looks really expensive," Ardena said.

He nodded, scribbled his signature on several pages, and limped away.

CHAPTER THIRTY-SEVEN

Tryg did a double take when Ardena came rushing into his office. The last time she hurried in looking as if she were trying to outrun a mustang, President Roosevelt had met with an untimely end.

"Mr. Howland," she said, "there's a Mrs. Corwin Braddingly on the line. Sounds pretty miffed if you ask me. She doesn't just want to talk to you, she's demanding it."

"Henrietta Braddingly? Calling during the noon hour?" Tryg swept up the receiver. "This is Tryg Howland. How may I help you?"

He held the receiver far from his ear to mute the angry explosion ripping up the wires, and then shot a querying brow at Ardena. During his short time in practice, he'd definitely had more pleasant and far less challenging exchanges.

Although she couldn't see him through the phone lines, he pulled back his shoulders and stated confidently, "Mrs. Braddingly, I'm sure there has to be a reasonable explanation. If you'd like, feel free to stop by my office any time, and we'll see what we can do to clear this matter up."

After enduring several more inflamed sentences, Tryg cradled the receiver. He would have preferred slamming it, but that would not be professional. Besides, Ardena was watching.

"That was certainly interesting," he said.

"What happened? What was she so irate about?"

"Was? You mean *is*. It appears that one Henrietta Braddingly appears to be having some problems with our legal counsel. Through her yelling, all I could make out were the words Jo Bremley, Marianne Glanz, and free advice. I don't recall having given Jo permission to give free advice to anyone, and now it looks as if this is the second time in a few short weeks that it's happened. What kind of advice could she have taken it upon herself to give out this time?"

"Uh-oh!"

Tryg shifted stiffly. "This is a lot more serious than uh-oh. What do you know about it?"

Ardena recoiled.

"Ardena?"

"I have no idea. Honest. But I'm sure Jo didn't do anything wrong."

Tryg honed in on Jo's words when she offered to quit over the Marianne Glanz washout. He'd beaten himself up for letting Jo's explanation stick in his craw. Couldn't shake it off. Maybe his instincts had been right after all. He looked up at Ardena. "I sure hope you're right. But she did say she couldn't guarantee that another incident like Marianne Glanz's wouldn't happen again."

"She said that?" Ardena asked doubtfully.

"Said that's who she is."

"Oh dear." Ardena folded her arms across her tailored navy suit. "I'm afraid I've heard her use those words myself. But I can't imagine her giving free advice without owning up to it. She's way too honest. We both know that."

Tryg glanced at his calendar. "Look, Mrs. Braddingly said she's on her way here now. Can you at least tell me where Jo is?"

"She had to take a late lunch hour. I think she'll be back in about another half hour or so."

"Thanks. Now would you please ask her to see me the minute she walks through that door?"

After Ardena left his office, Tryg crumpled a sheet of paper and flung it at the trashcan. It hit the inside wall and dropped in.

This was Jo's second major misstep since she started. She had always appeared gifted with common sense, presenting herself exceptionally well. What happened to her all of a sudden? Tryg had to hire her. Case deserved that. And she'd been so honest and repentant about the Glanz blunder. But after just a few short weeks, he'd lost one very important client and had another one ranting because of Jo's free advice. Maybe this was his fault. Maybe he hadn't given her enough formal training.

He crumpled another sheet of paper and pitched it at the trashcan. Missed.

This had nothing to do with formal training. This had everything to do with common sense and sound business protocol. He didn't need the aggravation of a runaway employee and a diminishing workload when he was trying to build up clientele. Yet it was so unlike the Jo he knew to be out of control.

Twenty minutes later, Tryg heard Ardena stirring in the outer office. "Well for heaven's sake!" she was murmuring to herself.

He got up and positioned himself in the doorjamb. Ardena was peering through the Venetian blinds. Someone or something had caught her attention.

"Excuse me," Jo cried.

The lady bustling up the sidewalk bore a striking resemblance to Henrietta Braddingly. Same cropped coarse gray hair, same wide girth, and thick at the ankles on equally thick black-heeled shoes.

"Mrs. Braddingly? Mrs. Henrietta Braddingly?" Jo called out again.

The woman wheeled around, caught a glimpse of her stalker, and gasped. "I see it's you, Mrs. Bremley."

Jo's stomach tightened at the unkind tone. "Is everything okay? You look awfully upset."

"No, everything is not okay. I'm on my way to see Mr. Howland about it now."

Jo clipped along faster, catching up with her a few doors shy of the law office, then gently reached for the elderly woman's arm. "Why? What's happened?"

"I don't want to discuss it with you. I want to talk to Mr. Howland directly," she snipped and turned to walk away.

Jo quickly stepped ahead of her. "Have I offended you in any way? I certainly didn't mean to."

"Well," Mrs. Braddingly spat, stopping dead center on the sidewalk, "I don't appreciate getting a bill when you provided exactly the same services to Mr. and Mrs. Glanz free of charge. That's a lousy way of doing business if you ask me."

Jo was not about to add more fuel to the woman's overheated fire, but she couldn't help wondering where Henrietta Braddingly got her information. "What services did we provide to the Glanzes free of charge? And how did you hear about that?"

"You know very well. *You* were the one who gave Mrs. Glanz the free advice."

"About?"

"The troubles they were having with their neighbor, of course. Word gets around."

Jo looked up and down the sidewalk, feeling uneasy. This was no place to carry on an upsetting conversation, but what else could she do? She needed to calm Mrs. Braddingly down before the woman had a chance to talk with Tryg.

"It isn't right for me to discuss the affairs of other clients," Jo said pragmatically, "but I can confidently tell you that your information is wrong. I did not have a formal consultation with Marianne Glanz, or with anyone else for that matter. But I did have a private chat with a new acquaintance on a personal level."

Mrs. Braddingly's face grew hard. She leaned in, constricting Jo's personal space. "You may not have given her a formal consultation, but you gave her valuable legal advice. And, what's worse, you didn't charge her one flimsy dime for it."

Jo tensed. *You got that part right.*

But while Jo was at the courthouse, she did some checking around. This woman had a history. She intentionally found ways to get out of paying her bills. And now she was repeating that history with Jo. Deliberately backing her up against a wall. Jo could not allow her to do that. Not to Jo. Not to Tryg. Not to Tryg's law practice.

"You asked Mr. Howland for help filing a lawsuit against your neighbors, isn't that right?" Jo asked.

"You know very well that's right."

"At any time have you felt intimidated by your neighbors?"

Shock flashed in Mrs. Braddingly's narrowing eyes. "Absolutely not," she boasted. "No one intimidates me."

Why am I not surprised? This was precisely what Jo expected and needed to know. "I understand. How much time did you spend with Mr. Howland when you discussed your case?"

"The greater part of an afternoon," Mrs. Braddingly said forthrightly. "You know that, too."

Jo ignored the slight. "Are you planning to move forward with a lawsuit?"

"You better believe I am."

"That's the difference," Jo said. "If you will recheck your billing, you'll find you weren't billed for the first hour of consultation, but we did bill you for Mr. Howland's time in excess of that. And, on a personal note, I can also assure you that my private chat with Marianne Glanz lasted far less than an hour. She never did meet with Mr. Howland."

Mrs. Braddingly looked as though someone just threw a cake in her face.

"If you still feel that you've been billed inappropriately," Jo said, "I'll see what we can do to adjust your account."

"See that you do. And you can be certain I'll be taking my business elsewhere."

Feeling relief at the revolting woman's words, Jo held back a smile. "Thank you. I do wish you well. And as for our bill, you might want to pay it right away. In the next billing cycle, our fees are going to be increasing. By the way, you also might want to check out the fee structures upfront when you approach other law firms. I'm sure you'd be much happier if you sought a firm that specializes in real estate."

"I'll be sure to do that, and immediately, if not sooner," Henrietta said before strutting off like a hen minus a few feathers.

CHAPTER THIRTY-EIGHT

Jo stopped short immediately inside the office door. Something in the air felt anything but right.

Tryg was heading toward her desk. He stopped and leaned back against it. Crossed his arms. His stance unyielding. His annoyed look directed at her.

She glanced back at the door, wanting to run through it, out onto East William, and a great distance away from the place she no longer felt welcome.

Ardena, meanwhile, sat quietly at her desk. Although her eyes were focused on her work, her attention was unquestioningly focused on Tryg and Jo and what was about to transpire.

"Do you have a minute?" Tryg asked, his tone brusque.

No. Not if you're going to browbeat me, I don't. "Yes, sir."

"Ardena, you might want to join us, too," he said, then led the way to his office at a fast lurching pace.

As if Jo and Ardena were unaware of the placement of the furnishings, he nodded, directing them to the two chairs opposite his desk. "Please. Have a seat."

Jo eased onto her chair. Trying to find a comfortable position to override the discomfort rending her insides, she extended one leg over the other and lightly interwove her fingers. "Is everything okay?" she asked, not that she needed to. His facial expression and tone said an emphatic no.

"Maybe you should tell me."

"Sir?"

"A short while ago, I got a phone call from Henrietta Braddingly. To say she was irate is an understatement. Ardena, here, took the call."

Jo's eyebrows yanked up involuntarily, but as the name registered, she found herself relaxing. Henrietta Braddingly. With Tryg's lack of particulars, no wonder he sounded irritated. Jo had tried to tell him about that woman before. Tried twice. But he dismissed her both times. Why be overbearing about it?

"You do know who she is, I assume," he said.

Jo nodded. "Yes, sir."

"She claims she was overcharged for an office visit. Mentioned something about Marianne Glanz and free advice." He paused, undoubtedly for dramatic effect. "That would be the Marianne Glanz with the beautiful ruby red pen, would it not?"

Again Jo nodded, but kept silent.

"She yelled so loud, I needed to shove the receiver away from my ear. Felt like my eardrum was about to burst. Through that firestorm all I could catch were a few words here and there—Jo Bremley, Marianne Glanz, free advice. She's on her way to the office now."

The air audibly whooshed out of Jo's lungs. "Oh! I'm so relieved that I didn't know that."

"Why in the world would you feel relieved?" Tryg asked dubiously. "First you gave free advice of your own volition, and now it's time to collect. People talk, Jo. How would you like me to handle this when she does get here?"

"There's nothing left to handle."

"Pardon me?"

Ardena's cherry lips jarred open, displaying a hole the size of a walnut. Quieter than a church mouse, she slumped deeper into her chair.

"I said there's nothing left to handle," Jo repeated. "We chatted for a few minutes. She was reluctant at first, but I think we both got a better understanding of each other. And now she's gone."

"We?"

"Yes, we. Henrietta Braddingly and me. She's fine. Well, on second thought, maybe she's not all that fine. She did strut off looking a bit miffed."

"Really? And where did *we* have this chat?"

Uncomfortable with Tryg's gruff tone, Jo straightened. "A couple of doors down our street here." Jo liked the sound of the word our—*our* street here. Made her feel like an integral part of things, negating her earlier feelings of repudiation.

"So that gray-haired lady with the moustache I saw you in a huddle with *was* Henrietta Braddingly," Ardena interjected.

Jo nodded.

Tryg reached for his shiny new black pen and tapped it nervously against his desktop. "Why did she leave? Why did she strut off looking a bit miffed?" He thought for a moment and then his eyebrows snapped together, the red in his cheeks rising from beneath the collar of his white starched shirt. "And how could you let that woman strut off disgruntled?"

Jo felt uncomfortable with either the seriousness of Tryg's expression or the guilt suddenly gnawing away at her, she wasn't sure which. She needed time to think things through. Maybe she inadvertently usurped his authority. She'd never seen him this angry before. Not many people had. But was it necessary for him to thump his shiny new black pen against his desktop to make his point? "She left after I asked her a few quick questions."

"You asked her a few quick questions," he repeated slowly and flatly.

Jo was beginning to feel as if she were on the witness stand, she the witness for the defense, he the attorney for the prosecution. "Yes, I did."

Tryg's eyes widened while his face registered unfeigned angst, and she could hear Ardena breathing. "Precisely what kinds of questions did you take it upon yourself to ask her?" he said.

Jo cringed at his choice of words, but only for a moment. She sat straighter. "I asked her if she felt intimidated by her neighbor. True to form, she let me know in no uncertain terms right out there on the sidewalk in front of God and the whole wide world that no one intimidates her."

"Wait a minute," Tryg said shy of a shout.

Jo squeezed the arms of her leather chair, bracing against a possible explosion.

"You did what?" he continued. "We aren't exactly knee-deep in work yet where we can afford to turn it away. Why on earth would you ask her such a thing?"

"Because she prides herself on being a bully."

Tryg's eyebrows pitched above his glasses. "What does that have to do with anything? When people seek legal counsel for a lawsuit, you can bet they've already felt a lot of frustration and intimidation...hence the lawsuit."

Jo gulped and squirmed. She wanted this conversation to be over with. Done. Kaput. "Because I did some checking after your initial consultation with her. I had a gut feeling and wanted to confirm it."

Jo looked at Ardena, hoping for a little visual help, which she was unsuccessful in getting. She then turned again to Tryg. He was steepling his hands, his attention still riveted on her.

"A gut feeling *you* wanted to confirm?" he repeated slowly and dramatically. "Not legal facts, but feelings?"

Jo was beginning to enjoy the courtroom-like conduct, so she paved the way to drop a nicely sized bomb. "Precisely," she announced.

"Excuse me?"

Jo leaned forward and held Tryg's gaze. "Did you know that Henrietta Braddingly systematically sues attorneys?"

The air whooshed out of Tryg's lungs this time. "She what?"

"I said Henrietta Braddingly sues attorneys," Jo repeated, looking down and smoothing a fold from her skirt. "She has a history of doing this. She intentionally oversteps her boundaries to get out of paying her bills. Seems to work for her."

"And how did you know about her history?"

"I didn't. Too bad you missed seeing the nasty attitude she brought with her the day of her initial meeting with you. She was a little too sour for my taste when she walked in the door. People usually aren't like that."

"That's true," Ardena piped up. "She was acting like a bully, but Jo defused her."

Jo smiled at Ardena, grateful to see she was finally sticking up for Jo.

"Why didn't you tell me about this before?" Tryg asked, incredulous.

"I guess I should have," Jo said. "It's just that her countenance melted so quickly with just a few kind words, I didn't see the need. She even chirped a cheerful goodbye when she left."

"And still you felt a need to check on her."

Jo nodded. "Absolutely. The more I thought about it, the more I questioned myself. You have to realize I was not looking to find her guilty of anything; I was looking to find her innocent."

Looking as though he suddenly understood, Tryg's anger melted like soft butter on a warm slice of toast. "Really?"

"That's right. So when I was at the courthouse anyway, I browsed through her files."

"Files?" Tryg asked, sounding surprised. "How many did she have?"

"Try five."

"Five?"

"That's right. I would have been surprised if there wasn't at least one thin file, but it shocked me to find that many. And they were all fat. I riffled through them pretty fast, but it didn't take long at all to find a recurring theme."

"She—"

"Sues people," Jo said, finishing his sentence for him, "and then turns around and sues her attorneys so she can get out of paying her legal bills. Even the attendant at the Clerk's office said, 'good luck with that woman.' Believe me, it wasn't hard to understand what she meant."

"But why didn't you tell me about this before, Jo?"

"I tried telling you a couple of times, but my timing wasn't very good. And I didn't feel comfortable either, because you didn't authorize my checking her out in the first place. I did it on a whim. I tried to tell you about it when we were discussing Sarah's case. I'm not meaning to be unkind here, but you did cut me off. You have to remember, Mrs. Braddingly was the first client I had any contact with."

Tryg looked at Jo, anything but certain.

"I'd feel a lot more comfortable if you checked her out yourself," Jo said. "Then you'd know for sure."

Tryg sighed. "I guess this meeting is adjourned."

"Before we go, could I have a private word with you?" Jo asked.

Ardena took her cue to leave. As soon as the door clicked behind her, Jo said, "It's about Big Ole. I'd like to ask your permission to go and talk with him."

"Why?"

"I want to clean up this mess somehow, or at least try, especially now that he knows about our talks with Sarah. I get the distinct feeling he isn't exactly pleased that we've gotten involved. I don't know. I might be overly sensitive here, but on Sunday morning when Brue and I were walking to church, I could swear he gave me the cold shoulder, and Sarah looked like she wanted to crawl into a hole when I said hello. I'm pretty sure what that was about—"

"That's not necessary, Jo."

"Why not?"

"Because I already talked with him."

Jo was dumbstruck. Her heart thumped. What if Big Ole told Tryg she'd stopped by to see if she could get another job at the boarding house? "You did?"

"Ran into him at Hotel Albert's coffee shop." Tryg looked at Jo questioningly. "Are you okay? You suddenly look like you're afraid of something."

"I'm fine."

Tryg nodded, but did not look convinced.

"So how did your discussion go?" she asked.

"Let's just say it could have gone better."

"I'm really sorry to hear that. I can't tell you how much I regret doing damage to our friendship with him. He's been so good to me. I'd still like to try to smooth things over from my end; that is, if you don't mind."

Tryg thought for a moment and then said, "Under normal circumstances, I'd say leave well enough alone. But since you used to work for the man, go ahead and say what you need to say on your behalf, but not on behalf of our firm. Understood?"

Ouch! "Understood."

Jo left Tryg's office with a feeling of dread. At five o'clock she would go home and face the night, trying to keep a lid on her thoughts again. Tryg's anger sliced deeply. She'd never heard him express his fury toward anyone, let alone exhibit it toward her. True, he calmed down considerably, but what if he had second thoughts? People typically rethink things. And she just had to push further by asking his permission to chat with Big Ole. *'Go ahead and say what you need to say on your behalf, but not on behalf of our firm. Understood?'* Understood!

Jo no sooner settled in at her desk when a question niggled at the back of her mind like the ringing of a distant bell. She looked up and stared out the window for a moment, wondering. Who on God's green Earth gave Henrietta Braddingly her information about Marianne Glanz? Jo doubted they moved in the same circles.

Tryg met Lauren at The Copper Kettle for a quick supper. "I'm really sorry," he said when she joined him at their booth. "I can't stay long. I've got way too much paperwork to do."

She smiled as she removed her brown gloves one dainty finger at a time. "I don't mind at all. It's just nice that you agreed to join me for a few minutes."

The waitress stopped and took their orders. Lauren ordered a hamburger and a Coke. Tryg ordered a bowl of vegetable beef soup and a coffee.

"That's all you're eating?" Lauren asked.

"I'm really not all that hungry tonight."

"Office problems again?"

He nodded.

"Don't tell me. Jo?"

Tryg nodded again.

"What did that awful woman do this time?" Lauren asked, irritation seeping through her voice.

"She's not an awful woman," Tryg said and then he shared briefly the problem with Henrietta Braddingly. "I think we got to the other side of it okay," he said.

Lauren appeared to withdraw. He studied her for a moment then said, "You're awfully quiet. What are you thinking?"

"Hmm?"

"I asked what you're thinking."

"Oh. I'm thinking you didn't get to the other side of it."

"What do you mean?"

"Just look at you. You can barely force down a bowlful of soup."

As Tryg picked up his spoon and began eating, Lauren grew quiet again. Then after he finished his first cup of coffee, she talked him into splitting a slice of angel food cake frosted with white icing and sprinkled generously with coconut. The moment the waitress placed it on the table, Lauren asked Tryg to begin eating while she made a quick trip to the ladies' room. Although not in there long, before returning to their table, she walked up to the owner. Ted appeared to be working into the night to look after things. They stood in a huddle, Lauren speaking animatedly while Ted smiled appreciatively. When she returned to their booth, Tryg asked, "What was that all about?"

"Oh, nothing much," was all she said.

CHAPTER THIRTY-NINE

D o you need that pillow, Brue?"

Brue shook her head. "You can have it."

Although Jo wedged the pillow behind her, she felt anything but comfortable.

The sweet air in the small Southern Minnesota town also seemed
to lose its freshness, and not because of the smokestacks from Wilson
& Company's meatpacking plant at the far side of the lake. Between the
Marianne Glanz blunder, Sarah's involving the firm with an unhappy
Big Ole Harrington, and Henrietta Braddingly's nasty tirade, Jo would
be foolish to assume her job was secure. She was too inexperienced and
too many things were happening in a far too brief period of time. She sat
on the sofa pondering how uneasy she felt—vulnerable in the workforce
and, with the exception of Marianne Glanz, through no fault of her own.

She glanced at Brue and sighed. Brue was sitting sidesaddle in the
easy chair with her nose hidden behind another book, one foot dan-
gling off the cushion, the other extending across the opposite arm of
the chair. Lost in her little world of books, she looked at peace, but that
peace was about to be disturbed.

Although it was painful to own, Jo's job had to be at risk. Coming up
with a backup plan was the responsible thing to do. A temporary move
to Minneapolis instead of New York might be more sensible. If gentle

push came to hard shove, Jo might stand a good chance of finding a job in the Cities. Brue had an aunt, uncle, and cousins there, as well as better opportunities at bigger schools, saying nothing about the possibility of gaining more friends.

Jo tossed her pillow aside, got up and picked up the receiver, but then looked at Brue and cradled the phone.

Jo returned to the couch. "Come here, sweetie," she said, patting the cushion. "Sit down with me for a minute. We need to have a little chat."

By the look on Brue's face, Jo's tone had caused her concern. Brue crawled up onto the sofa, knees first, looking anxious. "Why, Mom? What's the matter?"

"I don't know how to say this other than straight out. I think we might need to give moving a second thought."

Brue's eyebrows snapped together. "What do you mean?"

"I mean that at some point we may need to think about making a temporary move to Minneapolis."

Brue scrunched up her nose. "No, Mom. Not Minneapolis. I don't wanna live there."

"I don't want to leave Amber Leaf either, sweetheart, but we may not have any other choice. Wouldn't you like to live near Cousin Margaret?"

"Sure I would. But why can't they move here?"

"Because I may need to see if I can find a job in the Cities. With the war still on, it can't be all that hard to find one, but you just never know. I thought I'd call Margaret. See if we can stay with them for about a week or so, just in case. I'm sure she wouldn't mind."

"But I don't want to move to Minneapolis," Brue repeated. "If we have to move, why can't we go to New York?"

Jo smoothed Brue's hair, then pulled her close, lightly resting her chin on top of Brue's blond head. "We can still dream that dream and, someday soon, I hope we can go there, too. But if we move to Minneapolis first, that's close enough to Amber Leaf that we can always come back for a visit whenever we want."

"But I don't want to leave Poke and my friends at Ramsey School."

"I know." Jo let out a deep sigh. "I haven't wanted to involve you, Brue, but you do have a right to know that your world could turn upside down again any day now and you have a right to know why. I am trying to keep us here," she said. "And I promise I'll do everything I can to make that happen. But there's something you're still pretty young yet to understand."

"I'm not too young to understand," Brue said pleadingly. "Honest, I'm not!"

"Well, I guess maybe you're not at that. How do I say this? Let me think on it a minute. Hmm. Do you remember how you used to feel around Big Ole?"

Brue thought about it briefly and then nodded.

"I kind of feel that way around Tryg these days. Like I'm getting in his way. All kinds of things keep happening at the office, things I don't have any control over. It's like being in the wrong place at the wrong time. And I'm not sure how much longer I can hold onto my job."

Brue pulled back and asked, "Mr. Howland won't fire you, will he?"

"I don't know. I sure hope not. But I was thinking that if these uncontrollable things keep happening, it might be better if we did move away. Maybe our lives would get easier then."

"But why do we have to move? Why can't you just find another job here?"

Jo gave Brue's chin a gentle nudge upward. "Because there aren't any around for someone with my lack of skills. I'm not sure we need to go yet, and I'm also not sure I could get a job in Minneapolis anyway, so we may be worrying needlessly." Jo sat back and stared at the shafts of fading sunlight piercing through the sheer curtain like the shafts of pain piercing her heart, and once again drew Brue close. "For now, though, all I want to do is check our options. I don't want to force you against your will, but until we can come up with a better idea, Minneapolis seems like the only clear path to take. Like I said, things are getting much too complicated at the office, and I'm feeling like I'm becoming a real problem."

"Okay," Brue said resignedly and then she looked up at Jo. "Mom?"

"Hmm?"

"How come Cousin Margaret and Cousin Shirley don't call each other cousin?"

"That's because they're sisters."

"Then why don't they live in the same city?"

"They did. But Shirley moved to New York right after she got married."

"Why?"

"Because her husband got a job there. Now, if you'll excuse me." Jo pecked Brue on the forehead, then got up and picked up the phone. "Operator, would you connect me with Hennepin 3409, please?"

After several unsuccessful tries, the Operator said, "I'm sorry, ma'am, but I can't seem to get an answer at that number. Would you like to try again later?"

CHAPTER FORTY

J o downed the last of her coffee and winced at how little time it took for it to turn revoltingly cold. She rotated the empty cup in her hands. Brue was outside playing with her friends, which would make this an ideal time to go to the O.M. Harrington. Jo shivered at the idea. She rinsed out her cup and set it near the kitchen sink, then slipped on her wine-colored cardigan and drew her sleeves up to her elbows. She needed to face Big Ole and make things right. The thought alone of humbling herself again before that intimidating old man brought with it an invasion of nausea.

Rather than cutting through the park, Jo took the long way around, giving her a whole extra minute or so to steady her nerves. Other than a few wood ducks quacking by the lake, a wren chirping here and there, and stones crunching beneath her flats on the small stretch of gravel road, the neighborhood appeared quiet and serene. Sooner than she wanted, she smoothed a few loose strands away from her forehead and then rested her hand on the doorknob at the O.M. Harrington. She took a long, deep breath and stepped inside.

"Hello, Sarah."

Sarah, who was sitting behind the registration desk, looked up, the color instantly draining from her cheeks. "Hi."

Jo pasted on a reassuring smile. "I'm here to see your grandfather. I need to make things right with him."

The reluctant expression on Sarah's face took the form of a question.

"Don't worry," Jo said sympathetically. "This *is* the right thing to do. I need to give it a try anyway."

Sarah nodded, returning a smile that was anything but certain. "He's in his office."

Ole was riffling through a magazine when Jo rapped on his door-jamb. He didn't bother to breathe a word or even look up, for that matter. She knocked again, this time a bit harder. "Mind if I come in? Under the circumstances, I can't say as I'd blame you if you told me no."

"Come in," he said with a total lack of emotion.

"Mind if I close the door?"

"If you must."

Pulling the door closed behind her, Jo headed toward an overstuffed leather chair. "Mind if I sit down?"

"And if I said yes?"

"I would understand."

He did not reply, but at least the air in the room lacked enmity. Now to bring back the warmth. "I want to talk to you about Howard Rasmussen, to see if we can make things right. I understand you heard all about our possible involvement."

Ole rocked back in his heavy chair and cast his gaze toward the ceiling, his hiked up bushy eyebrows dominating his demeanor. "*Possible* involvement?"

"Yes, sir. Tryg asked me to do a little research to see if there was any way we might help Sarah."

"I see. So it's Tryg's fault, is that right? And?"

Jo cringed at his biting retort. "No, it's not Tryg's fault. I take full responsibility for my part in this. *And* we stopped just shy of going too far."

"That would be from your perspective," he added without the slightest hesitation.

Jo ignored his comment and went on. "We did go far enough to surmise we'd found out more than we felt comfortable knowing. We didn't think it would be right to take a position one way or another, and we knew it would not be right to share our findings with Sarah."

"How noble of you," Big Ole stated flatly. "I assume Tryg Howland neglected to tell you that he and I already had this little chat."

"No, not at all. He did tell me. He also let me know in no uncertain terms that under normal circumstances, he would prefer my not coming to see you. But with a little effort, I talked him into allowing it."

"And why would you bother to do that?"

"Out of respect for our friendship."

Big Ole shifted his heavy weight forward. "When were we ever friends, Jo? Character is consistent. Friends do not stop being friends. But undoubtedly that is a concept you've never fully understood."

Jo was dumbstruck. Engaging in a serious discussion with Big Ole was the equivalent of getting into the boxing ring with a heavyweight. That man could really pack a wallop. But then, so could Jo. "Sarah came to see us out of concern for you," she said.

"That wasn't her right."

"She told us about accidentally stumbling across a note when she cleaned your desk. In her words, she said the note smacked of blackmail. She felt uncomfortable going to the police. I was walking past her desk when she got one of Mr. Rasmussen's phone calls. She mentioned it in passing. Didn't know how to handle it. I suggested she talk to Tryg, see if there was anything to this, or if he could intercede. She did and that's when he involved me in the research."

Ole picked up a small piece of notepaper and fidgeted with its edges. "Is that a fact? And what did you learn about Howard Rasmussen?" he asked through a seriously clenched jaw.

Jo's eyes made a quick sweep of the floor. "That he had a son."

"And?"

"And that his son was incarcerated. From there we could only surmise."

"Surmise, you say?"

"That's right. We stopped our information gathering immediately; but before we could let Sarah down gracefully, she withdrew her request for our help."

Big Ole stood and, without his cane, strolled slowly toward the large French windows at the far wall. He dug his hands deep into his trouser pockets and stared out across Harrington Park.

Jo allowed him as much private time as he felt he needed, which was considerable. The quiet settled so completely, she heard the grandfather clock ticking in the great room—through his closed doors. Still she waited him out.

When he finally turned toward her, his countenance had transformed from a sniffing bulldog to a purring lap cat. "Where do we go from here?" he said.

"As far as Tryg and I are concerned, that's up to you. If you are being blackmailed, that's between you and the police. About Sarah, though, don't give that another thought. We won't breathe a word to anyone about our findings, especially to her. And as far as my doing research, I would apologize, but I'm not sure I did anything wrong. I'm only sorry that in trying to be helpful, my efforts only caused you grief. I don't think it's impossible for me to feel more filled with regret."

He studied the floor for another forever moment, and then said, "I can't tell Sarah who her dad is, Jo. I've never been able to tell her. That would be a curse no child should have to live with."

"I'm not so sure about that," Jo countered. "When we met with her at The Copper Kettle, my heart went out to her. You should have seen her just before she left."

"Why's that?" Ole said softly.

"She looked completely defeated. Said she knew she was causing problems, but had no idea why."

The tragic look in Big Ole's eyes indicated he was crushed. "She said that?"

"Yes, she did. Which brings me to ask the question, have you given any thought to getting counsel from anyone?"

"Can't say that I have. I know you mean well, but I'm not really what you'd call a counseling type of person."

"But what about Calvin Doherty? On the one hand, Sarah's finding out who her father is could cause her an awful lot of pain and make her feel less than good about herself. But on the other hand, don't we all have a right to know who our parents are? It would be wonderful if you could get out from under that bully who's trying to blackmail you, too. Calvin is a man of great wisdom. Maybe he could help."

Big Ole stroked his chin with his thumb and forefinger. "Maybe he could at that."

Jo stopped by the registration desk and smiled confidently.

"I take it that it went okay," Sarah said hopefully.

"I think it did. As a matter of fact, I think it may have gone very well."

Sarah's immediate smile looked as though the sun had broken through and shone on her for the first time in days. "Thank you," she said. "What a relief."

CHAPTER FORTY-ONE

On Wednesday evening, Jo settled into the back-row pew at Village Church. She smiled at the music flowing into the sanctuary from the basement below. A number of voices in the children's choir were in dire need of tuning, a job she did not envy the struggling new music director.

Jo sat quietly as she waited for Brue. Meditating. Praying. Meditating. Praying some more. Everywhere she turned these days, landmines appeared to dot the landscape. Every time things appeared to get better, they took another turn for the worse. Her emotional weight was crushing. She felt lost. And she felt alone.

As she prayed and twilight succumbed to darkness, a glow burgeoned from the back room. She was not alone after all. Calvin Doherty must be in his office, probably working on Sunday morning's sermon.

It would not be right to bother him.

Would it?

She got up, headed to the back, and knocked on his wide-open door. "Good evening! I saw your lights on."

"Jo!"

"Mind if I come in?"

"Not at all. Please do." Calvin stood long enough for her to get situated. "Brue's downstairs practicing with the children's choir, I take it."

"Yes, sir."

"That child has a wonderful little voice."

Jo acknowledged his comment with a faint smile and then crossed her legs, angling them to the side.

"You have something on your mind," he said.

Jo quickly shifted to a more erect position and swung her leg nervously back and forth.

"Something big," Calvin noted. "Do you want to talk about it?"

"Not really, but I guess I need to."

"So what's going on?"

"I don't know. Stuff, I guess."

He walked his pencil back and forth between his fingers, a feat few could do with such skill. "Stuff? What kind of stuff?"

"Stuff like I've given up on our dream of moving to New York, at least for the short term, but now I'm thinking about moving to Minneapolis instead. We have a few relatives there."

"Still tempted to run, are you?"

"Fast as I can."

"Really?"

"Yes, but not because I want to."

Calvin lightly tossed his pencil on his desk, sat back, and clasped his hands behind his head. "Why? What happened? You must be having some serious problems with Tryg. I'm surprised. I thought he'd be a pretty easy guy to get along with."

Taking her cue from Calvin's relaxed demeanor, Jo uncrossed her legs and quieted down. "He is, actually. But I'm afraid I'm making life more difficult for him than it needs to be."

"I find that hard to believe."

Jo examined the folds in her skirt, pressing them lightly with the tips of her fingers. How much should she say? What should she say? She hadn't figured that out yet. But since she started this conversation, she might as well finish it.

"I'm surprised, too. But through my naiveté and lack of experience," she admitted, "I've managed to drive away a potentially huge business opportunity for him. Then another one of his clients heard an exaggerated version of what happened and responded with an angry outburst. Not knowing where she got her information from unnerves me. A few other things have been happening, too. None that I care to mention if you don't mind. I've already been reprimanded twice, and I've only worked for the man for a month. I'm sure Tryg realizes by now he made a miserable investment in his business when he decided to hire me. He's too kind and responsible to let me go, but there's a strain in the air, and I don't know how to make it go away."

"Have you tried making things right with him?"

"Sure, I have. The problem is, I don't trust myself to not get into any more trouble. I can't stop being me. I'm thinking of doing him a favor by leaving voluntarily."

"I see," Calvin said. He sat back and interweaved his fingers. "I'm sorry I was so glib and accusatory when you first came in. Under the circumstances, I see now that I was wrong."

"Don't worry about it," Jo said thoughtfully. "So what do I do? Brue does not want to move to the Cities. Neither do I, really. Minneapolis is a great place, but our hearts are here. We can't afford a move to New York without a job waiting for me. When it comes right down to it, what other choice do we have? Too bad my negative memories here in Amber Leaf are accumulating faster than I can keep up with."

"I understand. So what should you do now, you ask? I'm thinking there are really only two things you can do."

"And they are?"

"First, realize you are new at your job, and you're navigating your way through the school of hard knocks."

Jo snickered. "The school of hard knocks, huh?"

"That's right. Nobody likes it, but it is a very effective way to learn. Happens to all of us. You should have seen how green I was when I first joined the military. It takes a while to figure things out, but eventually we all do."

"If this is what the school of hard knocks is like, I'm not sure I'll ever graduate. Okay, so that's the first thing. And the second?"

"And the second is to keep your backup plan in mind. Subscribe to the *Minneapolis Tribune*. That way you can check out the classifieds periodically."

Although Jo found Calvin's response appropriate, she also found it painfully validating. "That's probably a wise thing to do," she said reluctantly.

"I hope you'll give this situation with Tryg more time. See how it all shakes out. I wouldn't want you one day having to make peace with your past, Jo."

Jo chuckled. "These days I'm having to make peace with a past too painful to face, a present I somehow manage to keep messing up, and a future that holds little promise, if any at all."

"I understand. Whatever you do, though, just make sure you don't move too fast. You might live to regret it."

"That's fair, I guess," Jo said, feeling a sense of relief at Calvin's advice. Maybe it was getting his permission to stay that she found the most comforting. Although the well-intended counsel she received about not running away had seeped in, hanging tough was becoming a real chore.

"Calvin?"

"Hmm?"

"About my still being tempted to run."

"Yes?"

She lifted an eyebrow, feeling helpless to repress a growing knowing grin.

"What's going on inside that head of yours now?" he said. "Or dare I ask?"

"Nothing much. I had a thought, though."

"And?"

"You were the one who popped the lid on Pandora's box, so how about if we blow it off completely and see what's in there?"

Jo smiled at Calvin's groan, but did not envy him the challenge she was about to hurl his way. The window of opportunity for him to make peace with his past harbored a tight timeline.

"When I came in," she said, clasping her hands around her knee, "you asked if I was still tempted to run."

"I did. To run *to* is good, but to run *from* is very, very wrong."

"Not if you're running away from a rabid dog," she countered and grinned. "Anyway, now you said we need to make peace with our past. Right?"

"That's right."

"Have you made peace with your past?"

The white in Calvin's eyes grew prominent. Now it was his turn to give a reluctant answer. "What are you talking about?"

"Rainy."

"Huh?" Calvin looked as though Jo had just upended a barrel of ice water on him. With a stony look in his eye, Calvin shook his head. "Some things are better left alone. Remember, she's a married woman, and has been for quite some time. It would not be right for me to approach her. Besides, I have no idea where she is, and I wouldn't know how to reach her anyway."

Jo sat erect, a prideful grin cutting into her cheeks. "Then let me make this easy for you. She's staying at her parents' place in Clarks Grove and her husband died suddenly a few years ago, so that's no longer an issue either."

Calvin was unsuccessful in restraining a gasp. "Oh, but I couldn't," he blurted, his voice sounding uncharacteristically shaky.

"Why not? I thought you said it's very, very wrong to run *from*."

When Jo noticed Calvin's gaze clinging to a simple cross hanging on a far wall, she said, "I'm not meaning to be unkind here, but are you okay? You're looking a bit drained of color."

CHAPTER FORTY-TWO

Jo positioned a pork chop on each of their plates, then ladled mashed potatoes and gravy, peas, and applesauce alongside, and Brue carried them to the table. They bowed their heads, folded their hands, and Brue said grace, but her wee hands maintained their prayerful pose a bit too long after she finished praying.

"Looks like something's making you unhappy," Jo said softly. "Would you like to talk about it?"

Brue shrugged.

"Problems at school?"

Brue shrugged again.

"Poke?"

Brue nodded slowly.

"I see."

Brue stared at her plate and dropped the weight of her head on her hand, declining to say anything further.

"Brue?"

"Hmm?"

"Maybe it would be a good idea if you told me what's going on."

Brue sighed.

"I'm waiting, sweetie."

"It's Poke."

"What about him?"

"All the girls in our class are afraid of him," Brue said gloomily.

Jo mixed the gravy into her mashed potatoes, wondering for a moment what to do with this surprising bit of information. "Why are all of the girls in your class afraid of Poke?"

"Do I have to tell you, Mom?"

"I think you should, yes."

Brue lightly poked her pork chop with the tip of her fork. "It's cuz every time our teacher leaves the room, he grabs the girls by the hand and pulls them backward real fast. When he gets them to fall down, he drags them around the classroom."

"How can he possibly do that? He's got a broken arm."

"He gets a running start. Uses his good arm. Pulls them so fast, they can't keep up with him. This morning he started pulling them backward by their braids. Annie was yelling '*ouch, ouch, ouch*' all the way around the room. I could tell she was trying hard to keep from crying."

"I see. That is pretty serious. Has he done that to you?"

"Not yet."

Jo lifted a forkful of mashed potatoes and gravy, stopping just shy of her mouth. "And no one wants to be the one to squeal to the teacher about it, right?"

Brue nodded.

"So the rascal keeps getting away with it."

"What can I do about it, Mom?"

"Let's think on it, okay? Meanwhile, your supper's getting cold."

Jo considered the simple ironies of life—Poke not getting into trouble for his blatant transgressions; Jo getting into trouble for her accidental transgressions, saying nothing about the transgressions of others.

She sliced a wedge off her pork chop, lifted her fork, then placed it back on her plate. "Brue?"

"Hmm?"

"Have you thought about how you might handle Poke's behavior, other than just being afraid that he might pull you backward by your hair, too?"

Still looking distressed, Brue slowly shook her head.

"Come on. You're smart. You're good at figuring things out. Help me here. Give me some ideas."

"But none of the kids will do anything."

"That's not what I'm asking. Seems to me your classmates need a leader. Are the other boys encouraging him? Or are they trying to get him to stop?"

"They're all cheering for him."

"You mean that instead of questioning themselves, they're following the herd?"

It was obvious from Brue's blank expression that Jo had lost her.

"Let me say this differently," Jo said. "It sounds as if your classmates could use a good leader."

"What do you mean?"

"Give me some ideas, Brue. Come on. Be a leader. What can you do to help put a stop to Poke's bullying? I'm asking you to come up with something you would feel comfortable doing. It may be an idea that comes at the last minute, or even the last second. Think about it, okay?"

"Okay, Mom," Brue said, her confidence appearing to gain strength. "I'll think about it."

"That's my girl!"

"Mom, do you have any milk money? I need some for school."

"Oh, that's right. I better get it now while I'm thinking of it." Jo dropped her fork on the table and stood.

"But Mom, you aren't finished eating your supper yet."

"I'm not really all that hungry anyway, sweetie. I'll be right back."

Jo riffled through her handbag. No money left. She reached for the tin box in her bottom bedroom drawer to temporarily borrow from her emergency money supply. But as she reached for it, her fingers brushed against the handkerchief holding Marianne Glanz's pen.

That pen!

She extracted it from the drawer in a manner in which one would handle deadly poison.

If Brue needs to handle Poke, I need to handle Tryg.

She then seized her handbag and slipped the pen into it. She did not want the pen, and she did not want to look at it ever again. It was no good holding onto it. She needed to talk with Tryg, give him one more chance to accept it. If he didn't, into the trash it would go. She needed to get rid of Mrs. Glanz's thoughtful gift—permanently.

CHAPTER FORTY-THREE

In the wee hours of the morning, Jo hopped out of bed and snapped off the alarm long before it had a chance to ring. She lit a fire in the oil burner to take the chill out of the air, then poked around the house, completing a week's worth of chores, and still managed to be the first one in the office.

She perked a fresh pot of coffee. Tryg and Ardena would want a cup the moment they walked in the door. *Tryg. Ardena.* A feeling of dread washed through Jo, her grip on the coffee pot loosening. Coffee sloshed over the sides of her cup. Coffee all over the counter. Coffee dripping on the white marble floor. Coffee everywhere. She quickly mopped it up, carefully took a few healthy sips from her overfilled cup before picking it up, and sauntered back to her desk.

Ardena drifted in a minute before nine, the door easing shut behind her. Without so much as a 'good morning,' she said, "I saw you in church yesterday."

"You did?"

Ardena haphazardly draped her coat over a peg on the clothes tree, over-shooting the hook. Her coat plunged to the floor. "Honestly," she said. She picked it up and gave hanging it a second try. "In answer to your question, yes, I did."

"We didn't see you. Where were you sitting?"

"In the back row."

"You should have joined Brue and me."

"Couldn't. I had to leave early to pick up my neighbor at the train depot. Anyway, I'm a little confused about our debonair pastor. Can we go to The Copper Kettle at noon today? I'm hoping you might have some insight you could share with me."

Great! Ardena beat her to the Calvin punch. Now what was Jo going to do? Jo felt like a Benedict Arnold. Encouraging Calvin to get in touch with Rainy was the right thing to do. But she should have run the idea past Ardena first. If Ardena ever wanted to enjoy a healthy relationship with him, he needed to give up his obsession with Rainy. He needed to talk to the woman. If he did, though, would he see her character flaw, or even have the ability to see it?

She thought about the comical way Calvin's face drained of color when she manipulated him into contacting Rainy. But what if he chose not to see? What if he and Rainy got together again? Jo was the one who strong-armed him into it. Then what would Ardena think? What could she think?

At noon, they headed to The Copper Kettle for a quick bite and the chat Jo was anything but looking forward to.

Ted stood at the entrance with menus and a smile the size of Fountain Lake. It appeared as though he had been on the lookout for them. That seemed out of character for him. "I saved the best booth for you," he announced to Jo and then guided them toward the center of the restaurant. Something about the glint in his eye made Jo want to back away.

Although Ardena thanked him, he answered Jo. "It was my pleasure."

"What was that all about?" Ardena asked the instant he stepped away.

"I don't know, but it frightened me a little."

"Don't be afraid of him. He's really a nice guy."

Jo buried her face in her menu. "Easy for you to say."

"No, it's not. It's the truth. I wonder what's going on with him. He seems to be spending a lot more time around here these days. I mean, he used to let the place pretty much run itself."

"Maybe he's come across hard times."

"I doubt it. If he's ridden through the war up until now with his place still intact, I think he's doing fine. He must be a 4-F or something or I'm sure he'd be overseas." The lines in Ardena's forehead creased. "Why are you smiling?"

"You don't appear to need me for this conversation," Jo said.

"Of course I need you. Why would you say such a thing? Whatever his ailment, it must be legitimate. I haven't heard anything derogatory about him, ever. And speaking of easy for me to say," Ardena said, the pitch and volume of her voice taking a noticeable hike. "Let's talk about yesterday morning. What was that look about that Calvin shot your way in the middle of his sermon? You remember—when he was talking about facing your past."

"You noticed that, did you?"

"Yes. And I was sitting in the back row. The whole congregation noticed it. It was unmistakable."

Jo turned her menu upside down and slid it to the edge of the table. "Look, I've wanted to talk to you about something, but I didn't know what to say."

"What about? What kind of something?"

"I had a chat with Calvin last Wednesday night while Brue was at choir practice."

Ardena squirmed uncomfortably, then unfolded her napkin carefully onto her lap. "Your chat, was it about me?"

"Strangely, no."

Ardena's head snapped back. She looked disappointed. "Really?"

"It was about Rainy."

"Rainy?" slipped slowly through Ardena's lips as if flowing on thick syrup rather than dry air.

"She's in town for about a month, staying with family," Jo continued. "She's aged well. One of the loveliest creatures I've ever laid eyes on. Right up there with Lauren Albrecht."

"Great! Thanks! I really needed to hear that, Jo," Ardena said, her voice now edged with dread. "Why didn't you tell me about this?"

"Let me finish. You asked about her before, but all I knew at the time was that on their wedding day, she rejected Calvin at the altar in front of a packed church."

Ardena gasped.

Jo stopped long enough for the waitress to take their orders and then continued. "That's not all. It was at the height of World War I. While he was overseas risking his life for his homeland, she went off and married his best friend."

"That's terrible!" Ardena scoffed. "No wonder that poor man shied away from ever getting married again."

"I know. I met her for the very first time at a gathering in Hollandale a couple of weeks ago. You can imagine how shocked I was when I learned who she was. And you'll be interested to know that her veneer of perfection appears to be exceedingly thin."

The furrows in Ardena's forehead deepened. "What do you mean by that?"

"I mean Calvin Doherty needs to see and deal with Rainy's flaws or he will never be any good to you or anyone else."

"What kind of flaws?"

"Well, she obviously cheated on him before."

"And?"

"I'd rather not say."

"Jo!"

"Suffice it to say, if I saw what I think I saw, the ministry isn't a good fit for her unless she makes some serious changes. Anyway, he's been carrying her around for a good thirty years now. It's time for him to cut her loose."

"But how's that possible?" Ardena asked.

"He needs to see and face what's become of her."

Just then Ted approached their table, appearing to try overly hard to be a concerned gentleman. "Is everything all right, ladies? You've gotten your orders in okay?"

"Everything's fine," Jo assured him. "I'm sure we'll be getting our food any minute now. Thanks for asking." Not wanting to further encourage him, she looked away, and the moment he was out of range, she lowered her voice and said, "Any idea what all of this attention is about?"

"I have no idea, but he is coming on a little strong."

"I noticed that, too. Anyway, back to Calvin. You need to know that I was the one who suggested their getting together."

Ardena's jaw dropped. "How could you do that to me?"

"Look, Ardena, I feel awful about this."

"Not as awful as I do!" Ardena shot back.

"I know, but at the time it seemed like the right thing to do."

"Do you have any idea how hard it is to find someone you really care for?" Ardena asked, the pain in her voice seeping through her words. "Someone decent who fills up your insides? What if they get back together again? Have you given any thought to that?"

Jo glanced around the restaurant, making sure no one was listening to their conversation, and then said, "I know this hurts and it's scary, but you need to let go until Calvin gets to the other side of this. Give him all the room he needs. I don't know if he will see her. And if he does, I don't know if it will make a difference. But this is your best chance. "

"But—"

"That's the loving thing to do," Jo insisted. She leaned forward, holding Ardena's gaze. "If it means anything to you, I saw how he looked at you the day you met right here in this very restaurant."

"You did?" Ardena asked hopefully.

"I definitely did. And you of all people don't deserve to be haunted by a ghost from his past, or from any man's past, for that matter. He's a good man. I believe in him and hope you will, too."

Though tears welled in Ardena's eyes, she nodded appreciably. "You're right, Jo."

CHAPTER FORTY-FOUR

aving just finished eating, Jo gave the entirety of The Copper Kettle a brief and guarded glance. Ted was nowhere in sight. Good. Over the noon hour, he'd dropped enough subtle hints about his interest in Jo to call up a war party. "Let's get out of here, Ardena."

They had no more than stepped outside into the gray and overcast afternoon when the clap of decent-sized shoes pounded out onto the sidewalk behind them. To Jo's dismay, a masculine voice called her name. She hesitated before turning.

And there he stood.

Ted.

Ardena grinned mischievously before disappearing through the doors of the law office.

Whatever Ted wanted, Jo wanted no part of it.

He rammed his hands into his pockets and gazed at her with the innocence of a boy of about ten. "Some of my friends and I are going on an outing on Sunday," he said innocently. "I was wondering if you would like to come along. As my date, that is."

"This Sunday?"

He nodded.

Jo glanced up and down the sidewalk. Of all of the public places to handle her personal business...honestly! There were eyes everywhere. She did not want to go out with Ted and yet, with him looking as vulnerable as he did, she did not have the heart to turn him down. Why the sudden interest in her now? During her first few visits to The Copper Kettle, he never bothered to give her a second look.

She was about to respond, but hesitated when she heard someone else coming up from behind at a fast and markedly broken pace.

Tryg.

She tasted her food for a second time as it squeezed up her esophagus and into her throat. Why did she feel as if she needed to shrink or hide? After all, Tryg had a romantic interest of his own. For some odd reason, though, he flashed a disappointed look at them when he passed by. Why? Ted was a very nice-looking and quite successful businessman, *thank you very much*. She just happened to have no interest in him.

"Sunday would be fine," Jo said softly, feeling disingenuous for giving in to the pressure of Ted's vulnerability. "What time?"

"How about one?"

"One o'clock is fine."

He reached into his pocket and pulled out an order pad, a pencil from behind his ear, quickly scribbled down her address and telephone number, and then strutted back into the restaurant wearing an excessively pleased-with-himself grin.

Jo spent the rest of the afternoon jamming papers into her typewriter and pounding on its keys with a vengeance.

Ardena, meanwhile, snickered herself into a snort.

Jo glanced at her, shook her head, and burst into laughter. "Just for that, I promise I'm going to go and I'm going to have an *exceptionally* good time!"

Just then the phone rang. Ardena was still laughing too hard to answer.

Jo composed herself by the third ring and answered. It was Ramsey

School calling, requesting an immediate audience with her. Ardena sobered instantly and offered to cover at the office until Jo returned.

A crooked hopscotch outline etched with chalk by wee hands and an abandoned basketball lying on the asphalt merely yards away from a shredding basketball hoop were all that remained on the deserted playground as Jo rushed past. The children were all in their classrooms waiting for the closing bell—that is, with the exception of little Brue.

Jo ascended Ramsey Elementary's half-dozen or so concrete stairs and passed through its arched entry at a fast stride. Once inside the square redbrick building, with its ghostly quiet halls and wide hardwood floors, she slowed her pace to muffle the echo of her wedged heels. The occasional voice of a teacher with authoritative timbre filtered through the gaps beneath the opaque glass and wood classroom doors as she hurried on.

When she entered the principal's office, Poke, Brue, and another girl were standing near the far wall like little toy soldiers all in a row, looking more frightened than guilty.

The principal did not hesitate to invite Jo and Brue into her office.

"What happened?" Jo asked, taking a chair.

Looking more amused than concerned, the tall, thin, and graying woman said, "I'm hoping your daughter will answer that question for us."

Jo gazed at Brue. "What happened, sweetie?"

Brue stiffened and her eyes widened.

"I want you to forget about the principal being here with us," Jo said. "Just tell me what happened, okay?"

After an agonizingly protracted moment, Brue said, "I did what you told me to do, Mom."

Jo's insides suddenly seized. She was no longer sure she wanted to hear what her daughter had to say, especially in the company of the principal. "And?"

"Poke landed on his backside and skidded across the floor, but I caught Annie and kept her from falling."

Jo glanced at the principal whose laughter was in full restraint—a glint in her eyes giving her away.

Jo turned back to Brue. "That was kind of dangerous, wasn't it? And what about Poke's bad arm?"

"He landed on his backside because I think he was protecting his bad arm."

"Would you happen to have any idea why he skidded across the floor, Brue?"

Brue nodded.

"I'm waiting, sweetie."

"I sorta put my foot out quick and tripped him when he ran past me."

"Hmm," Jo said thoughtfully. "Then what happened?"

"After Poke hit the floor, everyone cheered."

"Cheered for Poke or cheered for you?"

"Cheered for me."

"I see." Holding her laughter in check as well, Jo asked the principal, "Will there be anything in the way of punishment against my daughter?"

"I don't think so," she said, and then she turned toward Brue, "Miss Bremley, that will be all. You may return to your class now."

Jo knelt and hugged Brue, whispering in her ear, "I'm proud of you, sweetie. We'll talk more about this tonight when we get home."

The moment Brue scooted out the door, the principal said, "I had hoped one of the children would take on that bully. Who would have thought it would take a little girl to do it? She's very courageous, Mrs. Bremley."

Jo nodded. "I just hope there won't be any repercussions from Poke."

"Rest assured, we'll keep an eye out."

Jo stood to leave, but then stopped and said thoughtfully, "There's something you might want to know about Poke."

"Really? What's that?"

"He's always been a handful, but it's gotten much worse since he learned about his dad."

The principal looked at Jo with concern-filled eyes. "What about his dad?"

"He's missing in action."

"Oh dear. I had no idea. Poke must be acting out then. Under the circumstances, who could really blame him?"

"That's right," Jo said. "I'm afraid he's one hurting little boy."

"I'll be sure to be gentle with his mother when she arrives. Maybe together we can come up with better ways to help him express himself."

"Thank you," Jo said. "I'm afraid Brue got lucky this time. Poke could have taken a bruising physically just as easily as he has emotionally."

"I'd say it was Poke who got lucky," the principal said. "He could have hurt one of those little girls every bit as bad."

Jo stepped into the outer office and, as she neared Poke, she hesitated, then extended her hand and lightly stroked his cheek. He flinched, but then relaxed, moisture welling in his guilt-ridden eyes. Jo said nothing as she walked away.

CHAPTER FORTY-FIVE

The following Monday morning, Ardena sat at her desk grinning. "How'd the big date go?"

Jo, unable to hide her accusing attitude as she marched toward Ardena's desk with every intention of fleshing out the truth, said, "You tell me."

Ardena's grin faded. "Huh? What are you talking about?"

"You wouldn't happen to know who would be brazen enough to put a bug in Ted's ear, telling him I was interested in him, would you?"

"What? How could you even *think* such a thing, let alone ask?"

"Let me tell you how. He said he was sure I was married until one of my *dear* friends told him I was a widow and *very* interested in him. That's why he asked me out. That's how I could think to ask. And he refused to tell me who that dear friend was."

Ardena shoved her chair back, deeply widening the space between them. "So you just assumed that friend was me? You think I told him that?"

"I'm a new face uptown, Ardena. Who else could it possibly be?"

Ardena slapped a manila folder onto her desk, then gave Jo a contemptuous glance. "I can't believe you'd think that. Consider us having our first tiff."

Suddenly unsure of herself, Jo sidled toward Ardena's desk. "Do you mean to tell me it really wasn't you?"

"That's precisely what I'm telling you."

"But...if it wasn't you, who else could it possibly have been?"

"How about Tryg?" Ardena asked, resentment still evident in her voice.

"No. It wasn't him. Absolutely not. You should have seen the look on his face when he walked past Ted and me out on the sidewalk last week, the day Ted asked me out."

"What kind of look?"

"I don't know. Disappointed. Disapproving, maybe."

Jo gently folded her arms across her pale blue sweater set and said, "Ardena?"

Silence.

"Will you forgive me?"

Ardena hesitated, undoubtedly wanting to make this punishing for Jo, not that she didn't have every right. "For what?"

"For falsely accusing you. I really am sorry."

Ardena's edge abated; her shoulders relaxed. "You're forgiven."

"Thank you," Jo said softly and sincerely.

"So Tryg looked disappointed, huh?" Ardena said.

"You can say that again. I didn't know what to think."

"Something else must have been bothering him."

"I don't think so. The look appeared to be directed at us."

Ardena tapped her pencil rhythmically against her desktop. "That's strange. I wonder why he'd do that. Regarding that friend, though, maybe one of the waitresses at The Copper Kettle put Ted up to it. You never know what they're saying about their customers behind the scenes."

"You know, I hadn't thought about that. You could be right. But which one? And why? I know them all on such a superficial level and I haven't told any of them about my marital status."

"You've got me!" Ardena blinked at Jo. "Well, all that aside, how did it go? Do you want to tell me about it? I'm champing at the bit here."

"It was a disaster. An utter and complete disaster."

Ardena laughed. "Okay. Now tell me the truth."

"I just did."

"What?" Ardena sobered. "No wonder you were so fired up when you came in. But why was your date an utter and complete disaster? What happened?"

Jo stepped forward and rested against Ardena's desk. "When Ted said we were going to the lake, I thought it was for a picnic. But he did tell me to bring a swimming suit along, just in case. I don't swim. Haven't tried since I was a kid. But back then at least I knew how to dog paddle.

"After we'd been at the lake for an hour or so, everyone, present company excluded, decided they wanted to take a walk out to the end of the dock, so I tagged along. One of Ted's buddies decided he needed some attention. At my expense, of course. All of a sudden, he came charging at me like a club-footed bull. He ducked his head down, and the next thing I knew, I was flailing around on the top of his shoulders. And he was a big man! You should have seen everyone double over with laughter. They thought it was hilarious. Not me. I have a problem with heights and was more into passing out, so I grabbed onto the only thing I could find for traction."

"Which was?"

"Try three thin strands of hair on top of baldy's head."

Ardena started snickering.

"It's not funny," Jo said. "Ted must have seen how scared I was. He reached up and grabbed my hand. Told his friend he might want to think about putting me down. I was embarrassed to death for spoiling everybody's fun. But it didn't stop there."

"What do you mean it didn't stop there?" Ardena asked, looking dubious.

"The next thing I knew, they all lowered themselves off the far end of the dock and into the lake for a swim. I thought, well, while they swim, I'll just dog paddle for a while. They made it look so easy, every last one of them, lowering themselves gently into the water just up to their shoulders. Again I thought to myself, I can do that. But when my turn came, instead of gently lowering myself into the water, I accidentally plunked my full weight in. Next thing I knew, I sank hard. Like 110 pounds of lead. Down. Down. Down. My arm pumping didn't do a bit of good. I couldn't get any traction or turn around until my feet sprung off the goo at the bottom of the lake."

Ardena exploded into laughter. When her snorts cut loose again, Jo finally saw the humor and burst into laughter, too.

CHAPTER FORTY-SIX

J ust outside Evelyn's front door, Jo lifted her hand to knock, but stopped instead and looked down at Brue, concerned. "Sweetie, are you sure you're ready for this?"

"I'm sure."

"You're absolutely, positively sure?"

"Uh-huh."

"Okay then. Let's get it over with."

A brief moment later, Evelyn opened her door and stepped back, her wondering eyes focused on Brue.

"We'd like to extend an olive branch," Jo said warmly. "Would you mind if we came in? We won't stay long."

"Not at all. Thanks for stopping by. Please. Have a seat on the sofa there," Evelyn said thoughtfully.

Leading Brue by her shoulder, Jo glanced around and asked, "Is Poke home? We really do need to include him."

Evelyn disappeared into her kitchen, then returned with a resistant young boy shuffling along with his hands stuffed in his pockets. He slumped onto the rocking chair and then lay back as if in total defeat while Evelyn stood by his side, her hands planted firmly on her hips.

"Brue," Jo said, taking the lead. "I believe you had something you wanted to say to Poke."

Poke cast petulant eyes toward the floor.

Brue got up and eased toward him. A foot in front of his chair, she stopped and said, "I want to apologize. It wasn't right for me to trip you."

His head snapped up, his wary gaze catching hers. "Huh?"

Evelyn turned to Brue with a line-creased forehead. "Why on earth did you trip Poke?"

"I didn't know how else to stop him."

"Oh yeah?" he scoffed. "Some friend you are."

"Wait a minute," Evelyn said, and then she looked at Poke. "Stop you from what?"

When he refused to answer, Evelyn turned to Brue. "Stop him from what?"

Brue wheeled around and looked pleadingly at Jo.

Jo got up and joined them. "It appears children are reluctant to tell tales," she said thoughtfully. "There's plenty of blame to go around, though."

"But what happened?" Evelyn asked.

"As I understand it," Jo said as she rested a light hand on Brue's shoulder, "your son was pulling little Annie backward so fast, Brue was afraid she was going to fall and get hurt. Annie started to cry. Brue felt sorry for her and thought she would be the best one to stop Poke, because they're friends."

Evelyn turned to Poke. "Do you mean you were actually pulling that little girl around backward? The principal said you'd gotten unruly and that Brue tripped you, but she didn't say anything else. So you were pulling her backward by the arm, then?"

Poke looked down, pouting.

"Poke? Answer me."

He shook his head.

"By the hand? Did you pull her by the hand?"

Poke still refused to answer, but his eyes revealed a fair amount of guilt.

"Don't tell me you pulled her by her hair." Evelyn raised her voice. "Poke, you answer me, and you answer me right now. Did you pull that little girl backward by her hair?"

Poke nodded.

"Honestly! How could you do such a thing?" Suddenly bafflement registered in Evelyn's eyes and she turned to Brue in disbelief. "Why in the world are you apologizing to Poke?"

"Because I tripped him and I knew that was wrong, too."

Evelyn glared at Poke. "What are you going to say to Brue? Come on," she insisted. "What are you going to say to Brue?"

He swung his feet back and forth.

"On your feet, young man."

Poke got up and, looking at the floor, stuffed his hands deep in his pockets. "I'm sorry."

"That's not good enough," Evelyn said. "What are you going to ask her?"

Poke kicked the tip of his shoe repeatedly against the Persian rug, then looked at Brue with his head tilted. "Will you forgive me?"

Brue nodded.

"Good. Now shake hands with her," Evelyn said.

After Poke and Brue shook hands, Evelyn turned to Jo. "I'm so sorry."

"I need to apologize, too," Jo said. "I was the one who encouraged Brue to take matters into her own hands before anyone got badly hurt. None of the kids wanted to snitch to the teacher. But it wasn't all Poke's fault, either. Brue tells me the boys were encouraging him. You know how kids can be."

Evelyn gave Jo a hug then lightly patted her arm. "Thank you. And thank you, too, Brue."

"Go easy on him," Jo whispered.

"I will," Evelyn said. "We're both hurting for his dad."

CHAPTER FORTY-SEVEN

Tryg pushed open the street-side door and peered into the office. The smile creasing his face reached for his ears. "Hey, Ardena. Jo. Do you have a minute?"

Jo glanced at Ardena who looked as bewildered as Jo felt.

"Come on," he said with a wave of his hand, then headed back outside with a sense of urgency.

"What's going on with him?" Ardena asked.

"I have no idea. But whatever it is, it must be awfully good."

Tryg stopped in the middle of the sidewalk and subtly pitched his head toward a parked car. "What do you think? Isn't she a beaut?"

"Whose is it?" Jo asked innocently.

Tryg looked and sounded hurt. "It's mine."

Jo immediately realized her faux pas. "Oh, but it is beautiful," she said. She dutifully looked over the shiny black car, wishing she could crawl under it. It was impressive looking, she had to admit. But it was Tryg's? He lived near the office and hadn't driven since his accident with Case. He couldn't have gotten over his fear of driving that quickly. No one could.

Ardena walked around the car, thoroughly admiring it. "It's absolutely gorgeous! When did you get it?"

"Saturday."

"Wow! What kind is it? A Buick, right?"

"That's right," he said. "A 1942 Buick Roadmaster, four-door sedan. I bought it off of a buddy of mine. When they start producing cars again after the war is over, I think I'll ante up and buy a new one."

Just then, the door of The Copper Kettle swept open and Ted stepped out on the sidewalk and joined them. "Hey, what's going on out here? What's the commotion all about?"

Jo's stomach tightened. Of the few people she did not care to encounter again until well into the twenty-first century, Ted topped the list. "This is Tryg's new car."

Ted gave the car an admiring glance. "Nice piece of metal, Tryg."

Tryg threw Ted an easy smile. "Thanks!"

"How does she do out on the open road?"

"I don't know. I haven't taken her out there."

Jo noticed that Tryg recoiled at the question and also hadn't mentioned the word *yet*. He must only feel comfortable driving in town, she decided.

Tryg opened the front and back doors while Ardena leaned in, patting the seats and inhaling the scent of fine leather that Jo also smelled, but from a distance.

Meanwhile, Ted poked his nose through the front door and ogled the dash. "Not too bad, Tryg."

The faint ringing of the telephone from inside the office begged for attention, bringing with it an immediate opportunity for escape. Jo quickly excused herself.

When Tryg and Ardena re-entered the office several minutes later, Jo said, "Congratulations on your purchase, Tryg. It really is a beautiful car."

He acknowledged her compliment with a reluctant smile.

"By the way," she added quickly, "that was Lauren on the phone. She said she'd stop by later this afternoon to pick up the keys to your home. She mentioned something about needing to take measurements for something. Said you'd know what that was all about."

Tryg looked hard to read. He thought for a moment then pulled out his keychain and handed it to Jo. "Here. Give these to her when she comes in. Harry Anderson should be here in a few minutes. I'm afraid our meeting could last a while. It probably wouldn't be a good idea to interrupt us."

Twenty minutes later, Lauren arrived. Although she emitted a flicker of disappointment in not being able to see Tryg, when she walked off with his set of keys, she did raise her chin exceptionally high.

When the door closed behind her, Ardena said, "That woman needs to wise up."

Surprised by Ardena's comment, Jo asked, "Why did you say that?"

"Those are the keys to Tryg's house, for crying out loud. They are anything but the keys to his heart."

Jo thought about Ardena's profound words and had to agree. "Speaking about the keys to a man's heart."

"Yes?"

"I'm embarrassed to admit it, but I felt an aversion toward Ted when he joined us out on the sidewalk. I sure hope it wasn't obvious. He's been so kind. I know our date was an utter and complete disaster, but he doesn't deserve to be rebuffed."

"Do unto others, right?" Ardena said.

Jo nodded.

"What are you going to do about it?"

"You mean other than hunt down and destroy the person who set us up?" Jo glanced at the clock. Twenty-five past three already. "I'll be back in a few minutes."

There were more customers holed up in The Copper Kettle than Jo thought at this time of day. She looked around just the same and found Ted lurking behind the counter. When he glanced up, she waved, indicating a private booth. He nodded and joined her immediately.

"What's going on?" he asked as he slid onto the seat across from her.

"Me."

He looked uncomfortable and taken aback for a moment, but then smiled and said, "You?"

"That's right, Ted. I'm afraid I could have been more of a lady on Sunday. I want to apologize for my behavior. I really embarrassed myself with my lack of—"

"You were just fine."

"No," she said thoughtfully. "It's more than that."

"Us?" he asked, somewhat defensively.

Jo nodded. "I'm fond of you, Ted. I really am. And I enjoy coming in here." She glanced around the well-kept upscale restaurant. "Seeing you so caught up in your work. But I'm not interested enough in dating to give too many men a chance. I'm not meaning to be presumptuous, but you deserve better than I have to offer."

Ted laughed and reached for Jo's reluctant hands. "Don't worry about a thing," he said warmly. "I had a serious relationship up until a couple of months ago. Thought it was over forever, but then she called last night. Caught me completely off guard. She wants to get back together again. Looks like this conversation works well for the both of us."

Jo smiled appreciably, yet somehow she felt an unexpected sense of loss. "I'm glad I stopped by. You're a good man, Ted. I sure hope your relationship works well for you."

CHAPTER FORTY-EIGHT

C alvin stood by the window, watching the rain flow as gently and evenly down the pane as the tears flowed down Mrs. Sorbo's rosy cheeks. She was sitting beside his desk, delicately blowing her reddening nose.

Fortunately for Calvin, he enjoyed counseling even more than preaching. He found himself most fascinated by common complaints, and people's inability to see the obvious. He loved witnessing that unmistakable look of relief when they finally understood. As for Mrs. Sorbo, he'd heard her story one too many times. *Why didn't women get it?*

"It's always like this," she said, her voice breaking. "He takes me so for granted."

Calvin turned and strolled back to his chair, pulling it up close to his desk. "I'm curious. How, specifically, does your husband take you for granted? From what I've seen, he's amazingly responsible. He appears devoted to you and your family. Does a fabulous job helping around the church here, and we know that if there's anyone we can consistently depend on, it's him."

Mrs. Sorbo's response was not buried deep. "Well, for starters, he never acknowledges or says thank you for a thing. Never remembers my birthday, either. I bore his children, cook his meals, do his dishes, do his dirty laundry, iron his clothes, do his shopping, do his cleaning, and make his bed. I even mow and rake and shovel snow. I do everything for that man. Yet not once have I ever gotten a thank you. I'm surprised he even remembers me at Christmastime."

"I see. That is a problem," Calvin admitted.

Mrs. Sorbo sighed, looking utterly relieved to find a man who understood.

"Do you really want to handle the problem?" Calvin asked matter-of-factly.

"Of course I do, Pastor Doherty. That's why I'm here."

"Good. Then I have an idea."

When Mrs. Sorbo's relieved look withered, Calvin questioned himself. Did he appear too eager?

"What's that?" she asked apprehensively.

"Have you tried setting him up to succeed with you?"

Her eyebrows pinched into a V-shape. "What do you mean by that?"

"Have you ever said anything like, 'Did I do a good enough job of mowing the lawn today or raking the leaves or shoveling the snow'? Or how about this one... 'there are only seven more shopping days until my birthday'? You don't strike me as being one of those women who waits it out and then gives her husband the cold shoulder when he doesn't remember."

Mrs. Sorbo fidgeted with a button on her paisley dress, her gaze cast downward. Calvin must be getting through to her. Either that, or she was shocked that he would be so blunt.

"I'm sure you've asked him on occasion how your meals taste." Calvin smiled inwardly. He was on a roll. "And if he likes the way you do his laundry. But have you ever asked him if he appreciates you...as much as you appreciate him?"

"Well—" Mrs. Sorbo said, looking as though she would prefer passing out to answering. "I guess not, exactly."

She hadn't gotten defensive. Good. This was going exceptionally well. "Now, since your husband isn't here to defend himself, let's take a minute to discuss what life might be like from his perspective."

Mrs. Sorbo winced. "Okay," she said reluctantly.

Calvin sat back in his chair, interwove his fingers, and cast his gaze toward the ceiling as though he were reaching deep into a dark cavern to find answers to address this difficult problem, which he was not. "Every week when your husband brings home a paycheck," he said, slowly tapping his fingertips together, "do you tell him how much you appreciate how hard he works? And when he gives you spending money, brings out the trash, or carries in heavy groceries, do you take the time to say 'thank you'?"

Mrs. Sorbo's face turned the deepest shade of crimson. "I get it, Pastor Doherty," she said, her tone unmistakably contrite. "You don't have to say any more. I better not take up any more of your valuable time." As she stood and approached the door, she stopped short and looked back. "By the way, your sermon yesterday was excellent, absolutely excellent." She then added with a raised brow and a mischievously playful yet warm and grateful grin, *"Thank you!"*

The moment the door closed, a smile played at Calvin's cheeks. "I'm pretty good at this," he muttered to himself. "Too bad I can't charge for these sessions." But then he flashed on Mrs. Sorbo's comment about the excellence of Sunday morning's sermon and his generous ego took a quick trim. It hadn't been one of his best. He knew that. Oh, the words were okay. But he read them, he hadn't delivered them.

Looking out over the congregation, he'd seen Jo Bremley sitting in her usual fourth row pew. She unintentionally yet uncannily made him brutally aware of his weaknesses. Although she did not have it in her to be judgmental or unkind, he respected her too much to play loose with her approval.

He thought of Ardena. She was the best thing that happened to him in quite a long time. She deserved all of his attention, not just a part of it. But who was he kidding? She was competing with Rainy in his heart, and that was not right.

Rainy. She was in the area. What if she had shown up at church, too? Would Calvin have been able to open his mouth at all?

He peered at the phone.

"*Rainy*," he whispered.

He inhaled a deep breath. He picked up the receiver. He cradled it down. Actually, he would have preferred throwing the thing. After all, he was the preacher. He was the beggar showing the other beggars where the bread was. That was his calling. If he could not face his past, how could he have the power to help those in his congregation face theirs? How dare he judge the women who came to him for counsel? He was no better than any one of them.

But he was not ready to call Rainy. Not yet. He needed to go for a walk. Maybe a nice long stroll through Harrington Park would help. No. Not with the gloom and sopping wet out there. Besides, he needed to get this over with.

He noticed a slight tremor in his hand as he picked up the receiver one more time. Ignoring it, he forced himself to talk. "Operator, would you put me through to the Christiansen residence in Clarks Grove, please?"

CHAPTER FORTY-NINE

Through the office window, Jo caught a glimpse of the back end of Tryg's new used car. Since buying it, his mood seemed more upbeat. Jo was also in a lighter mood after clearing the air with Ardena and Ted.

Returning to her work, she two-hole punched an onionskin copy of a document, slipped it over the prongs in a folder, and then glanced back at Tryg's open door.

The sight of the entry alone made her insides crawl.

Like the document she was filing away, it was time to put to rest her unfinished business with him, too. She opened her lower right-hand drawer, plucked the ruby red pen out of her handbag, and lightly buffed it.

A skittish moment later, she raised her chin before tapping lightly on Tryg's doorjamb. "Mind if I come in?"

He glanced up, a questioning look wriggling across his face, and then he laid aside a document he'd been reading. "Not at all. Please do."

Tryg's gaze locked on Marianne Glanz's shiny pen, his questioning look deepening as Jo rhythmically tapped it across her hand and strolled toward his desk.

"What's going on?" he asked.

"I know I'm being silly, but I've been having trouble sleeping lately. I thought it might be a good idea to talk with you about it once and for all."

He eased his forearms onto the arms of his chair and lightly interweaved his fingers. "I'm sorry to hear about your trouble sleeping," he said, his tone serious. "There's nothing worse than insomnia. You have my attention. Please, go ahead."

She glanced out his windows and watched a few cars motor by. She recalled briefly the effective way Calvin Doherty paused before he prayed each Sunday morning. He always maintained silence for a good five seconds or so to settle the congregation down and better prepare them to receive his message. Jo's message was also important. Important to her, at least. So she waited a drawn-out moment.

"We both know that I made a mistake with Marianne Glanz," she said finally. "A huge mistake. Obviously, that has me feeling vulnerable. And we both know there is no way for me to undo what I did, but I wish with all my heart that I could.

"Then there's that situation with Henrietta Braddingly coming from out of nowhere. I don't understand that one or where she got her information. It doesn't make any sense."

Tryg, an exceptional listener, let her continue without interruption.

Jo then lifted Marianne Glanz's pen to eye level for him to comfortably view. "Now we're playing a cat-and-mouse game with this pen. That would not be a problem, except I noticed you've been using a shiny new black pen lately that I haven't seen before."

"It was a gift," he said, without hesitation or hint of a flinch.

Jo felt subtly rebuffed, but she needed to finish what she started. "Like I said, I'm feeling awfully silly having this discussion with you, but I'm just not sure where I stand in this office. I can't read you or your motives. I'm constantly worrying that I'll make another misstep. And that's not good for any of us."

"So that's what this is all about," he said, his expression nondescript. He reached for the paper he'd been reading on his desktop and fingered it, plucking lightly at its corners. "About Marianne Glanz…"

"Yes?"

"Lauren and I ran into the Glanzes at a concert the other night. They were both very polite and friendly, but neither of them breathed a word about Mrs. Glanz's visit with you."

Tryg set the document aside, got up, strolled over to the window, and peered through the Venetian blinds as if he were looking for someone, and then looked back, his expression grim. "As far as Henrietta Braddingly is concerned, she is known to be a walking nightmare. As to whether she would have acted that way with us or turned around and sued us, that, I'm afraid, we'll never know."

Jo suddenly saw Tryg with blinding clarity. No wonder sleep escaped her. He was having doubts about her. Serious doubts. Doubts that lacerated to the marrow in her bones.

"Like I said about the shiny new black pen, it was a gift. And about your ruby red pen there," he said, for the first time breaking a slight grin, "I rather enjoyed the exchange."

"You did?"

He nodded.

"Thank you," she replied, but not without the bile in her stomach pressing far up into her throat. "And thank you for the chat. I appreciate it."

Jo did not find out what she wanted to know, but she did find out what she needed to know. Clearly their conversation had not gone well. Tryg's lack of encouragement regarding Marianne Glanz and Henrietta Braddingly left her feeling even more vulnerable than before. And he merely tossed her a bone when he said he rather enjoyed the pen exchange. She sat still, collecting her thoughts, and then looked at Tryg as emotionlessly as he looked at her earlier. She purposely rolled Mrs. Glanz's pen slowly in her hand, then placed it carefully in the middle of his desk the way one would place an overfilled cup of hot liquid, and left the room as deliberately as she'd entered.

CHAPTER FIFTY

Tryg watched the door close behind Jo, and then picked up his shiny black pen and held it in one hand and Mrs. Glanz's ruby red pen in the other. He studied them. Weighing them. Comparing them. Marianne Glanz's pen definitely had an edge when it came to class.

He thought about Jo and how hard she tried to smoke him out. Tried to get a feel for what he was thinking. Tried to get a feel for where she stood in his office. He couldn't blame her, really. That was wise. It took decency and courage.

He shook his head. *And I gave her little to no support.*

That evening, Tryg stopped by Lauren's house to pick her up for a quick and casual supper somewhere. It was getting late. When he strolled up the sidewalk, Lauren was already outside locking her door, struggling with her skeleton key. It was stuck in the keyhole. She looked flustered when Tryg offered his help, but succumbed when she couldn't get it out.

Carefully maneuvering it back and forth, Tryg removed the key and handed over her keychain. "You've got an awful lot of keys on that chain for such a delicate little lady," he said caringly. "Doesn't it weigh your handbag down?"

Tryg noticed that she appeared to ignore his comment.

They headed out to the truck stop east of town on old Highway 65. Tryg ordered a hamburger, French fries, and a Coke; Lauren ordered green pea soup, coleslaw, and a glass of water.

Lauren eyed Tryg as he ate. And after a short while she expressed concern about his preoccupation.

He gazed across the Formica table, feeling a sheepish smile begin to form. "It's nothing, really." He then told her about Jo's talk with him, how she gave the pen back, how guarded his response was, and how he felt regret.

Lauren reached for his hands and lightly stroked them with her thumbs as she held them. "This really bothers you, doesn't it?"

Tryg nodded.

"Because of Case?"

"I don't know. That probably enters into it."

"Are you wondering what he would have thought?"

"I'm not sure," Tryg answered with a strained sigh. "All I know is that I could have said more, but I just didn't know what to say."

"Why don't you give the pen back to her?"

"I have. I know this sounds crazy. It's just a silly pen. But I feel guilty keeping it, and I don't feel right about throwing it away."

"Think about it, Tryg," Lauren said, her tone resolute. "Jo knows she did wrong. To her, the pen is payment for services she preempted. She's probably feeling guilty about keeping the pen, too. The two of you need to find a way to break out of this cat-and-mouse game."

"I know. But how?"

"I don't know. How about giving it back to her and including a pithy note that says something like, '*Case would want you to have this*'?"

"Are you sure?" Tryg asked. "That would be kind of insensitive, wouldn't it? I mean, bringing her husband into it?"

"At this point, it's probably what you need to do. That way she'll definitely know the pen belongs to her. She might back off."

"Maybe you're right. Let me think about it."

They called it a short night, just supper and the ride home. When Tryg walked Lauren to her door, she quickly said, "Let's see if I can get my door unlocked without the key getting stuck again."

This time she was successful.

CHAPTER FIFTY-ONE

J o hung her coat, glanced across the room at Tryg's closed door, and said, "Is he in?"

Ardena stopped typing. "Good morning to you, too."

"I'm sorry."

"Don't worry about it. And yes, he is in. I can't read him, though."

"What's to read?"

"He slipped something into your desk drawer." Pulling back her return carriage, Ardena eyed her typing and said distractedly, "I think it might be that pen again."

Jo squeezed down a backed-up taste of breakfast. Walking to her desk, her feet took on a heavy feel, weighing her down. Did she anger him when she placed it neatly in the center of his desk?

"What's the matter?" Ardena asked.

"Oh, nothing much." Jo opened her desk drawer. Ardena was right. The pen was there again, but this time with a short note that said, '*Case would want you to have this. Tryg.*'

Jo buried her face in her hands. How could Tryg bring Case into this? What on earth was he thinking?

For the rest of the morning, she listened as the clock ticked in slow motion. Tryg holed up in his office, and the steady thump of the keys on

Ardena's Corona pounded like drums in Jo's ears. Neither helped ease her angst. She wanted to go home. She just wanted out.

At precisely ten minutes before twelve, what was left of Jo's world collapsed when the perfectly groomed Miss Albrecht swept in the door, smelling fresher than the late-morning breeze rushing in behind her.

"I'm here to have lunch with Mr. Howland," she announced.

Jo glanced at his open door. "Yes, ma'am. I'll be happy to get him for you."

"He usually leaves at twelve sharp, doesn't he?" Lauren asked.

"Usually, unless he's working on a case."

"Fine. Don't bother him, then. I'm a few minutes early, so I'm happy to wait."

Jo glanced at the waiting area. "Great. Feel free to have a chair. Can I get anything for you while you're waiting?"

"No, thank you. I'm fine."

As Lauren Albrecht's peppy little body floated on her trendy heels to the waiting area, Jo glanced down at her own scuffed-up shoes and slid her feet as far under her desk as they would go. There was something about Miss Albrecht that made Jo feel like a walking advertisement for the local thrift store.

A couple of minutes before noon, Lauren gathered her handbag and approached Jo's desk.

Reading her thoughts, Jo slipped into Tryg's office, announced Miss Albrecht's arrival, and then returned saying, "He'll be out in just a minute."

Miss Albrecht pressed her gloves on tightly, one finger at a time, smiling reticently. "While I'm waiting, I thought you might appreciate knowing that Mr. Howland has told me so much about you," she said, looking at Jo as if she actually had value.

"Really?" Jo said, pleased to feel a surprising and genuine connection with Lauren for the very first time. Was it possible they might actually become friends?

"It was awfully generous of him to give you a job when you didn't have any experience," Lauren said innocently.

"Pardon me?"

"I said it was awfully generous of him to give you a job when you didn't have any experience," she repeated. "He really is a very kind and patient man."

What is that supposed to mean?

Tryg must have heard their conversation. He bounded out of his office and whisked Miss Albrecht off, his fingers lightly guiding her by the small of her back. Without making eye contact, he turned and said, "I should be back in about an hour or two."

Ardena, who had been retrieving a folder from the file drawers, returned to her desk and plopped heavily onto her chair. She roughly sandwiched carbon papers between a sheet of stationery and several sheets of onionskin paper, stuffed them onto the platen, slammed the carriage, and then hammered the keys of her typewriter.

"That's quite some deadline you have there," Jo said with a smirk.

Ardena grunted.

"If I'm reading you correctly," Jo said, "Miss Lauren Albrecht isn't worth breaking your fingernails over."

Ardena nodded. "You're right about that." Her shoulders relaxed and her typing returned to a normal rhythm, but then she stopped. "Honestly! I can't believe that woman. And I can't imagine how awful hearing those words must have been for you. You handled it like a real lady, Jo. How in the world are you still able to smile?"

"I think I'm still in shock. Besides, I don't have much choice. She is Tryg's lady friend."

"You might want to start building an arsenal of responses. She's out to get you."

"That's what I've been thinking, too. But why?"

"I have no idea. She doesn't even know you."

Jo had difficulty resuming her work. Ardena was right. There was more to Lauren's barb. Whatever it was could not be all that mysterious. First Henrietta Braddingly, then Lauren Albrecht. Jo thought for a moment. *No! Couldn't be.* She got up and crossed the room, riffled through the directories, and then turned to Ardena. "Any idea where the phone book is?"

"I have it right here. Help yourself."

Jo returned to her desk with the phone book in hand. She opened it and flipped a few pages until she found the 'A' listings. She looked down the column and searched for Lauren Albrecht's address. Finding it, she then turned the page and looked down the column again searching for Henrietta Braddingly's address. She buried her head in her hands and exhaled.

They were next-door neighbors.

CHAPTER FIFTY-TWO

J o searched the pantry rummaging through cans and jars to find something for supper. These decisions she found difficult under normal circumstances, but deciding when she had no appetite was next to impossible.

"Brue, what would you like to eat?"

"A cheese grill sandwich and canned plums, please."

Jo smiled emptily at Brue. "Thank you. *Grilled cheese* sandwiches and canned plums, it is."

The conversation at supper was uncharacteristically one-sided due to Jo's preoccupation, with Brue sharing her experiences at school while Jo tossed in an occasional, distracted '*uh-huh*.'

After they finished eating, Jo finished the dishes, prepared brown bags, and set aside tomorrow's clothing. She and Brue then gathered near the radio. Even with listening to *The Lone Ranger*, Jo found it difficult to concentrate.

The grandfather clock chimed eight times. In less than twelve hours it would be time to get ready for work again. Jo shoved that anything-but-cherished idea out of her mind as quickly as it came. At eight-thirty, she tucked Brue into bed and kissed her lightly on the forehead before heading out to the porch for some much-needed introspection.

Staring out through the porch windows, Jo listened intently to the creaking of her rocking chair against the well-worn floor. Darkness had all but swallowed the twilight, dusting the sky with a sliver of a moon and countless stars that arrested her attention, but not her heart. She could not get past feeling numb and betrayed.

In this less than perfect world, she'd experienced her share of unkind looks, angry voices, snubs, and slights. Everyone had. Yet this was her first real taste of blatant evil.

Tryg's lady friend, no less.

Lauren Albrecht had definitely set her up, but how many times?

Lauren's unkind words about Tryg's having hired Jo; the timely gift of his black pen, no doubt from Lauren; the less than sensitive note on Marianne Glanz's pen referencing Case; the good friend telling Ted that Jo was very interested in him—how many of these exploits had Lauren Albrecht's fingerprints spread all over them? And then there was Henrietta Braddingly, who just happened to live next door to her.

A negative pattern of behavior was actively in play. Ardena noticed it, too. She'd made one too many comments about Lauren's actions lately, none of them complimentary.

Tryg deserved better. But he needed to find out on his own that Miss Albrecht was not the sophisticated and kind young lady she pretended to be.

In the meantime, Jo's job was being threatened. She needed to watch her back and stand up against further less-than-kind deeds. But how?

As the rockers of her chair moaned against the wooden floor, Jo's angst moaned against her spirit. It was not her nature to stand up to anyone. The times she had, she found herself overreacting. And her conscience never did let her get away with it, chewing at her for days on end.

She gazed up at the star-studded sky and then stopped rocking. In the end, her choices for handling Lauren were really quite simple: handle Lauren Jo's way, or put a smile on God's face by handling Lauren His way.

Jo gazed out across the park and toward the O.M. Harrington to find Big Ole and Sarah walking up the porch steps together. *Must have gone out for a nice supper somewhere,* Jo mused, and then she broke into a smile. On Sunday morning at Village Church, Sarah sang a solo for the very first time. Her alto voice was every bit as remarkable as Big Ole's baritone, and the lyrics were taken directly from the pages of the Book of Zechariah. *"'Not by might, not by power, but by My Spirit,' says the Lord of Hosts."*

Jo slowly rocked back and forth while the sound of Sarah's voice and the lyrics she sang played once again in her mind. Not by might. Not by power. But by *My Spirit.*

Jo stopped rocking and looked up.

God's Spirit.

Taking a moment to consider Lauren through the filter of God's loving eyes, a welcome peace suddenly enveloped her, a peace that not only neutralized her anger and fear, but replaced them with compassion and concern.

Compassion and concern for Lauren Albrecht.

What must it be like living in the shadows of Lauren's mind? Jo did not want to imagine. Did Lauren learn that unfortunate pattern of behavior in her home while she was growing up? Why did her parents tolerate it? Didn't they love her enough to establish healthy boundaries? What a sad and deeply troubled childhood she must have had. And what a deep and troubled life she continued to live.

After Jo turned off the lights and crawled into bed, she whispered a heartfelt prayer for Lauren. That unfortunate woman was destroying her own life—never able to feel secure, never able to feel good about herself. If she didn't push past it, she would never get a decent grip on lasting peace and happiness.

CHAPTER FIFTY-THREE

Tryg slipped out of his blazer and hung it up in his closet. He untied and kicked off his shoes, first one and then the other, and placed them on the closet floor. He gazed at his bed. It sure looked good. He was dog-tired. He pulled off the paisley tie his parents gave him last Christmas and hung it on a tie peg, but as he started to unbutton his shirt, the phone rang. He glanced at the clock. Nearly eleven. That was odd. Who could be calling this late? He dashed to the living room and picked up the receiver. "Hello?"

"Tryg Howland?" the deep male voice asked.

"This is Tryg."

"Chief Stout here."

"Chief Stout?" Tryg repeated, suddenly overcome with alarm.

"Yessir! Sorry to call so late, but I was sure you'd want to know that I just found your office door wide open."

"The place was broken into?"

"I can't be sure yet. All I know is that it's wide open."

"I'm on my way."

Tryg stepped out into a night darker than pitch, and fog heavy and thick. He could only assume the streets were empty by an eerie absence of sound. His tired and weary eyes strained to focus.

His left shoe straddled the grass and sidewalk as he sensed his way up the half dozen or so blocks to town. He slowed at the corners where sidewalk met sidewalk, his feet carefully feeling for the curbs. He listened to the constant dull clap and drag of his shoes against the wet pavement as he crossed the streets. The dim glow of distant streetlights and the counting of blocks served as his compass.

He shivered at the moisture clinging to his face and clothing. Large drops of dew pelted his hat as he passed beneath trees hovering like canopies over the sidewalks of the town that should be sleeping.

The brighter lights of uptown cut through the fog, making the trek up the last block much easier. Tryg arrived to find Chief Stout standing beneath Tryg's shingle, his imposing height and demeanor an asset in a town where hard-working farmers and factory workers preferred peace and quiet.

"Any foul play?" Tryg asked.

"None that I can see. With the fog as thick as it is, though, it would be an ideal night for a burglary, that's for sure. Thought you might want to go in and take a look at your place. I checked the lock. Doesn't appear to have been tampered with."

Tryg flipped on the lights and stepped inside, the chief at his heels. They strolled through the office, carefully searching for any signs of vandalism. Nothing apparent. Tryg glanced at the waiting area. The cover of a *Life* magazine with a picture depicting the devastation at Iwo Jima caught his eye. "The Picasso!" he said. Maybe someone saw it through his window and thought it was an original. He rushed into his office. But the Picasso was still hanging on his wall precisely where he'd hung it. He checked everything over. Surprisingly, all appeared in good order.

"Do you have a petty cash box of some sort around?" the chief asked.

"Ardena does. It's in her desk."

Tryg pulled out her drawer. The box was still there. He unlocked it and rummaged through the bills and change. The cash appeared to be accounted for.

Tryg rubbed his forehead. "This is the strangest thing."

"It is strange, isn't it? We'll be sure to keep an eye on the place, just in case we caught a burglar or two in the process of breaking and entering and they were able to get away."

"Thanks. And thanks for the call, and for looking things over with me. I'll talk with the ladies first thing in the morning and let you know what I find out. Maybe one of them forgot to lock the door and it slipped open somehow. But that seems unlikely with the door being as heavy as it is."

"I didn't take into consideration the heaviness of the door," Chief Stout said thoughtfully. "You might be right, Tryg. That could be why it swung open. Let's check it out."

Tryg pulled the door closed and unlatched it enough for the lock not to hold.

"Well, would you take look at that?" the chief said. "It's off plumb enough to fall open on its own."

Tryg shook his head and relocked the door.

Chief Stout stepped out onto the sidewalk, slipped his large hands into his pockets, and gazed at the cloud cover swirling skyward. "Looks like the fog's lifting. That sure was fast. Come on. Let me give you a lift home."

As Tryg undressed again for bed, he mulled over the unlocked door. There were only three people who possessed keys to the office—Jo, Ardena, and him.

Then for some strange reason, he thought about Lauren.

But she only borrowed his keys and gave them back the same evening he'd loaned them to her.

CHAPTER FIFTY-FOUR

J o's chest felt as though it were about to explode with the volume of air pressing against the walls of her lungs. "I was the last one to leave," she said breathlessly. "And I know I locked the door. I always double-check it."

"Look, I'm not accusing anyone of anything here," Tryg insisted.

But his sincerity wasn't working. He looked and sounded as tense and irritated as the times he'd queried Jo about Mrs. Glanz and Mrs. Braddingly. She questioned herself again. She could not be wrong. Not about a locked door.

"All I'm saying," Tryg continued, "is that Chief Stout called me around eleven o'clock last night. Said our office door was wide open, and the lock didn't appear to have been tampered with. We checked the place out. Didn't find anything out of the ordinary." Tryg's gaze shifted from Jo to Ardena. "You ladies might want to check everything over with a magnifying glass. See if anything's been damaged, or is out of place or missing. Other than that, I'm not sure what to make of this. It's never happened before."

Tryg nervously rubbed the nape of his neck and then, with a pained expression, he disappeared into his office.

The instant his door closed, Jo turned to Ardena and said softly, "He thinks I did it, but I didn't. I know I locked that door."

"I know," Ardena said reassuringly. "I believe you."

Jo shook her head. "Tell that to Tryg."

"He's got to believe you, Jo. He's just got to. You don't lie. We all know that."

Jo wanted to believe Ardena, but there was no way for Jo to prove her innocence. Why should Tryg believe her? She'd had one too many negative incidents. It was Jo's word against one more disparaging reality. And what a disparaging reality that had become with Chief Stout's involvement now, too.

Jo squeezed her eyes closed, remembering only too well the urgent phone call about the need for Tryg's house key for an interior decorator. How the keychain jangled when Jo handed it over, the keychain that held not only Tryg's house key, but also held the skeleton key to the office. Then there was that smug expression. And a locksmith nearby...a locksmith who makes keys. Jo shook her head.

Lauren.

Checkmate.

Tryg's breakfast was not behaving in his stomach all that well. He meandered to his desk and slumped into his chair.

Jo does not lie. If she said she always double-checks the door after locking it, she always double-checks the door after locking it.

He leaned heavily back in his chair and mulled things over.

Lauren called last night at about seven. Her words, although benign, suddenly took on grim meaning. "Don't tell me you were the last one to leave the office again tonight," she'd said in that voice she always uses when she's subtly digging for information. "No," Tryg had said. "I'm afraid Jo had to lock up. Ardena and I were both at the courthouse and headed straight home from there." When Lauren replied, "Ohh," she sounded as though she was singing.

Tryg disliked what he was thinking and how he was feeling. What if he was wrong? What if he was right? This was a road he did not care to walk down. He wasn't sure he wanted to see what might be waiting for him at its end.

CHAPTER FIFTY-FIVE

Several minutes before noon. First came the familiar sound of uneven footsteps—one distinct, the other a hit-and-miss scrape against the floor. Then came the acute sensing of the masculine presence. But this time Jo was not about to acknowledge Tryg. She needed to keep focused on her work until he left the office. The moment he did, she turned to Ardena. "He didn't ask if we found anything."

"I noticed that."

"He's had plenty of time to think about it. I guess his mind is made up."

"I'm sorry, Jo. I'm really, really sorry."

"Not as sorry as I am," Jo said mournfully.

Ardena got up and pulled her chair along with her as she walked to the far side of Jo's desk. "I've been giving this some serious thought. You and I both know that door being found wide open last night was no accident."

"What do you mean?"

"You know precisely what I mean. Who are we kidding? Too many things keep happening around here lately, too many things that implicate you. I'm not blind, Jo. We both know who did this."

Jo looked Ardena square in the eyes. "But what can I do about it? She's Tryg's romantic interest. He's got to figure this out for himself."

"How can you stay so calm?" Ardena asked, a crease wedging her forehead. "If it were me, I'd be nose-to-nose and toe-to-toe with that dame."

"I can't do that."

"Why not? You can't let her get away with this. She'll never respect you."

"I don't care about her respect, Ardena. That doesn't mean a thing to me."

"You can't be serious!"

"Oh yes I am. Last night, you have no idea how much I wanted to get in her face. The more I thought about the mean-spirited things she's been doing, the angrier I got. It took a while, but I finally got past it."

"What are you talking about?" Ardena countered, agitation bubbling through her words.

"Lauren knows precisely what she's doing. I don't have to tell her. But she also has no idea what she's doing. She's so focused on reaching a goal, she isn't giving an inkling of thought to the ramifications for either of us. What's worse, she isn't thinking about what she's doing to her relationship with Tryg. If I back her up against a wall, she's only going to dig in deeper. From what I can see, she's crying out to be loved, and through that twisted and upside-down mind of hers, she must see me as standing in her way somehow. Why she would feel that way is beyond me."

Ardena shook her head and rolled her chair back to her desk. *"Unbelievable!"*

"No, Ardena. Not unbelievable. You need to know that I'm not playing victim here. I've made a decision."

"What's that?"

Realizing she may have spoken prematurely, Jo backed off. "I'll tell you about it in a little while."

Jo rolled a sheet of stationery into her typewriter and then stared at the blank piece of paper.

No words would come.

She typed '*Dear Tryg*,' and then stared at the paper a while longer, waiting for the words frozen in her mind to thaw, and thaw they did. Before long, words poured onto the paper like fresh paint dripping onto an easel.

She told Tryg how much she appreciated her job. With her lack of experience, it was an opportunity few would have considered giving her.

She told him how much she appreciated learning what the business world was like, and how she admired his ambition and professionalism.

She praised his selection of Ardena as the best of the best stenographers, and told him how much she was going to miss her.

And then she said that, effective two weeks from this coming Friday, she was resigning her position for an opportunity to find employment in the Cities.

She signed the letter '*Respectfully, Jo.*'

She folded the sheet of paper, placed the ruby red pen inside, and tucked it into an envelope. She knew the pen was taking things a step too far. But it was a statement, an act putting a defined end to any further association with T.W. "Tryg" Howland, III, Attorney-at-Law. She wrote *Tryg* on the outside of the envelope, along with the words "*Personal and Confidential*," and placed it at the center of his desk.

"I'll be out for the rest of the day," Jo said.

Ardena's head snapped up. "Where are you going?"

"Home."

"Home? But why?"

"I just placed my letter of resignation on Tryg's desk. Please don't make me say anything more."

Pain crushed her chest and tears flooded her eyes like a dam about to burst. Not able to look at Ardena or even mumble a quick goodbye, she dashed out the door and drove home, having no idea what tomorrow might bring.

CHAPTER FIFTY-SIX

A t five past three the phone rang. Jo hesitated. She was not in the mood to chat with anyone. With no small measure of reluctance, she picked up the receiver after the third double ring.

"Jo?" a booming male voice said.

"Yes?"

"It's Big Ole Harrington. Why people call me 'Big Ole' is beyond me," he said as though he were talking to himself. "I don't know if it's because of my generous girth, or because they think I have a fat head." He chuckled, sounding as if he really enjoyed his own humor. "Anyway, I called for you at the office, but the young lady there said you weren't in this afternoon. Is everything okay?"

No. "Everything's fine."

"You're sure?"

No. "I'm sure."

"Good! Then I was wondering if you might join me in the park for a few minutes. It's too nice out not to feed the squirrels. Besides, I'd like to have a little chat with you."

What dreadful timing. Jo was not presentable for speaking with anyone, let alone Big Ole Harrington. Not five minutes ago, she took a good look at her face in the mirror. Countless tears. Red and swollen eyes. "Thanks," she said, "but I'm afraid this isn't a good time for me."

"So something is wrong, then."

Yes. "I'm fine."

"Meet me in the park in five minutes. You'll find me at my usual bench."

The phone clicked and the line went dead. Big Ole was not the kind to hang up by accident.

Jo smeared on enough powder, rouge, and mascara to frost a birthday cake, and still the swelling around her eyes showed. She should have been more forceful with her no. Oh well. He was a man, and men didn't pay any attention to those sorts of things. Besides, she could never turn Big Ole down.

She stepped out into the bright afternoon and immediately shielded her vulnerable eyes. Although the sun warmed her cheeks, it was blinding. After her eyes adjusted, she ventured on. Big Ole was right. Having been so upset earlier, she didn't pay attention to the weather when she drove home. The walk through Harrington Park was beyond beautiful, the temperature ideal, the breeze light and dry. A robin flew overhead, its red breast contrasting beautifully against the clear blue sky. A fly buzzed past. The aroma of freshly baked bread permeated the air. Mrs. Wilder must be baking again.

Big Ole was sitting at his favorite bench in the middle of the park tossing peanuts to a squirrel when Jo walked up. Rather than bothering to say hello, he said with a mischievous grin, "So, young lady, did you load your face up with war paint on my behalf, or do you always wear that much ungodly stuff when you're alone in the house?"

"Now, Mr. Harrington!"

The way Big Ole looked at Jo, there was no question he saw through the war paint, but didn't ask about the source of the tears. At least, not today—not yet.

"Please," he said, "have a seat."

As Jo lowered onto the hard bench, she watched Big Ole's lone squirrel quickly scamper up a tree.

"He'll be back," Ole noted convincingly. "Just needs to adjust to more company. He's only used to me, you know."

Jo nodded and looked out across the park. "You were right about the weather. It sure is beautiful out here. I'm glad the humidity finally subsided."

"Me too. Sure has been miserable the past couple of days. It's nice to see the sun again." Ole pressed his large hand into his brown paper bag, pulled out a mitt full of peanuts, and slowly lobbed them out onto the grass, one at a time. "Believe it or not," he said, glancing at her with an appreciative grin, "I didn't invite you out here for a discussion about the weather."

"I was sure you hadn't. Whatever you wanted, you made it sound important."

He nodded, his deep gray eyes sparkling. "It is important. Important to me, anyway. I wanted to tell you that I did precisely what you suggested."

"What's that?"

"I had a chat with Calvin Doherty."

Jo brightened. "You did? I can't tell you how happy I am to hear that."

"You were right about him. That man has wisdom well beyond his years, and he's not exactly a youngster anymore."

"I know. He is pretty amazing, isn't he? So you talked about—"

"Sarah. Actually, Sarah's dad."

"And?"

"Calvin has a way of viewing life from fifty miles up. He has a much broader perspective than the rest of us. And to think I thought I was the only one gifted with keen insight," he said with a light and self-deprecating chuckle. "It appears to be a way of life for him, though. But then, I guess you already knew about that."

"You're right. I did."

"As I was saying, when I told him about the circumstances of Sarah's birth and that her dad was in prison, he didn't hesitate. Told me she had a right to know who her dad was. I guess deep inside I've always known that, but I didn't know how to handle it."

"Couldn't that cripple her emotionally?" Jo asked.

"Well, that's what I was worried about. But like Calvin says, she's a grownup now. Has been for quite some time. She's turned out very well, too, I'm pleased to say. Calvin thinks she'll feel betrayed and angry at first, but she'll get over it. She'll understand why I kept this information from her, and in time, he's sure she'll forgive me. I think he's right. She is an awfully good girl."

Jo nodded.

"There's one other thing," he said with a widening grin.

"What's that?"

"Calvin asked if I'd mind if he went to the prison in his capacity as a man of the cloth to see what he can find out about Butch. He thought it would ease the blow if Sarah heard something positive about the man."

A loud commotion interrupted their quiet. They turned and watched two teenaged boys tearing through Harrington Park on their bikes, hooting and hollering. One of them tore after a squirrel, looking as though he wanted to run it down. "Hey!" Ole shouted. The young tough immediately turned and re-aimed his bike, making an unmistakable statement by whipping past within an inch of Big Ole's knee.

Ole shook his head as he watched the boys ride out of sight. "Where are those boys' parents?"

"Kind of makes you wonder."

"Anyway," he continued, "there are a lot of toughs in prison, but Calvin insists there are a lot of good people there, too, people who happened to be at the wrong place at the wrong time, and involved with the wrong company. Kind of reminds me of those young hoodlums that just rode by."

"I know. It's a real shame." Jo thought for a moment. "How do you feel about Calvin having a word with Butch?"

Big Ole reached for his cane and rested his hands on it, slowly shifting it back and forth. "Mixed, I guess. I decided years ago that I had no choice but to forgive him. It nearly tore my heart out when he violated my only daughter. Then when she died during childbirth, the bitterness exploded. I didn't think it would be possible to ever forgive him. But for as much as that infuriated me, it didn't make sense to let the mere thought of him keep eating away at my bones. Why give him a piece of my flesh, too? So I reluctantly chose to let the past die a complete death. It was one of the toughest decisions I've ever made."

"First Butch, then the doctor," Jo said.

Big Ole reached for another handful of nuts and tossed them onto the sidewalk. Several squirrels finally scampered down the side of the thick trunk, gathered them until their cheeks filled, and skittered back up the tree.

"After I forgave him, I saw things differently, more rationally," Ole continued. "My daughter's death really wasn't his fault. It was one of those things that just happened. And then one day, I realized how much joy our granddaughter was giving the missus and me. Obviously, Sarah wouldn't have been here without him, so something good did come out of that tragedy."

"I commend you. That was a healthy way to handle it."

Ole picked up his walking stick again and tapped it lightly yet repeatedly against the sidewalk, the way one would hammer a nail. "Oh, I don't know. If I had a healthy attitude, I might have found an excuse to go to the prison myself a long, long time ago—with a magnifying glass, of course," he said with an impish grin. "Maybe I could have found at least a trace of decency in that good-for-nothing."

"But what about the blackmail?" Jo asked. "Will you confront Howard Rasmussen?"

"You bet I will!"

"And you'll call in the police?"

"No. No police."

"Why not?"

Ole gazed up at the sky and sighed. "Because I want this behind me. It's too dark and unpleasant to trawl around in. It's just too dark and unpleasant."

"But I hate to see him get away with it," Jo said.

"In the greater scheme of things, he's not getting away with a thing. Mark my word, we all have to live with our trespasses. And one day, like it or not, believe it or not, we'll all stand before our Maker to give an accounting."

CHAPTER FIFTY-SEVEN

On Friday evening, Tryg looked up from the file cabinets and watched Jo as she walked out the door and headed for home, looking like a seriously whipped cocker spaniel. Sadness swept over him. Sadness for Jo. Sadness for himself. The conflicts in the office hadn't all been her fault.

Neither were his nightmares.

Tryg had never been in business before. Never had anyone work for him before Ardena and Jo. Never fired anyone. Never wanted to. But what could he do about Jo? He had to admit feeling relief when he read her letter of resignation, but why did he accept it? That was wrong. He could feel it in the depths of his belly. When he did that to Jo, he wronged Case and little Brue, too.

He stood for a moment, wishing he could make his problems disappear. But that was impossible, so he decided to take a lesson from Jo— stop by her place over the weekend and make things right.

Not more than two minutes later, the phone rang. Ardena, who was staying late to catch up on a project, picked up the receiver after the second ring.

"It's for you, Mr. Howland," she said excitedly, waiting for him to respond. When he didn't, she said, "You'll want to get this one. It's Marianne Glanz."

"Marianne Glanz?" Tryg asked, as if he feared for a moment he was hearing strange voices.

"Yes, sir."

"I'll take it in my office."

After several minutes of an unusually pleasant chat, he cradled the phone and then rested his elbows on his desk, the full weight of his chin in his hands. Now what was he going to do? Del and Marianne Glanz decided to transfer all of their family business to Tryg's law firm. Their reason? Jo Bremley's professional generosity. They wanted to work with a firm they knew they could trust.

"What have I done?" he muttered beneath his breath.

Memories of Case's devotion to Jo suddenly surfaced, memories Tryg had never been able to understand. During Case's short time on Earth, that man had never been able to say enough good about her. Now, finally, Tryg understood why. She was unspoiled, thoughtful, generous, kind, hardworking, and honest to a fault, even when it cost her.

Unfortunately, Tryg's understanding arrived after the stroke of midnight.

He plucked Jo's resignation letter out of his in-box and read it one more time.

After not so much as acknowledging her letter, and after fearing she'd been a liability, he knew full well he had rescinded any right to ask her to stay. His motives stood a chance to pass muster before Marianne Glanz's phone call. But afterward? That didn't smell right, especially to Tryg.

How could he have been so wrong about someone he'd known so long? Reality reached in and wrung his insides with a vice-like grip. If Tryg had seen the deer on time, Jo's husband would still be alive. If he hadn't looked the other way, she would not have been fair game for Lauren. Something wasn't right with Lauren, and it was time he faced it. He felt uncomfortable receiving her black pen; the timing wasn't right. Then there was her insistence on decorating his office. The skeleton key.

The unlocked door. Lauren's silence. How many other schemes was she behind? Her little chat with Ted? Is that why he asked Jo out? If Tryg had given Jo his full support, she would know she still had a job. He deserved the raw pain wrenching his throat, the air that refused to fill his lungs.

How many more times would it be possible for him to violate a family—a family he cared for so deeply?

CHAPTER FIFTY-EIGHT

C alvin was surprised yet pleased that Rainy insisted on meeting him at Stables Supper Club rather than having him drive all the way to Clarks Grove to pick her up. On the one hand, he would have preferred it. But facing her family would have been even more difficult. When he arrived at twenty past seven and announced his seven-thirty reservation, the hostess indicated that his friend was already there and waiting for him in the upstairs lounge. His friend. That had a nice sound. They would be called to supper in five to ten minutes.

He mopped his forehead with his handkerchief as he ascended the staircase. He was strangely pleased he hadn't seen the lounge before, allowing him to concentrate on what it would look like rather than what was awaiting him. But that fantasy was a fool's errand. He could not get his mind off of Rainy. Would she be pleased to see him? Or would she be repulsed? Did she age well? Would they have anything to talk about? Would the conversation flow? Would the crippling memories of the past gain free rein once again? Memories of what could have been but never got the chance to be? Would he walk away once again feeling inadequate?

As he rounded the top of the staircase, his eyes immediately met Rainy's. He wanted to turn and run—run to preserve what was left of his life, what was left of his heart. Unfortunately, she was as beautiful as ever, if not more so. Wearing a simple black sheath with a string of pearls and smart black pumps, she stood and extended her hand, looking surprisingly pleased to see him.

Before he had a chance to join her at her small table for two, the hostess called his name. He stepped back, allowing Rainy to take the lead. She weaved a bit as she descended the top step, giving the illusion of being a bit unstable. Calvin understood. Occasionally heights did that to him as well. Or maybe she was just nervous.

After being seated and handed their menus, Rainy said, "How about if we enjoy supper first, and then go for a ride and a talk later? I think it's pretty obvious we both have a lot of ground to cover, but I don't think this is the right venue."

"Agreed," Calvin said.

After a relatively uncomfortable though excellent supper of prime rib, baked potatoes, string beans, and hot rolls, Rainy excused herself to go powder her nose while Calvin paid the bill. He glanced at his watch. It was taking an inordinate amount of time for her to return to their table. He wondered for a moment whether she might have slipped out a back door.

Several minutes later, Rainy reappeared. She nearly tripped on a chair leg as she hurried back, but caught herself just shy of coming face-to-face with the floor. "How embarrassing," she said as she reached their table. "That was a close call. How clumsy can I be?"

"You were fine. I just felt bad that I couldn't get to you on time." Calvin helped her slip her coat over her narrow shoulders. "Where would you like to go for a chat?"

"How about if we head out of town? Find a nice country road somewhere. It's a beautiful night. I'd love to see the moonlight glowing on the fields. We don't get to see much of that in New York City."

His tires whirred against the asphalt as Calvin drove north. The moment they crossed over onto the gravel roads, bits of stone pelted the undercarriage of his '38 Ford, a cloud of dust chasing close behind them. He soon found a remote entrance to a barren field where no farms could be seen from any direction for miles. "How is this?"

"Perfect."

Calvin switched off the engine, switched off the lights, and then turned toward Rainy.

She kicked off her shoes and leaned her back against the passenger door, facing him head on. "You haven't changed much."

"Neither have you. Ray was one very lucky man," Calvin managed to say. "You're just as beautiful as ever."

Rainy laughed, perhaps a bit too gaily. "You're wrong. He was anything but lucky."

Moo.

Rainy's head snapped in the opposite direction. "There are cows close by," she exclaimed. "I haven't heard a cow moo in ages. It sounds wonderful!"

Right now Calvin could not care less about cows, but he let her enjoy the sounds for a short while before asking, "Why did you say Ray was anything but lucky?"

She looked back at Calvin with a near-wicked smirk. "Because we were married to each other...and to our guilt."

"What's that supposed to mean?"

"That was a pretty awful thing we did to you. We paid for it dearly," she said, her tone tinged with regret, her eyes gazing down toward the floorboard. "I swear you were an integral part of our lives every day until Ray..." Her voice trailed off. She caught herself and turned away again, gazing out toward the deep ditch on the north side of the car. "When God set up the world, He laid out a strong yet invisible set of rules, rules that can never be violated."

"How so?"

She turned again toward Calvin, the moon reflecting off the

moisture pooling in her eyes. "He doesn't allow us to build our happiness on anyone else's unhappiness—*your* unhappiness."

"But that wasn't entirely your fault."

She snickered. "Right!"

"I'm serious," he insisted. "I knew something wasn't right between us, but I didn't want to face it. I kept silent, and I have to own that. That was definitely not your fault."

She smiled a guarded smile. "There's something you need to know, as if you didn't already."

"What's that?"

"No one gets away with anything, Calvin. Back then, I was in love with three men."

"You were what?" he asked, feeling the humiliation of violation as if he were standing alone in a tuxedo in front of that packed church again.

"You heard me. I was in love with three men."

"Ray, me, and who else?" Calvin asked incredulously.

"Johnnie Walker Red. "

"Johnnie..." Calvin said, his mouth freezing open.

"When we were engaged, I was tortured with thoughts of Ray. To be honest, I never felt good enough for you. And then the day Ray and I said 'I do,' I was tortured with thoughts of you. You never left my heart. You never left my mind. But I could never have married you. I should have put an end to our relationship long before our wedding day, but I didn't know how."

"But why not?"

"Come on. I just told you. I think you've always known."

Calvin quickly turned away, gazing out onto the open field, wanting to be out there, wanting to distance himself from the woman who brought fresh pain to his heart.

"You're doing it again," she said.

"Doing what again?"

"You don't want to face it. Look at me, Calvin." She lifted her chin and leaned across the bench seat toward him. "Smell my breath. Can you honestly tell me you didn't smell Johnnie on my breath when you were standing at the altar on our wedding day? How could I possibly marry a chaplain?"

"If you loved me, really loved me, why couldn't you break the habit? Why couldn't you have at least tried?"

Rainy looked at Calvin incredulously. "Because I didn't want to."

"What kind of answer is that?"

Rainy's next words exploded in Calvin's ears like the loud clashing of cymbals, jolting him out of his world of fantasy and into the world of reality where he belonged.

"Because I love Johnnie Walker Red too much. I don't want to give him up."

"But—"

"Ever!" she said, her tone emphatic.

CHAPTER FIFTY-NINE

While Tryg's car was in the shop for a few days for minor repairs and improvements, the rattletrap taxi he was riding in pulled into Lauren's driveway at twenty-five past seven. Tryg handed the driver both cab fare and a tip, stepped out into the drizzle, and quickly ascended her front steps. The aroma of pot roast drifting from her oven had been well worth the ride. He started to lift his hand to knock, but hesitated. A car pulling into the adjacent driveway invited his attention. An elderly man stopped his car long enough to let his wife out and then continued on into their garage.

The wife climbing the side steps of their home looked strangely familiar, so much so that Tryg paused on Lauren's front porch to steal a better look. He was right. He was too right. All of the things he feared fell neatly into place. And it grieved him.

The door opened as he again lifted his hand to knock. After pecking Lauren dutifully on her cheek, he entered her immaculate and beautifully decorated home—one last time. The ambience was lovely. He could feel Lauren watching him as he looked around, actually seeing the place rather than seeing her. That was a first. A warm fire danced in the fireplace. Candlelight flickered on the living room end tables and coffee table, as well as the table in the dining room. Her home was outfitted with the finest furniture money could buy. A rainbow of fresh flowers and plants cheerfully filled her large living room in all the right places. Tasteful paintings covered the walls. Waterford crystal and fine Wedgwood dinnerware glistened in a cherry wood china cabinet. Yes, he would definitely miss this home.

After several bites into his food, Lauren asked, "Are you okay? You look as if something's bothering you."

How many times had Lauren spoken those words before? Too many to count. "We can talk later," he said thoughtfully.

"No, we'll talk now," she insisted, her tone inconsistent with that of the perfect lady he thought he knew.

He hesitated, subdued further by lingering disbelief. Yet even her insistence made sense. He wiped his mouth with his cloth napkin and folded it back into a triangle before sprawling it over his lap.

"Okay. You want to talk, we'll talk." He held the napkin in place as he shoved his chair back. Right now there was something about space that he felt in need of. "I overheard you talking with Jo at the office the other day. From what I could tell, you told her it was awfully kind of me to give her a job when she didn't have any experience. When did I tell you she didn't have any experience? And what did you mean by, 'He really is a very kind and patient man?' Can you imagine how Jo must have felt hearing that?"

"It *was* kind of you to give her a job," Lauren said matter-of-factly, not addressing the rest of the questions.

"And what about the black pen? Why did you feel you needed to buy that for me?"

Lauren laughed dismissively. "Because of that night when we were at the drugstore, silly. Don't you remember? You wanted to write a check, but you didn't have a pen on you. I thought you could use a new one. What's wrong with that?"

"The timing, that's what's wrong with that. If you will recall, I told you about Marianne Glanz and how she'd given Jo a new ruby red Parker pen. And I told you that Jo passed it on to me."

Lauren pulled back, furrows pleating her forehead. "Yes, and if you will recall, you also told me that you gave it back to her. Why are you doing this to me, Tryg? And what's worse is why are you doing this to us? Why all of the accusations?"

With too many instances to overlook, too many subtle instances, he leaned forward in his chair. "Because if we are going to continue any kind of relationship at all, it has to be built on solid ground. Not on suspicion. Not on fear. Not on jealousy. Not on possessiveness."

"Are you saying—?"

Tryg cut her off. "The last time we ate at The Copper Kettle, you mentioned that it would be good if Jo started to date again. The next thing I knew, you left to powder your nose, and on your way back, I saw you getting into a huddle with Ted. When I asked what that was all about, you dismissed me. A couple of days later, I watched Ted calling after Jo—out on the sidewalk of all public places. She looked wanting-to-crawl-out-of-her-skin uncomfortable. You didn't happen to encourage him to ask her out, did you?"

"What's wrong with that? She has to be lonely."

"You're not her friend. That's what wrong with that. You hardly know her. Why would you do a thing like that?"

Lauren's face turned hard. "Is this supper about you and me? Or is it about you and Jo?"

"What's that supposed to mean?"

Lauren's chest heaved visibly, and with tear-filled eyes and trembling lips, she said, "It means that I can't compete with your dead friend's wife."

It took all Tryg had to stay seated. "What are you talking about? You aren't competing with Case's wife. You never have. You aren't competing with anyone. I gave Jo a job because she needs to make a living."

"Right," Lauren said sarcastically.

"If you will recall, I was the one driving the car that claimed her husband's life." Tryg felt helpless to stop the switch turning off inside his heart. He stared at Lauren, frightened by his sudden indifference toward her. His lack of interest. Numbness. "I almost wish you were right about me having feelings for Jo," he said finally.

"Why would you say that?"

"Because then maybe, on a very small scale, at least, I could justify to myself some of the cruel shenanigans you've been pulling."

Lauren gently patted away a spill of tears with the tip of her napkin and sat quietly for a moment before carefully realigning the silverware she had yet to use.

Tryg listened to the silence and then thrummed the table. "Why didn't you tell me about Henrietta Braddingly?"

"What are you talking about now?" Lauren asked softly, managing an innocent look.

"You neglected to tell me that she's your next-door neighbor."

Lauren bristled, her eyes signaling guilt like a red light signals stop. "What does that have to do with anything?"

"I was wondering who told Henrietta about the advice Jo unthinkingly gave to Marianne Glanz. No one else knew about that. It hadn't made any sense—that is, not until I saw Henrietta getting out of their car when I arrived tonight."

"Her being my neighbor doesn't make me guilty of anything. How could you think that?"

Tryg exhaled deeply. "Believe me, I don't want to. Do you have any idea how hard this conversation is for me?"

"Then why are you doing it?" Lauren asked, tears pooling again in the corners of her eyes.

"Because..." Tryg replayed in his mind Lauren having been possessive with her keychain the night her skeleton key got stuck in her door. He remembered feeling an unusually long key in his hand when he held it, the kind of key he used for his office. He finger-combed his hair then shook his head, his chest crushing with foreboding. "That night I got the call from Chief Stout, what time did you stop by the office and unlock the door?" he asked, not really wanting to hear the answer.

Lauren jerked back, but then looked at Tryg indifferently. She said nothing.

He felt his eyes narrowing, his jaw clenching. "You set Jo up," he said angrily.

Staring down at her plate, Lauren disconnected. "My sister lives in California," she said coldly. "A place called Perris. She called recently. Said she wants me to come for a visit. I think I could use a change of scenery for a few weeks."

Tryg stood. "That might be a good idea." He tossed his napkin on the table near his plate, gathered his blazer and hat, and limped out her front door.

Tryg stomped down Lauren's steps and headed deep into the blackness. With few streetlights and a thick cloud cover, seeing the road ahead was a challenge, but he didn't care.

He didn't care that he didn't have a ride.

He didn't care that with every step, a shockwave of pain shot up and down his bad leg.

He didn't care that the light drizzle was turning into a steady rain, saturating his best blazer and shoes.

He was irked that he hadn't seen who Lauren Albrecht really was until he was in too deep.

He was galled that she willfully chose to do evil, giving no thought to the pain it was inflicting on others.

But mostly he was incensed that he still cared.

He pulled the collar of his blazer up around his neck, pressed his hands deep into his pants pockets, and limped on. At least his hat kept his head dry. A few blocks farther up the street, moisture bled through his hat, and the backs of his shoes cut painfully into his heels. So be it. He was not about to walk barefooted, carrying his shoes in his hands like he was some kind of sissy.

An occasional car drove by, lighting his path here and there. He concentrated on the rain and kept walking. It felt good. Cleansing.

When he reached the south side of Fountain Lake, he kept an eye out for a park bench. Through the darkness and pouring rain, he thought he saw one in the distance on the opposite side of the street. He crossed over. Five minutes later, he sat down for a short rest. He pulled off his shoes and placed them on the bench beside him. Inhaled a deep breath. Raised his chin. Felt the erratic puffs of wind brushing against his cheeks, beads of moisture stinging his cheeks and trickling down his face. He smiled at nature's kind diversion, and then hiked his pants up a few folds, pulled off his socks, and headed off again with shoes and socks in hand—amazed at how good the grass felt beneath his bare feet.

When he arrived home, his wet clothes were pasted to his body, his feet white with cold, and he was exhausted both physically and emotionally. The rain had washed away much of his anger, but it could never wash away his grief.

CHAPTER SIXTY

J o cradled the phone and simply stared at it. Tryg sounded too professional, too businesslike, and his request far too inappropriate. It lacked in good taste; it lacked in good judgment. To her, he was no longer the same Tryg who had been her husband's best friend.

Brue, who was playing jacks in the middle of the living room floor, looked up. "Who was that, Mom?"

"Tryg."

"What did he want?"

"He invited me out for supper."

Brue caught her bouncing ball and held it in her hand. "When?"

"Tonight."

"But it's Saturday night. I thought he had a girlfriend."

Jo gazed at Brue. Even a child could see the inappropriateness of Tryg's invitation. "As a matter of fact, he does."

Brue scrunched up her face.

"It's okay, sweetie," Jo said. "I'm sure she'll be coming along. This is probably a last-minute going-away supper for me."

The late notice bothered Jo. She told Tryg no. Said she'd be coming back to Amber Leaf from time to time, and they could celebrate her departure then. Celebrate. What a misplaced word. Yet Tryg insisted he would not take no for an answer.

Under the circumstances, having to be a third wheel with Lauren Albrecht, on a Saturday night no less, was the most uncomfortable way to spend an evening Jo could possibly imagine. She could not let Tryg do this to her. She could not accept the late notice, and she could not sit through an evening with Lauren Albrecht acting as if everything was okay. Far off in the future, absolutely. But right now, Jo's insides were far too tender.

She eyed the phone and quickly snatched up the receiver. Without an inkling of thought, she called Tryg's home, but there was no answer. She called the office. No answer there either. She was stuck.

Tryg knocked at the door at seven o'clock sharp, smelling as if he'd swum a few laps through a pool of aftershave. Jo invited him in while she gathered her coat and handbag.

"Where's Brue?" he asked.

"Next door at the Wilders's."

"She could have come with us. I'm sorry. I didn't think to say anything."

"That's okay. I thought about that, too, but didn't want to be presumptuous."

"My fault," he insisted.

"Don't give it another thought," she said softly. He helped her slip her coat over her shoulders. She gathered her handbag and led the way out the door, already wishing the night could be over.

Tryg looked relatively comfortable behind the wheel of his Buick Roadmaster. Jo was surprised. She wondered if he was feeling any trepidation at all. If he was, he certainly hid it well.

Surprised, too, that Lauren wasn't in the car, Jo asked, "Where does Lauren live?"

"Shoreland Heights. Why do you ask?"

"I guess I just figured you'd pick her up first."

Tryg shook his head. "She's not coming, Jo."

"She's not?"

Or was she? Would Lauren and Ardena be waiting for them at the restaurant? They had to have planned a little surprise party. Ardena, Tryg, Lauren, and Jo. She shivered at the thought. At least she would have Ardena to lean on for support. Hmm. Would Calvin be there, too? *Oh no. The five of us, with me the odd one out? What could possibly feel more miserable?*

"No, she's not. I hope that doesn't make you feel too uncomfortable."

"But why, if you don't mind my asking?"

"She flew to Perris for a couple of weeks."

"Paris? I'm not sure I'd want to set foot in France until after the war is over."

Tryg smiled at the remark, which Jo found rather strange. She then swallowed her pride and shared a generous truth. "I have to tell you that Lauren is one of the loveliest women I've ever seen. I can't imagine how happy the two of you must be."

Tryg nodded impassively, but said nothing further.

"May I ask where we're going?"

"I thought Stables Supper Club. Sound okay?"

Jo nodded.

Silence fell between them like a dark and invisible veil as the tires spun along Amber Leaf's winding roads. Tryg looked ill at ease. The confidence and professionalism surging through the wires when he phoned earlier had all but vanished. This get-together felt as uncomfortable as their dinner on Christmas Eve day when he finally got a chance to talk to her about Case's death.

Jo felt relieved when the car wheeled into the parking lot at the Supper Club. Soft music flowed down from the piano bar when they entered. She looked around the restaurant to see only a sprinkling of empty tables. Lots happening on a bustling Saturday night.

The hostess seated them promptly at a table for two. Jo was wrong. No Lauren, and no Ardena either. Tryg and she read their menus and briefly discussed their choices. Several minutes later the waitress appeared. "Are you ready to order?"

"Yes. The lady will have prime rib, please," Tryg said, and then turned to Jo. "Medium?"

She nodded.

"Medium," he confirmed. "I'll have the same, and we'd like the coleslaw and baked potatoes, please."

Jo wasn't sure she wanted prime rib. Or coleslaw. Or the baked potato. Fried chicken had more appeal, for some reason.

"Do you have any interviews lined up in the Twin Cities yet?" Tryg asked after a long and uncomfortable pause.

Feeling violated by the question, Jo did not care to answer, but she did just the same. "No, not yet."

Tryg brightened at her response.

That was certainly rude.

"If you'd like, I'd be happy to write a letter of reference for you before you leave."

"You can't do that, Tryg."

"I can't? Why not?"

"Well, in the first place, I haven't worked for you long enough. Haven't even made it through my three-month probationary period," she said matter-of-factly, refusing to admit to him how severely her confidence had been crushed. "And it seems I've made one too many bad decisions. I'll take my lumps. It's only right."

He ignored her, as though he didn't hear a word she said. "I can also put a feeler out for job opportunities, if you'd like. I know a few people in Minneapolis."

Jo did not want or need his help. She'd tried that when she accepted his job offer, and she ended up out on the street in record time. Why couldn't he leave well enough alone? Regardless of how insensitive he was capable of being, Jo chose to be gracious no matter what. "I'm sure

I'll be fine. But thank you anyway. There are a number of employment agencies up there. I thought I'd start with them."

Tryg gave Jo a conciliatory nod.

They ate their meal in silence. By the way Tryg was poking at his food, he did not appear to have much of an appetite.

"I'm not meaning to be rude here, Tryg, but there are a lot of hungry people in this world, especially now with the war raging. I notice you're leaving quite a bit of food on your plate."

"So are you."

Jo sighed. "I guess I am. Everything is happening so fast."

"Let's get out of here. There's something I want to talk with you about, but not in a crowded restaurant."

He suddenly came to life as he summoned the waitress, but didn't breathe another word until he parked his car near Northside Drug.

"What are we doing here?" Jo asked.

"I thought we could use some air. Besides, I'd like us to take a walk. Would you indulge me?" Tryg appeared to ignore the fact that Jo did not respond. He stepped around his car and opened her door. "This way, please."

He guided her by the elbow across the bridge and onto Katherine Island. He then slipped his hands into his pockets and glanced up at the sky. "It's gotten awfully dark," he said. "The number of stars you can see is dizzying. It would be impossible to count them all."

"I had no idea these sorts of things interested you."

"Lots of things interest me."

Jo felt uneasy with Tryg's choice for a walk. The alluring island felt too intimate. He was in a serious relationship. Jo was a widow. She had no idea what Tryg was up to. How awkward it felt being alone with him on a Saturday night. She just wanted to go home.

Tryg kicked at the grass as they strolled slowly around the perimeter of the small island. Crickets chirped and soft waves lapped steadily against the shoreline.

Tryg was quiet as usual. After one full lap, he stopped and peered down at her. "Look," he said, "I know I don't have the right to ask this of you, but I'd like you to think seriously about staying with my firm. Before you make your decision, though, there's something you need to know."

Jo was taken aback. "What's that?"

"Marianne Glanz."

Huh? Of all the people... "What about her?"

"I got a call from her yesterday a couple of minutes after you left the office. Seems she was so pleased with your good business sense that she and her husband want us to take over all of their legal issues. I understand they've been unhappy with their current attorney for quite some time. This will be a huge and on-going account. I doubt the other law offices in town are going to be happy we're taking them on."

Words caught in Jo's throat at the news. "What kind of business are they in?"

"Let's just say they own an ample amount of land."

A twinge of anxiety twisted Jo's insides. She never did get a chance to find out who Tryg really was professionally, and that bothered her. Might as well find out. She inhaled a subtle yet sizable breath. "Tryg?"

"Yes?"

"If the Glanzes had come into the office as originally planned, no handbag and no blunder on my part, how would you have handled their case?"

"Why are you asking?"

"I guess I'm just curious."

Tryg shoved his hands deep into his pockets and looked up, thinking. "I wouldn't have suggested they plant an apple orchard, if that's what you're wondering."

Jo smiled at the comeback. "But what would you have done?"

"I would have laid out the facts," Tryg said confidently. "Told them where the law served them best versus where the law served their neighbor best. Regarding your idea of a tree line, that would have been something I would have recommended before the fact, not afterward. After explaining the options available to them, the decision about how to proceed would have been entirely up to them."

"I see."

"Jo?"

"Hmm?"

Tryg broke into a grin. "Your idea of planting an apple orchard really was very creative."

"Maybe. But if Marianne Glanz didn't already want to plant an apple tree, it wouldn't have mattered."

"But she did, and in the end, it worked to our advantage."

Jo looked up toward heaven and smiled. She then exhaled and closed her eyes for a quick moment, while in her heart she expressed a soulful *Thank you, Lord*. Something good had come out of the Marianne Glanz blunder after all.

But as swiftly as her gratitude came, it was snatched away by a niggling thought. It was Marianne Glanz who called. What if her husband didn't follow up? Jo and Tryg would be back to square one. What if this was nothing more than wishful thinking on Mrs. Glanz's part?

"Del called a few minutes after I hung up with his wife," Tryg said. "I was surprised. He asked if they could stop by on Monday afternoon to get things rolling."

Tryg slipped his hands inside his coat pockets and lifted his shoulders. In the moonlight, his eyes had grown intense and forlorn. Why? He had everything now. His business was back to thriving mode. He had a relationship. He had a car and was driving again. He had done right by offering Jo a job, and she had done right by letting him off the hook. Why bother to ask her to come back? Not because of Marianne Glanz. Please, no!

"You look upset about something," Jo said after a quiet and slow stroll toward one of the maples.

"Not really." Tryg stopped and rested, leaning his back against the trunk of the tree. "I don't know when I've ever felt so ashamed of myself, though," he said softly.

"What are you talking about?"

"I should have given you my complete support from the very first day you started working for me. I knew your incident with Mrs. Glanz was accidental. To be honest, I was more concerned about losing the income so I could pay your salary than I was about you."

Why did he have to say that?

"And about Henrietta Braddingly?" he continued, "Like I told you before, you did save us a major headache by following your instincts. And I did what you asked me to do."

"Which is?"

"I checked her background. You were right. She would not hesitate to sue us to get out of paying her bill. You had the courage to face that fact up front. What's unconscionable about this whole thing is that you were set up."

He did know. He was paying attention.

"I had a feeling," he said, "but I just needed to confirm it. If it's okay with you, I'd rather not say anything more about that. At least, not now." He turned to Jo and added, "You asked if I was okay. Well, I will be, but only if you agree to stay with my firm."

"But, Tryg, I can't. Don't you see? These sorts of things are going to keep happening. I can't seem to help myself. It's who I am."

Tryg shook his head and grinned appreciatively. "I know. That's why I believe in you. That's why I want you to stay."

Jo shook her head forcefully. "You only believe in me because Marianne Glanz called and made things right."

"No," he countered. "That's not true. She was merely my wake-up call."

"But they're only promising to bring their work to you. What if they find they aren't happy with your firm either?"

"Our firm, not my firm. And if they do, that wouldn't have anything to do with you. It would have everything to do with me. You just happened to make that outcome less likely."

Jo did not know what to do with herself. She needed to get away from Tryg. She stepped up to the shore and looked out across the water. He had been a gentleman, at least. He didn't follow her. Just gave her the time she needed. After collecting herself, she turned and glanced back at him.

Tryg took his cue. He strolled over and joined her by the water's edge. "I wouldn't blame you if you told me to take a hike," he said, "but I want you to know that I couldn't possibly be surer about wanting you to stay."

She folded her arms across her spring jacket.

"Jo?"

"Hmm?"

"Why did you decide to move to Minneapolis?"

"What other choice did I have?"

He nodded and then smiled at her warmly. "I understand. But you do have another choice now. Hopefully, you'll find it to be the best and wisest choice."

Jo felt her will begin to break as she reconsidered his offer. If she stayed, she still had to contend with her feelings of infatuation. Could she handle that? Did she even want to? And what about Lauren? Maybe if Jo did choose to stay, she might at least be instrumental in calming Lauren's insides, so she wouldn't be so tortured. Or was that wishful thinking on Jo's part? "What about Lauren? Won't she be upset if I come back?"

"Lauren is no longer an issue," Tryg said, a hint of finality evident in his tone.

Jo's heart fluttered involuntarily. She turned and looked up at the silvery moon, hoping it wasn't casting a glow on the tears welling in her eyes. She nodded. "Okay then."

"Good." He reached into his inside coat pocket. "I also wanted to give this back to you. I know we've been playing quite a cat and mouse game with Mrs. Glanz's ruby red Parker pen, and like I told you before, I've rather enjoyed the exchange."

"I was so sure I was irritating you."

"Not at all. But this is yours. Enjoy it." As Tryg placed the pen in Jo's hand, he said, "Be forewarned, Jo. Your acceptance seals the deal."

CHAPTER SIXTY-ONE

Calvin stood at the door of Big Ole's office with two steaming cups of coffee. "Would you consider allowing entry to the bearer of interesting news?"

"Depends. Good news or bad?"

"I'm afraid you're going to have to make that judgment call yourself."

Ole lifted his chin and eyed Calvin with a quintessential poker face. "I already had my coffee."

"You look like you could use another cup." Calvin slipped around Big Ole's desk and placed it immediately in front of him. "Careful. It's hot."

"So, out with it. What did you find out?"

"Whoa! Wait a minute. How about giving me a little time to get to my chair?" Calvin sat down. As he warmed his fingers with his cup, he broke into a smile. "Butch Rasmussen really did love Sarah's mother."

"He did, did he?" Ole asked skeptically.

"Yes, sir. He did. Said he turned his life around before he went to prison. Your daughter did that to him—her influence."

Ole inhaled a loud breath before swiveling away from Calvin.

"He did his time," Calvin said.

"What's he doing now?"

"That's the best part. Seems he involved himself ministering to his fellow inmates when he was in prison. Since he got out, he's been going back regularly for pastoral-type visits. Brings Bibles, and ministers to anyone who is willing to listen to him."

"What's he do for money these days? Or doesn't he work?"

"He said he sells used cars for now. New cars when they become available again."

"How's he planning to pull that off with a criminal record?"

"He knows the owner. Says they've been pals since they were kids."

Ole turned back. "Anything else?"

Calvin nodded. "After he got out of prison, I understand he took a vital interest in your granddaughter's life. He's been seeking her out. Following her. Watching from afar. Wanting to make sure she's okay."

"How long has he been doing that?" Big Ole asked indifferently.

"Ten, twelve years maybe. Even followed her all the way to California and back."

"Or so he says."

Calvin sobered as he rested his cup on Ole's desk. "Does the name Alvin Braunlough ring any bells?"

"Alvin Braunlough?" Ole asked, finally engaging.

Calvin nodded. "About eight or nine years ago—"

"He was busy pestering Sarah," Ole said, finishing Calvin's sentence for him.

"Did you happen to notice that one day he magically disappeared?"

Ole lifted his cup, but paused just short of his lips. "I've always wondered about that."

"Butch got wind of it. Said he tapped Alvin on the shoulder one night. I think Alvin had a latent fear of ex-cons. He hightailed it out of town and never did come back."

Ole set his cup down and thoughtfully stroked his chin. "You don't say. Butch did that?"

"Yes. Your Butch did that."

Big Ole broke into a proud grin and then thought for an extended moment. "Say, do you think after all these years the lad would be amenable to a get-together with his crusty old father-in-law?"

Calvin's eyes sparkled. "Turn around, Ole," he said. "Take a look out your window. Tell me what you see."

Ole turned and looked out into the park where a middle-aged man with graying hair wandered beneath the trees. Ole's heart skipped a beat. "That's him? That's Butch?"

"That's him. What do you say? Are you up for a little reunion?"

On their way past the registration desk, Ole stopped. "Sarah? Would you mind coming with us? There's someone I think you might want to say hello to. It's a meeting that's long been overdue."

CHAPTER SIXTY-TWO

In the Sunday morning reception line at Village Church, Calvin squeezed Jo's hand. "Can you wait a few minutes? I'd like to have a word with you after everyone leaves." His expression was unreadable, more neutral than anything.

Jo had no difficulty getting Brue to play in the park until Jo could meet up with her later. She did, however, ask Brue to be especially careful with her Sunday clothes. Jo then slipped into the sanctuary and waited for Calvin.

She looked back when his footsteps finally echoed from the vestibule. "Thanks for waiting," he said, lowering himself onto the pew next to her and positioning his hands comfortably on his thighs.

"I was happy to. So what did you want to talk to me about? It's not like you to call me out on a bright and cheery Sunday morning."

"This is about Rainy, Jo."

Jo caught her breath, the cadence of her heart gaining momentum. "Rainy, huh?"

"Yes, ma'am." A hint of a grin reached his eyes. "There was a reason why you conned me into meeting with her, wasn't there?"

Jo nodded. He knew, but did he finally understand? "So you did meet with her, then?"

"Yes, I did."

"And you figured out the reason?"

"I did."

"I hope it wasn't too painful."

Calvin chuckled lightly. "At my age, a man finally grows up."

Jo smoothed the rough wood of the pew lightly with the tips of her fingers, feeling the ripples and the smoothly planed surface, but mostly feeling compassion for a true friend. "Don't be so hard on yourself," she said.

"I'm not," he replied confidently. "If there's one thing I've learned in my advancing years, it's that there are few things more refreshing and freeing than having the courage to face and own the truth."

"Do you mind if I ask how things went?"

"Not at all. It went as well as it could have. Rainy is heading back to New York in a few days, and I doubt we'll ever see one another again."

"But I thought you said it went as well as it could have?"

Calvin grinned sheepishly. "I guess I could have used a better word choice, couldn't I? What I do know is that we all have our demons. But it's one thing to have them, and it's another thing entirely to want to keep them."

"What do you mean by that?"

He frowned and turned toward Jo, pulling up and resting his elbow on the back of the pew. "Rainy told me that Johnnie Walker Red was and is her first love."

"You have to respect her honesty."

"And she wants to keep it that way."

Jo slowly shook her head and, with a heart filled with compassion, she said, "Oh my! That must have hurt."

"It didn't hurt. It made me angry."

"What?" Jo blurted. "Why on earth would that make you angry?"

"Because it's a direct insult to God. I don't begrudge anyone their vices. We all have them. Look at all the years I wasted being angry with

God over that woman. I'm no better than anyone else. But I lost respect for her."

"That's an awfully harsh statement, isn't it? A little judgmental for a man of the cloth?"

Calvin shook his head. "She's blatantly choosing the wrong path, and she refuses to change. It's one thing to try, to keep on tripping and falling and repeatedly getting up again. It's another thing completely to refuse to try at all." He paused, looking around at the walls and ceilings of the small church as if he was inspecting them the way he was inspecting his own heart. "God clearly tells us in the Book of Revelation that we are to be overcomers. To me, that means we need to overcome the demons that hound our lives, not willfully nurture them."

Jo studied Calvin. To a degree, she bought his explanation, but not entirely. Unlike Calvin, Jo admired Rainy. Owning her vices took raw courage. "Is that really what your anger is all about?"

Calvin centered his confusion-lined eyes on Jo then shook his head.

"There are ways to compete with another man," she said, "but how do you compete with a bottle? That's what's really going on with you, isn't it?"

A roomful of air whooshed out of Calvin's lungs, his eyes suddenly sad. "I knew I was out of line, that I wasn't being honest with myself. I felt it in my gut. It's just that she makes me feel small, Jo, like I'm just not good enough," he confessed. "Always has, I guess."

"I understand. I feel badly for her, but for your sake I'm also pleased that you're finally free of her."

"Me too. It just pains me something awful to see her ruin her life. It's as if she's trying to punish herself over something."

"I know. But what about you? You're okay?"

Calvin smiled, warm and confident. "I couldn't be better. Especially now that I stand a good chance of having Ardena in my life." He then reached for Jo's arm, lightly touching it. "There's something else I'd like to share with you."

"What's that?"

"Butch Rasmussen. I'm sure that name has a familiar ring."

Thinking she saw a glint in Calvin's eyes, Jo's hopes spiraled. *Please. Let this news be good, too.* "Very familiar. Have you had a chance to have a chat with him yet?"

"Day before yesterday."

"And?"

"He's a good man, Jo. Very good. And, on second thought, maybe it would be better if Big Ole told you the news himself."

"He knows?"

"I stopped by yesterday morning. Told him all about it." He grinned. "I had Butch waiting out in the park. They had a nice reunion. Butch. Big Ole. And Sarah."

Jo squealed. "Sarah got to meet her dad?"

"Yes, and it couldn't have gone better."

"But what about Butch's dad and the blackmail?"

"Butch didn't know anything about it. He and his dad haven't spoken since before Butch went to prison. His dad disowned him."

"Disowned his son who ended up in prison while he, himself, indulges in blackmail? That doesn't make any sense."

"Butch says theirs is a situation of like father, like son. He wouldn't be surprised if his father is blackmailing Ole out of sheer desperation. Butch heard some time ago that he had a half-sister who's been gravely ill. He's sure the money is for her medical expenses."

"Oh my."

"Oh my is right."

CHAPTER SIXTY-THREE

Like a freshman on her first day of high school struggling with that do-I-really-belong-here feeling, Jo lingered outside the office door. Saturday night felt surreal, like a dream, a reality that hadn't really happened.

When she finally entered, she smiled at the aroma of fresh coffee perking in the back room. Just then, Ardena peered around the door-jamb. "I thought I heard something out here. Good morning to you! And is that a starry look I see in your eyes? Is there anything you want to tell me?"

Jo plucked Marianne Glanz's pen from her handbag and nodded. "Look!"

Ardena lifted her hand to her mouth, tears forming in her eyes. "Don't tell me. All is well then? Does this mean you've made peace with Tryg and you're staying?"

Jo nodded and they hugged. "He figured out what was going on. Felt pretty bad about it. I've got to get something black and bitter and strong to shock my emotions or I'm afraid I might go over an emotional cliff," Jo said, making a beeline for the coffee pot. "I'm so relieved, I feel like crying."

At fifteen past nine, Tryg entered the office grinning. "Morning,

Ardena. Jo." When his gaze met Jo's, warmth radiated from his big brown eyes. "It sure is good to have you back again."

Jo didn't say anything. She didn't need to. The glow emanating from her heart undoubtedly radiated through her eyes. She smoothed the Parker pen with her fingertips and recalled her grandfather's favorite scripture. Now that her trial had reached a favorable end, she felt humbled. Her grandfather was right after all. *All things had worked together for good.*

At ten o'clock, the phone rang. Calvin Doherty was calling an extraordinarily delighted Ardena.

At precisely twelve o'clock noon, Calvin entered the office clear-eyed and beaming. Jo was thrilled. He'd made his choice, and it was definitely the right one.

Ardena turned to Jo with an equally wide grin, and as she and Calvin headed toward the door, she said, "I may be away a bit longer than an hour. Would you mind covering for me?"

Jo shook her head and grinned. "You don't even need to ask."

But as Jo watched the door close behind the happy couple, the surprising sting of feasting only on memories cut her to her center. It felt as though she were looking through the windows of a beautiful home, where people were waltzing and laughing and living blessed lives while she was standing alone in the cool of evening, feasting only on memories of her past.

And that could never change.

Or had it already changed?

She glanced at Tryg's door. There was no denying their deep and strong bond. He felt it, too. She sensed it. And then she remembered those closest to her.

She thought about Brue, and how happy and blessed she was to have such a delightful and caring daughter, and how deeply Brue needed her love, acceptance, and guidance. What a privilege to provide them.

She thought about Marianne Glanz, and how playing it straight had inadvertently given Tryg more business than if Jo kept silent.

And she thought about Henrietta Braddingly, and how Jo had found the courage to take a risk, conceivably saving Tryg's firm from an immense headache, saying nothing about a possible lawsuit.

She reflected on her conversation with Calvin and her heart fluttered. He had gotten beyond his past, and she'd played an integral part in his breaking free. That was no small privilege.

Jo reconsidered her plight. Between her strengthening bond with Tryg and playing a vital role in the lives of others, maybe she was living on far more than memories after all. And that felt very good indeed.

CHAPTER SIXTY-FOUR

Jo placed her gardening tools on the grass beside Case's grave. All was quiet. No one around. She plucked the first pot from the wagon wheel, removed what was left of the stem and hard soil, replaced the black soil, and then carefully pressed the red geranium tightly into its pot. It looked healthy and beautiful once again.

She replaced the first pot and reached for the second, thinking for a moment that she might have heard a disturbance. But she was far too absorbed with replacing stolen geraniums to give the strange sound any further thought. The flowers were healthy and beautiful. They made the wagon wheel look colorful and impressive once again.

Well into replanting the third geranium, the sound of steps swishing through tall grass and the snap of a twig caught her breath. She sat frozen, too frightened to look past her peripheral vision. No car had pulled in. If it had, she would have heard it. She sensed a strange presence, as though eyes were watching her. Feeling a puff of breath close to her ear, the fine hairs at the nape of her neck stood erect. She clenched the trowel so tightly that it caused pain. Hoping her imagination wasn't playing cruel games with her while she was alone out in this lonely setting, she turned slowly to see who was there.

"Well, I'll be," she whispered. She slowly let out a lungful of air, then laughed softly. "If it isn't the flower thief. I caught you red-handed, didn't I? If Case could only see you." She then, little by little, held out a geranium. "Come here. Don't be afraid. Come on. I brought some fresh flowers this morning. I think you're going to like them."

Jo held out her hand until the wide-eyed deer took a step forward and lopped off the cardinal-red flowers with one swift bite. The doe then bolted over the fence, through the freshly planted field, and disappeared into a far-off grove.

"Thank you for keeping Case such good company," Jo called after the gentle creature. Her gaze then dropped to the gravesite and she announced proudly, "I caught the flower thief red-handed, Case. The most beautiful deer I've ever seen. After all my complaining about thieves absconding with flowers from cemeteries, I'm pleased to know I was wrong, and that such pleasant company is keeping watch over you."

A breeze shivered the leaves. Jo gazed up at the clouds billowing eastward across the sky. "Looks like it's about to rain again." Just then a raindrop fell, and all was still until a subtle movement caught her eye. She looked up and watched a herd of deer roam gracefully through the fields, exuding warmth with their gentle presence. Then another raindrop splashed down and the wind kicked up again. "Hmm. And here I am, sitting somewhere between raindrops." She smiled at the thought.

Jo nestled in on the ground next to Case's grave and tugged at some wild clovers threaded through the grass. "There's something I haven't told you. It's about Tryg. He offered me a job at his law office. That's where I've been working all this time. I never felt comfortable telling you about it before. Guess I was fearful about what you'd think. I'm really happy there, Case. It didn't start out that way, though. I only took Tryg up on his offer because of our canceled trip to New York. Since I couldn't get my old job back and couldn't find another one anywhere else, I figured that working for Tryg was the fastest way out of Amber Leaf.

"It didn't go well with us at first—not at all. I lost his trust right out of the chute, and then his lady friend pulled a few fast ones on me. It's been tough going, to say the least. Tryg and I have made our peace, and I honestly believe we've become good friends. At least I think he's behind me now.

"I've been doing a lot of thinking lately, too," she confided, and then caught herself smiling widely. "Brue and I don't have a pressing need to move to New York after all. We belong here, Case. Here with you. Amber Leaf is our home."

Finally feeling at peace, warm tears rolled down Jo's cheeks and splashed onto her lap. The breeze picked up again, and the rain began to fall.

Though raindrops fall from darkened skies
On soil thirsty or parched by heat
Though weathervanes spin and the wild winds blow
O'er fields barren or golden with wheat
There whispers a warm new hope for one
In the rustle above the trees
That there is no storm that can't be outrun
If one hopes and only believes

QUESTIONS FOR DISCUSSION

1. Did you feel well grounded in time and setting? Is Amber Leaf a place you would like to visit or live?

2. Jo's mind was made up from the beginning. She could never give her heart to Tryg out of loyalty to Case. He would always come between them. Did you find her dilemma believable?

3. Who was your favorite character, and why?

4. Did you pick up on Lauren's jealousy when she was first introduced? And did you see Jo as a victim or as in control of the situation?

5. The Marianne Glanz pen exchange springboarded from a true story. Did you find it believable and were you inspired to turn little annoyances in your own life to your advantage?

6. Calvin could see Rainy's weakness, but was not able to see his own. Did Jo do an effective of job of leveling the playing field when she confronted him?

7. Calvin, Big Ole, and Jo are equals when it comes to making others accountable. Did you feel the way they challenged one another was appropriate, believable, and helpful?

8. What was your favorite scene in the book and why?

9. We all make snap judgments. Did the flower thief inspire you to re-evaluate yours?

10. What was the book's greatest weakness and strength?

CPSIA information can be obtained at www.ICGtesting.com
Printed in the USA
LVOW081235261112

308820LV00004B/474/P